The Guide

Indian Thought Publications

Other works by Narayan in this imprint

Novels

Swami and Friends
The Bachelor of Arts
The Dark Room
The English Teacher
Mr. Sampath – The Printer of Malgudi
The Financial Expert
Waiting for the Mahatma
The Man-eater of Malgudi
The Vendor of Sweets
The Painter of Signs
A Tiger for Malgudi
Talkative Man
The World of Nagaraj
Grandmother's Tale

Short Stories

Malgudi Days
Under the Banyan Tree and Other Stories

Autobiography

My Days

The Guide

R. K. NARAYAN

INDIAN THOUGHT PUBLICATIONS

INDIAN THOUGHT PUBLICATIONS
New No.38, Thanikachalam Road,
T. Nagar, Chennai - 600 017

The Guide

ISBN: 978-81-85986-07-4

First published in Great Britain in 1958 by Methuen &Co. Ltd., and in the U.S. by Viking Reissued in 1970 by The Bodley Head Ltd. Reissued in 1980 by William Heinemann Ltd.

First Indian Edition 1958
78th Reprint 2011

Printed in India at
Sudarsan Graphics Private Limited
27, Neelakanta Mehta Street,
T.Nagar, Chennai - 600 017

I

RAJU welcomed the intrusion—something to relieve the loneliness of the place. The man stood gazing reverentially on his
face. Raju felt amused and embarrassed. 'Sit down if you like,'
Raju said, to break the spell. The other accepted the suggestion
with a grateful nod and went down the river steps to wash his
feet and face, came up wiping himself dry with the end of a
chequered yellow towel on his shoulder, and took his seat two
steps below the granite slab on which Raju was sitting cross-
legged as if it were a throne, beside an ancient shrine. The
branches of the trees canopying the river course rustled and
trembled with the agitation of birds and monkeys settling down
for the night. Upstream beyond the hills the sun was setting.
Raju waited for the other to say something. But he was too
polite to open a conversation.

Raju asked, 'Where are you from?' dreading lest the other
should turn round and ask the same question.

The man replied, 'I'm from Mangal.'

'Where is Mangal?'

The other waved his arm, indicating a direction across the
river, beyond the high steep bank. 'Not far from here,' he
added. The man volunteered further information about himself. 'My daughter lives near by. I had gone to visit her; I am
now on my way home. I left her after food. She insisted that I
should stay on to dinner, but I refused. It'd have meant walking
home at nearly midnight. I'm not afraid of anything, but

[5]

why should we walk when we ought to be sleeping in bed?'

'You are very sensible,' Raju said.

They listened for a while to the chatter of monkeys, and the man added as an afterthought, 'My daughter is married to my own sister's son, and so there is no problem. I often visit my sister and also my daughter; and so no one minds it.'

'Why should anyone mind in any case if you visit a daughter?'

'It's not considered proper form to pay too many visits to a son-in-law,' explained the villager.

Raju liked this rambling talk. He had been all alone in this place for over a day. It was good to hear the human voice again. After this the villager resumed the study of his face with intense respect. And Raju stroked his chin thoughtfully to make sure that an apostolic beard had not suddenly grown there. It was still smooth. He had had his last shave only two days before and paid for it with the hard-earned coins of his jail life.

Loquacious as usual and with the sharp blade scraping the soap, the barber had asked, 'Coming out, I suppose?' Raju rolled his eyes and remained silent. He felt irritated at the question, but did not like to show it with the fellow holding the knife. 'Just coming out?' repeated the barber obstinately.

Raju felt it would be no use being angry with such a man. Here he was in the presence of experience. He asked, 'How do you know?'

'I have spent twenty years shaving people here. Didn't you observe that this was the first shop as you left the jail gate? Half the trick is to have your business in the right place. But that raises other people's jealousies!' he said, waving off an army of jealous barbers.

'Don't you attend to the inmates?'

'Not until they come out. It is my brother's son who is on duty there. I don't want to compete with him and I don't want to enter the jail gates every day.'

'Not a bad place,' said Raju through the soap.

'Go back then,' said the barber and asked, 'What was it? What did the police say?'

'Don't talk of it,' snapped Raju and tried to maintain a sullen, forbidding silence for the rest of the shave.

But the barber was not to be cowed so easily. His lifelong contact with tough men had hardened him. He said, 'Eighteen months or twenty-four? I can bet it's one or the other.'

Raju felt admiration for the man. He was a master. It was no use losing one's temper. 'You are so wise and knowing. Why do you ask questions?'

The barber was pleased with the compliment. His fingers paused in their operations; he bent round to face Raju and say, 'Just to get it out of you, that is all. It's written on your face that you are a two-year sort, which means you are not a murderer.'

'How can you tell?' Raju said.

'You would look different if you had been in for seven years, which is what one gets for murder only half-proved.'

'What else have I not done?' Raju asked.

'You have not cheated in any big way; but perhaps only in a small, petty manner.'

'Go on. What next?'

'You have not abducted or raped anyone, or set fire to a house.'

'Why don't you say exactly why I was sent to jail for two years? I'll give you four annas for a guess.'

[7]

'No time now for a game,' said the barber and went on, 'What do you do next?'

'I don't know. Must go somewhere, I suppose,' said Raju thoughtfully.

'In case you like to go back to your old company, why don't you put your hand in someone's pocket at the market, or walk through an open door and pick out some trash and let the people howl for the police? They'll see you back where you want to be.'

'Not a bad place,' Raju repeated, slightly nodding in the direction of the jail wall. 'Friendly people there, but I hate to be awakened every morning at five.'

'An hour at which a night-prowler likes to return home to bed, I suppose,' said the barber with heavy insinuation. 'Well, that's all. You may get up,' he said, putting away the razor. 'You look like a *maharaja* now'—surveying Raju at a distance from his chair.

The villager on the lower step looked up at his face with devotion, which irked Raju. 'Why do you look at me like that?' he asked brusquely.

The man replied, 'I don't know. I don't mean to offend you, sir.' Raju wanted to blurt out, 'I am here because I have nowhere else to go. I want to be away from people who may recognise me.' But he hesitated, wondering how he should say it. It looked as though he would be hurting the other's deepest sentiment if he so much as whispered the word 'jail'. He tried at least to say, 'I am not so great as you imagine. I am just ordinary.' Before he could fumble and reach the words, the other said, 'I have a problem, sir.'

'Tell me about it,' Raju said, the old, old habit of affording

[8]

guidance to others asserting itself. Tourists who recommended him to one another would say at one time, 'If you are lucky enough to be guided by Raju, you will know everything. He will not only show you all the worth-while places, but also help you in every way.' It was in his nature to get involved in other people's interests and activities. 'Otherwise,' Raju often reflected, 'I should have grown up like a thousand other normal persons, without worries in life.'

My troubles would not have started (Raju said in the course of narrating his life-story to this man who was called Velan at a later stage) but for Rosie. Why did she call herself Rosie? She did not come from a foreign land. She was just an Indian, who should have done well with Devi, Meena, Lalitha, or any one of the thousand names we have in our country. She chose to call herself Rosie. Don't imagine on hearing her name that she wore a short skirt or cropped her hair. She looked just the orthodox dancer that she was. She wore saris of bright hues and gold lace, had curly hair which she braided and beflowered, wore diamond ear-rings and a heavy gold necklace. I told her at the first opportunity what a great dancer she was and how she fostered our cultural traditions, and it pleased her.

Thousands of persons must have said the same thing to her since, but I happened to be the first in the line. Anyone likes to hear flattering sentiments, and more than others, I suppose, dancers. They like to be told every hour of the day how well they keep their steps. I praised her art whenever I could snatch a moment alone with her and whisper in her ear, out of range of that husband of hers. Oh, what a man! I have not met a more grotesque creature in my life. Instead of calling herself Rosie, she could more logically have called him Marco Polo.

[9]

He dressed like a man about to undertake an expedition, with his thick coloured glasses, thick jacket, and a thick helmet over which was perpetually stretched a green, shiny, waterproof cover, giving him the appearance of a space-traveller. I have, of course, no idea of the original Marco Polo's appearance, but I wanted to call this man Marco at first sight, and I have not bothered to associate him with any other name since.

The moment I set eyes on him, on that memorable day at our railway station, I knew that here was a lifelong customer for me. A man who preferred to dress like a permanent tourist was just what a guide passionately looked for all his life.

You may want to ask why I became a guide or when. I was a guide for the same reason as someone else is a signaller, porter, or guard. It is fated thus. Don't laugh at my railway associations. The railways got into my blood very early in life. Engines, with their tremendous clanging and smoke, ensnared my senses. I felt at home on the railway platform, and considered the stationmaster and porter the best company for man, and their railway talk the most enlightened. I grew up in their midst. Ours was a small house opposite the Malgudi station. The house had been built by my father with his own hands long before trains were thought of. He chose this spot because it was outside the town and he could have it cheap. He had dug the earth, kneaded the mud with water from the well, and built the walls, and roofed them with coconut thatch. He planted papaya trees around, which yielded fruit, which he cut up and sold in slices: a single fruit brought him eight annas if he carved it with dexterity. My father had a small shop built of dealwood planks and gunny sack; and all day he sat there selling peppermint, fruit, tobacco, betel leaf, parched gram (which he measured out in tiny bamboo cylinders), and whatever else the wayfarers on the Trunk Road demanded. It was known as the 'hut shop'. A crowd of peasants and drivers of bullock-wagons were always gathered in front of his shop. A very busy man indeed. At midday he called me when he went in for his lunch and made a routine statement at the same hour. 'Raju, take my seat. Be sure to receive the money for whatever you give. Don't eat off all that eating stuff, it's kept for sale; call me if you have doubts.'

And I kept calling aloud, 'Father, green peppermints, how many for half an anna?' while the customer waited patiently.

'Three,' he shouted from the house, with his mouth stuffed with food. 'But if he is buying for three-quarters of an anna, give him . . .' He mentioned some complicated concession, which I could never apply.

I appealed to the customer, 'Give me only half an anna,' and gave him three peppermints in return. If by chance I had happened to take four greens out of the big bottle, I swallowed the fourth in order to minimise complications.

An eccentric cockerel in the neighbourhood announced the daybreak when probably it felt that we had slept long enough. It let out a shattering cry which made my father jump from his bed and wake me up.

I washed myself at the wall, smeared holy ash on my forehead, stood before the framed pictures of gods hanging high up on the wall, and recited all kinds of sacred verse in a loud, ringing tone. After watching my performance for a while, my father slipped away to the back-yard to milk the buffalo. Later, coming in with the pail, he always remarked, 'Something really wrong with that animal this time. She wouldn't yield even half a measure today.'

My mother invariably answered, 'I know, I know. She is

[11]

getting wrong-headed, that is all. I know what she will respond to,' she said in a mysterious, sinister manner, receiving the pail and carrying it into the kitchen. She came out in a moment with a tumblerful of hot milk for me.

The sugar was kept in an old tin can, which looked rusty but contained excellent sugar. It was kept on a wooden ledge on the smoke-stained wall of the kitchen, out of my reach. I fear that its position was shifted up and up as I grew older, because I remember that I could never get at that rusty can at any time except with the co-operation of my elders.

When the sky lightened, my father was ready for me on the *pyol*. There he sat with a thin broken twig at his side. The modern notions of child psychology were unknown then; the stick was an educator's indispensable equipment. 'The un-beaten brat will remain unlearned,' said my father, quoting an old proverb. He taught me the Tamil alphabet. He wrote the first two letters on each side of my slate at a time. I had to go over the contours of the letters with my pencil endlessly until they became bloated and distorted beyond recognition. From time to time my father snatched the slate from my hand, looked at it, glared at me, and said, 'What a mess! You will never prosper in life if you disfigure the sacred letters of the alphabet.' Then he cleaned the slate with his damp towel, wrote the letters again, and gave it to me with the injunction, 'If you spoil this, you will make me wild. Trace them exactly as I have written. Don't try any of your tricks on them,' and he flourished his twig menacingly.

I said meekly, 'Yes, Father,' and started to write again. I can well picture myself, sticking my tongue out, screwing my head to one side, and putting my entire body-weight on the pencil: the slate pencil screeched as I tried to drive it through and my father ordered, 'Don't make all that noise with that horrible pencil of yours. What has come over you?'

Then followed arithmetic. Two and two, four; four and three, something else. Something into something, more; some more into less. Oh, God, numbers did give me a headache. While the birds were out chirping and flying in the cool air, I cursed the fate that confined me to my father's company. His temper was rising every second. As if in answer to my silent prayer, an early customer was noticed at the door of the hut shop and my lessons came to an abrupt end. My father left me with the remark, 'I have better things to do of a morning than make a genius out of a clay-head.'

Although the lessons had seemed interminable to me, my mother said the moment she saw me, 'So you have been let off! I wonder what you can learn in half an hour!'

I told her, 'I'll go out and play and won't trouble you. But no more lessons for the day, please.' With that I was off to the shade of a tamarind tree across the road. It was an ancient, spreading tree, dense with leaves, amidst which monkeys and birds lived, bred, and chattered incessantly, feeding on the tender leaves and fruits. Pigs and piglets came from somewhere and nosed about the ground, thick with fallen leaves, and I played there all day. I think I involved the pigs in some imaginary game and even fancied myself carried on their backs. My father's customers greeted me as they passed that way. I had marbles, an iron hoop to roll, and a rubber ball, with which I occupied myself. I hardly knew what time of the day it was or what was happening around me.

Sometimes my father took me along to the town when he went shopping. He stopped a passing bullock-cart for the trip. I hung about anxiously with an appealing look in my eyes

(I had been taught not to *ask* to be taken along) until my father said, 'Climb in, little man.' I clambered in before his sentence was completed. The bells around the bull's neck jingled, the wooden wheels grated and ground the dust off the rough road; I clung to the staves on the sides and felt my bones shaken. Still, I enjoyed the smell of the straw in the cart and all the scenes we passed. Men and vehicles, hogs and boys—the panorama of life enchanted me.

At the market my father made me sit on a wooden platform within sight of a shopman known to him, and went about to do his shopping. My pockets would be filled with fried nuts and sweets; munching, I watched the activities of the market—people buying and selling, arguing and laughing, swearing and shouting. While my father was gone on his shopping expedition, I remember, a question kept drumming in my head: 'Father, you are a shopkeeper yourself. Why do you go about buying in other shops?' I never got an answer. As I sat gazing on the afternoon haze, the continuous din of the marketplace lulled my senses, the dusty glare suddenly made me drowsy, and I fell asleep, leaning on the wall of that unknown place where my father had chosen to put me.

'I have a problem, sir,' said the man.

Raju nodded his head and added, 'So has everyone,' in a sudden access of pontificality. Ever since the moment this man had come and sat before him, gazing on his face, he had experienced a feeling of importance. He felt like an actor who was always expected to utter the right sentence. Now the appropriate sentence was 'If you show me a person without a problem, then I'll show you the perfect world. Do you know what the great Buddha said?' The other edged nearer. 'A woman once went wailing to the great Buddha, clasping her dead baby to her bosom. The Buddha said, "Go into every home in this city and find one where death is unknown; if you find such a place, fetch me a handful of mustard from there, and then I'll teach you how to conquer death." '

The man clicked his tongue in appreciation and asked, 'And what happened to the dead baby, sir?'

'She had to bury it, of course,' said Raju. 'So also,' he concluded, while doubting in his mind the relevance of the comparison, 'if you show me a single home without a problem, I shall show you the way to attain a universal solution to all problems.'

The man was overwhelmed by the weightiness of this statement. He performed a deep obeisance and said, 'I have not told you my name, sir. I am Velan. My father in his lifetime married thrice. I am the first son of his first wife. The youngest daughter of his last wife is also with us. As the head of the family, I have given her every comfort at home, provided her with all the jewellery and clothes a girl needs, but . . .' He paused slightly before bringing out the big surprise. But Raju completed the sentence for him, 'The girl shows no gratitude.'

'Absolutely, sir!' said the man.

'And she will not accept your plans for her marriage?'

'Oh, too true, sir,' Velan said, wonderstruck. 'My cousin's son is a fine boy. Even the date of the wedding was fixed, but do you know, sir, what the girl did?'

'Ran away from the whole thing,' said Raju, and asked, 'How did you bring her back?'

'I searched for her three days and nights and spotted her in a festival crowd in a distant village. They were pulling the temple chariot around the streets and the population of fifty villages was crowded into one. I searched every face in the crowd and at last caught her while she was watching a puppet show. Now, do you know what she does?' Raju decided to let the other have the satisfaction of saying things himself, and Velan ended his story with, 'She sulks in a room all day. I do not know what to do. It is possible that she is possessed. If I could know what to do with her, it'd be such a help, sir.'

Raju said with a philosophic weariness, 'Such things are common in life. One should not let oneself be bothered unduly by anything.'

'What am I to do with her, sir?'

'Bring her over; let me speak to her,' Raju said grandly.

Velan rose, bowed low, and tried to touch Raju's feet. Raju recoiled at the attempt. 'I'll not permit anyone to do this. God alone is entitled to such a prostration. He will destroy us if we attempt to usurp His rights.' He felt he was attaining the stature of a saint. Velan went down the steps meekly, crossed the river, climbed the opposite bank, and was soon out of sight. Raju ruminated. 'I wish I had asked him what the age of the girl was. Hope she is uninteresting. I have had enough trouble in life.'

He sat there for a long time, watching the river flow into the night; the rustle of the peepul and banyan trees around was sometimes loud and frightening. The sky was clear. Having nothing else to do, he started counting the stars. He said to himself, 'I shall be rewarded for this profound service to humanity. People will say, "Here is the man who knows the exact number of stars in the sky. If you have any trouble on that account, you had better consult him. He will be your night guide for the skies."' He told himself, 'The thing to do is to start from a corner and go on patch by patch. Never work from

the top to the horizon, but always the other way.' He was
evolving a theory. He started the count from above a fringe of
palmyra-trees on his left-hand side, up the course of the river,
over to the other side. 'One ... two ... fifty-five ...' He
suddenly realised that if he looked deeper a new cluster of
stars came into view; by the time he assimilated it into his
reckoning, he realised he had lost sight of his starting point and
found himself entangled in hopeless figures. He felt exhausted.
He stretched himself on the stone slab and fell asleep under the
open sky.

The eight o'clock sun shone fully on his face. He opened his
eyes and saw Velan standing respectfully away on a lower step.
'I have brought my sister,' he said and thrust up a young girl
of fourteen, who had tightly braided her hair and decorated
herself with jewellery. Velan explained, 'These jewels were
given by me, bought out of my own money, for she is after all
my sister.'

Raju sat up, rubbing his eyes. He was as yet unprepared to
take charge of the world's affairs. His immediate need was
privacy for his morning ablutions. He said to them, 'You may
go in there and wait for me.'

He found them waiting for him in the ancient, pillared hall.
Raju sat himself down on a slightly elevated platform in the
middle of the hall. Velan placed before him a basket filled with
bananas, cucumbers, pieces of sugar-cane, fried nuts, and a
copper vessel brimming with milk.

Raju asked, 'What is all this for?'

'It will please us very much if you will accept them, sir.'

Raju sat looking at the hamper. It was not unwelcome. He
could eat anything and digest it now. He had learned not to

B
[17]

be fussy. Formerly he would have said, 'Who will eat this? Give me coffee and *idli*, please, first thing in the day. These are good enough for munching later.' But prison life had trained him to swallow anything at any time. Sometimes a colleague in the cell, managing to smuggle in, through the kindness of a warder, something unpalatable like mutton-puff made six days ago, with its oil going rancid, shared it with Raju, and Raju remembered how he ate it with gusto at three in the morning— a time chosen before the others could wake up and claim a share. Anything was welcome now. He asked, 'Why do you do all this for me?'

'They are grown in our fields and we are proud to offer them to you.'

Raju did not have to ask further questions. He had gradually come to view himself as a master of these occasions. He had already begun to feel that the adulation directed to him was inevitable. He sat in silence, eyeing the gift for a while. Suddenly he picked up the basket and went into an inner sanctum. The others followed. Raju stopped before a stone image in the dark recess. It was a tall god with four hands, bearing a mace and wheel, with a beautifully chiselled head, but abandoned a century ago. Raju ceremoniously placed the basket of edibles at the feet of the image and said, 'It's *His* first. Let the offering go to Him, first; and we will eat the remnant. By giving to God, do you know how it multiplies, rather than divides? Do you know the story?' He began narrating the story of Devaka, a man of ancient times who begged for alms at the temple gate every day and would not use any of his collections without first putting them at the feet of the god. Half-way through the story he realised that he could not remember either its course or its purport. He lapsed into silence. Velan patiently waited for the continuation. He was of the stuff disciples are made of; an unfinished story or an incomplete moral never bothered him; it was all in the scheme of life. When Raju turned and strode majestically back to the river step, Velan and his sister followed him mutely.

How could I recollect the story heard from my mother so long ago? She told me a story every evening while we waited for Father to close the shop and come home. The shop remained open till midnight. Bullock-carts in long caravans arrived late in the evening from distant villages, loaded with coconut, rice, and other commodities for the market. The animals were un-yoked under the big tamarind tree for the night, and the cartmen drifted in twos and threes to the shop, for a chat or to ask for things to eat or smoke. How my father loved to discuss with them the price of grain, rainfall, harvest, and the state of irrigation channels. Or they talked about old litigations. One heard repeated references to magistrates, affidavits, witnesses in the case, and appeals, punctuated with roars of laughter— possibly the memory of some absurd legality or loophole tickled them.

My father ignored food and sleep when he had company. My mother sent me out several times to see if he could be made to turn in. He was a man of uncertain temper and one could not really guess how he would react to interruptions, and so my mother coached me to go up, watch his mood, and gently remind him of food and home. I stood under the shop-awning, coughing and clearing my throat, hoping to catch his eye. But the talk was all-absorbing and he would not glance in my direction, and I got absorbed in their talk, although I did not understand a word of it.

After a while my mother's voice came gently on the night air, calling, 'Raju, Raju,' and my father interrupted his activities to look at me and say, 'Tell your mother not to wait for me. Tell her to place a handful of rice and buttermilk in a bowl, with just one piece of lime pickle, and keep it in the oven for me. I'll come in later.' It was almost a formula with him five days in a week. He always added, 'Not that I'm really hungry tonight.' And then I believe he went on to discuss health problems with his cronies.

But I didn't stop to hear further. I made a swift dash back home. There was a dark patch between the light from the shop and the dim lantern shedding its light on our threshold, a matter of about ten yards, I suppose, but the passage through it gave me a cold sweat. I expected wild animals and supernatural creatures to emerge and grab me. My mother waited on the doorstep to receive me and said, 'Not hungry, I suppose! That'll give him an excuse to talk to the village folk all night, and then come in for an hour's sleep and get up with the crowing of that foolish cock somewhere. He will spoil his health.'

I followed her into the kitchen. She placed my plate and hers side by side on the floor, drew the rice-pot within reach, and served me and herself simultaneously, and we finished our dinner by the sooty tin lamp, stuck on a nail in the wall. She unrolled a mat for me in the front room, and I lay down to sleep. She sat at my side, awaiting Father's return. Her presence gave me a feeling of inexplicable cosiness. I felt I ought to put her proximity to good use, and complained, 'Something is bothering my hair,' and she ran her fingers through my hair and scratched the nape of my neck. And then I commanded, 'A story.'

[20]

Immediately she began, 'Once upon a time there was a man called Devaka . . .' I heard his name mentioned almost every night. He was a hero, saint, or something of the kind. I never learned fully what he did or why, sleep overcoming me before my mother was through even the preamble.

Raju sat on the step and watched the river dazzling in the morning sun. The air was cool, and he wished he were alone. His visitors sat patiently on a lower step, waiting for him to attend to them, like patients in a doctor's room. Raju had many problems of his own to think of. He suddenly felt irritated at the responsibility that Velan was thrusting on him, and said frankly, 'I am not going to think of your problems, Velan; not now.'

'May I know why?' he asked humbly.

'It is so,' Raju said with an air of finality.

'When may I trouble you, sir?' he asked.

Raju replied grandly, 'When the time is ripe for it.' This took the matter from the realms of time into eternity. Velan accepted his answer with resignation and rose to go. It was rather touching. Raju felt indebted to him for the edibles he had brought, so he said pacifyingly, 'Is this the sister you told me about?'

'Yes, sir; it is.'

'I know what your problem is, but I wish to give the matter some thought. We cannot force vital solutions. Every question must bide its time. Do you understand?'

'Yes, sir,' Velan said. He drew his fingers across his brow and said, 'Whatever is written here will happen. How can we ever help it?'

'We may not change it, but we may understand it,' Raju

replied grandly. 'And to arrive at a proper understanding, time is needed.' Raju felt he was growing wings. Shortly, he felt, he might float in the air and perch himself on the tower of the ancient temple. Nothing was going to surprise him. He suddenly found himself asking, 'Have I been in a prison or in some sort of transmigration?'

Velan looked relieved and proud to hear so much from his master. He looked significantly at his difficult sister, and she bowed her head in shame. Raju declared, fixedly looking at the girl, 'What must happen must happen; no power on earth or in heaven can change its course, just as no one can change the course of that river.' They gazed on the river, as if the clue to their problems lay there, and turned to go. Raju watched them cross the river and climb the opposite bank. Soon they were out of sight.

2

WE noticed much activity in the field in front of our house. A set of men arrived from the town every morning and were busy in the field all day. We learned that they were building a railway track. They came to my father's shop for refreshments. My father inquired anxiously, 'When shall we have the trains coming in here?'

If they were in a good mood, they answered, 'About six or eight months, who can say?' Or if they were in a black mood, 'Don't ask us. Next you will tell us to drive a locomotive to your shop!' and they laughed grimly.

Work was going on briskly. I lost to some extent my freedom under the tamarind tree, because trucks were parked there. I climbed into them and played. No one minded me. All day I was climbing in and out of the trucks, and my clothes became red with mud. Most of the trucks brought red earth which was banked up on the field. In a short while a small mountain was raised in front of our house. It was enchanting. When I stood on the top of this mound I could see far-off places, the hazy outlines of Mempi Hills. I became as busy as the men. I spent all my time in the company of those working on the track, listening to their talk and sharing their jokes. More trucks came, bringing timber and iron. A variety of goods was piling up on every side. Presently I began to collect sawn-off metal bits, nuts and bolts, and I treasured them in my mother's big trunk, where a space was allotted

[23]

to me amidst her ancient silk saris, which she never wore.

A boy grazing his cows approached the spot just below the mound on which I was playing a game by myself. His cows were munching the grass right below the mound on which the men were working, and the little fellow had dared to step on the slope where I played. I was beginning to have a sense of ownership of the railway, and I didn't want trespassers there. I frowned at the boy and barked, 'Get out.'

'Why?' he asked. 'My cows are here, I'm watching them.'

'Begone with your cows,' I said. 'Otherwise they will be run over by the train, which will be here shortly.'

'Let them be. What do you care?' he said, which irritated me so much that I let out a yell and pounced on him with 'You son of a . . .' and a variety of other expressions recently picked up. The boy, instead of knocking me down, ran screaming to my father, 'Your son is using bad language.'

My father sprang up on hearing this. Just my misfortune. He came rushing toward me as I was resuming my game and asked, 'What did you call this boy?' I had the good sense not to repeat it. I blinked, wordlessly, at which the boy repeated exactly what I had said. This produced an unexpectedly violent effect on my father. He grabbed my neck within the hollow of his hand, and asked, 'Where did you pick that up?' I pointed at the men working on the track. He looked up, remained silent for a second, and said, 'Oh, that is so, is it? You will not idle about picking up bad words any more. I will see to it. You will go to a school tomorrow and every day.'

'Father!' I cried. He was passing a harsh sentence on me. To be removed from a place I loved to a place I loathed!

A tremendous fuss was made before I started for my school each day. My mother fed me early and filled up a little aluminium vessel with refreshment for the afternoon. She carefully put my books and slate into a bag and slung it across my shoulder. I was dressed in clean shorts and shirt; my hair was combed back from the forehead, with all the curls falling on my nape. For the first few days I enjoyed all this attention, but soon developed a normal aversion; I preferred to be neglected and stay at home to being fussed over and sent to a school. But my father was a stern disciplinarian; perhaps he was a snob who wanted to brag before others that his son was going to a school. He kept an eye on my movements till I was safely on the road each morning. He sat in his shop and kept calling every few minutes, 'Boy, have you left?'

I walked endlessly to reach my school. No other boy went in my direction. I talked to myself on the way, paused to observe the passers-by or a country cart lumbering along, or a grasshopper going under a culvert. My progress was so halting and slow that when I turned into the Market Street I could hear my classmates shouting their lessons in unison, for the old man, our master, who taught us, believed in getting the maximum noise out of his pupils.

I don't know on whose advice my father chose to send me here for my education, while the fashionable Albert Mission School was quite close by. I'd have felt proud to call myself an Albert Mission boy. But I often heard my father declare, 'I don't want to send my boy there; it seems they try to convert our boys into Christians and are all the time insulting our gods.' I don't know how he got the notion; anyway, he was firmly convinced that the school where I was sent was the best under the sun. He was known to boast, 'Many students who have passed through the hands of this ancient master are now big officials at Madras, collectors and men like that . . .' It was purely his own imagining or the invention of the old man who taught me. No one could dream that this was in any sense a school, let alone an outstanding school. It was what was called a *pyol* school, because the classes were held on the *pyol* of the gentleman's house. He lived in Kabir Lane, in a narrow old house with a cement *pyol* in front, with the street drain running right below it. He gathered a score of young boys of my age every morning on the *pyol*, reclined on a cushion in a corner, and shouted at the little fellows, flourishing a rattan cane all the time. All the classes were held there at the same time, and he bestowed attention on each group in turn. I belonged to the youngest and most elementary set, just learning the alphabet and numbers. He made us read aloud from our books and copy down the letters on our slates, and looked through each and gave corrections and flicks from the cane for those who repeated their follies. He was a very abusive man. My father, who wanted to save me from the language of the railway trackmen, had certainly not made a safer choice in sending me to this old man, who habitually addressed his pupils as donkeys and traced their genealogies on either side with thoroughness.

The thing that irritated him was not merely the mistakes that we made but our very presence. Seeing us, such short, clumsy youngsters, always fumbling and shuffling, I think got on his nerves. Of course, we made a lot of noise on his *pyol*. When he went into his house for a moment's nap or for his food or for any of a dozen domestic calls, we rolled over each other, fought, scratched, bleated, yelled. Or we tried to invade his privacy and peep in. Once we slipped in and passed from room to room until we came to the kitchen and saw him sitting before the oven, baking something. We stood at the doorway and said, 'Oh, master, you know how to cook also!' and giggled, and a lady who was standing near by also giggled at our remark.

He turned on us fiercely and ordered, 'Get out, boys; don't come here; this is not your classroom,' and we scampered back to our place, where he found us later and twisted our ears until we screamed. He said, 'I am admitting you devils here because I want you to become civilised, but what you do is . . .' and he catalogued our sins and misdeeds.

We were contrite, and he softened and said, 'Hereafter let me not catch you anywhere beyond that threshold. I will hand you over to the police if you come in.' That settled it. We never peeped again, but when his back was turned confined our attention to the drain that flowed beneath the *pyol*. We tore off loose leaves from our notebooks, made boats, and floated them down the drain, and in a short while it became established practice, and a kind of boat-racing developed out of it; we lay on our bellies and watched the boats float away on the drainwater. He warned us, 'If you fall off into the gutter, you will find yourselves in the Sarayu River, remember, and I shall have to tell your father to go out and look for you there, I suppose!' and he laughed at the grim prospect.

His interest in us was one rupee a month and anything else in kind we cared to carry. My father sent him every month two cubes of jaggery, others brought in rice and vegetables and anything else he might demand from time to time. Whenever his store at home ran out, he called one or another to his side and said, 'Now if you are a good boy, you will run to your house and fetch me just a little, only so much, mind you, of sugar. Come, let me see if you are smart!' He adopted a kindly, canvassing tone on such occasions, and we felt honoured to be able to serve him, and pestered our parents to give us the gifts and fought for the honour of serving him. Our parents showed an excessive readiness to oblige this master, grateful probably because he kept us in his charge for the major part of the day, from morning till four in the afternoon, when he dismissed us and we sprinted homeward.

In spite of all the apparent violence and purposelessness, I suppose we did make good under our master, for within a year I proved good enough for the first standard in Board High School; I could read heavier books, and do multiplication up to twenty in my head. The old master himself escorted me to the Board School, which had just established itself, and admitted me there; he saw me off in my new class, seated me and two others, and blessed us before taking leave of us. It was a pleasant surprise for us that he could be so kind.

Velan was bursting with news of a miracle. He stood before Raju with folded hands, and said, 'Sir, things have turned out well.'

'I'm so happy. How?'

'My sister came before our family gathering and admitted her follies. She has agreed . . .' He went on to explain. The girl had all of a sudden appeared before the assembled family that morning. She faced everyone straight and said, 'I have behaved foolishly all these days. I will do what my brother and the other elders at home tell me to do. They know what is best for us.'

'I could hardly believe my ears,' explained Velan. 'I pinched myself to see whether I was dreaming or awake. This girl's affair had cast a gloom on our home. If you left out our partition suit and all the complications arising from it, we had no worry to equal this. You see, we are fond of the girl, and it pained us to watch her sulk in a dark room, without minding her appearance or dress or caring for food. We did our best to make her cheerful and then had to leave her alone. We had all been very miserable on account of her, and so we were surprised this morning when she came before us with her hair oiled and braided, with flowers in it. Looking bright, she said, "I have been a bother to you all these days. Forgive me, all of you. I shall do whatever my elders order me to do." Naturally, after we got over the surprise, we asked, "Are you prepared to marry your cousin?" She did not answer at once, but stood with bowed head. My wife took her aside and asked whether we might send word to the other family, and she agreed. We have sent the happy message around, and there will soon be a marriage in our house. I have money, jewellery, and everything ready. I will call the pipers and drummers tomorrow morning and get through it all quickly. I have consulted the astrologer already, and he says that this is an auspicious time. I do not want to delay even for a second the happy event.'

'For fear that she may change her mind once again?' Raju asked. He knew why Velan was rushing it through at this pace. It was easy to guess why. But the remark threw the other into a fit of admiration, and he asked, 'How did you know what I had in mind, sir?'

Raju remained silent. He could not open his lips without provoking admiration. This was a dangerous state of affairs. He was in a mood to debunk himself a little. He told Velan sharply, 'There is nothing extraordinary in my guess,' and promptly came the reply, 'Not for you to say that, sir. Things may look easy enough for a giant, but ordinary poor mortals like us can never know what goes on in other people's minds.'

To divert his attention, Raju simply asked, 'Have you any idea of the views of the bridegroom? Is he ready for you? What does he think of her refusal?'

'After the girl came round, I sent our priest to discuss it with him, and he has come back to say that the boy is willing. He prefers not to think of what is gone. What is gone is gone.'

'True, true,' Raju said, having nothing else to say and not wishing to utter anything that might seem too brilliant. He was beginning to dread his own smartness nowadays. He was afraid to open his lips. A vow of silence was indicated, but there was greater danger in silence.

All this prudence did not save him. Velan's affairs were satisfactorily ended. One day he came to invite Raju to his sister's marriage, and Raju had to plead long and hard before he could make him leave him alone. However, Velan brought him fruit on huge trays covered with silk cloth, the sort of offering which Raju would conjure up for the edification of his tourists when he took them through an ancient palace or hall. He accepted the gift gracefully.

He avoided the girl's marriage. He did not want to be seen in a crowd, and he did not want to gather a crowd around him as a man who had worked a change in an obstinate girl. But his aloofness did not save him. If he would not go to the wedding, the wedding was bound to come to him. At the earliest possible moment Velan brought the girl and her husband and a huge concourse of relatives to the temple. The girl herself seemed to have spoken of Raju as her saviour. She had told everyone, 'He doesn't speak to anyone, but if he looks at you, you are changed.'

His circle was gradually widening. Velan, at the end of his day's agricultural toil, came and sat on the lower step. If Raju spoke, he listened; otherwise he accepted the silence with equal gratitude, got up without a word when darkness fell, and moved away. Gradually, unnoticed, a few others began to arrive very regularly. Raju could not very well question who they were; the river bank was a public place, and he himself was an intruder. They just sat there on the lower step and looked at Raju and kept looking at him. He didn't have to say a word to anyone; he just sat there at the same place, looking away at the river, at the other bank, and tried hard to think where he should go next and what to do. They did not so much as whisper a word for fear that it might disturb him. Raju was beginning to feel uncomfortable on these occasions, and wondered if he could devise some means of escape from their company. Throughout the day he was practically left alone, but late in the evening, after doing their day's work, the villagers would come.

One evening before the company arrived, he moved himself to the back-yard of the temple and hid himself behind a gigantic hibiscus bush full of red flowers. He heard them arrive, heard their voices on the river step. They were talking in low, hushed voices. They went round the building and passed by the hibiscus bush. Raju's heart palpitated as he crouched there like an animal at bay. He held his breath and waited. He was already planning to offer an explanation if they should discover his presence there. He would say that he was in deep thought and that the hibiscus shade was congenial for such contemplation. But fortunately they did not look for him there. They stood near the bush talking in a hushed, awed whisper. Said one, 'Where could he have gone?'

[31]

'He is a big man, he may go anywhere; he may have a thousand things to do.'

'Oh, you don't know. He has renounced the world; he does nothing but meditate. What a pity he is not here today!'

'Just sitting there for a few minutes with him—ah, what a change it has brought about in our household! Do you know, that cousin of mine came round last night and gave me back the promissory note. As long as he held it, I felt as if I had put a knife in his hand for stabbing us.'

'We won't have to fear anything more; it is our good fortune that this great soul should have come to life in our midst.'

'But he has disappeared today. Wonder if he has left us for good.'

'It would be our misfortune if he went away.'

'His clothes are still all there in the hall.'

'He has no fears.'

'The food I brought yesterday has been eaten.'

'Leave there what you have brought now; he is sure to come back from his outing and feel hungry.' Raju felt grateful to this man for his sentiment.

'Do you know sometimes these Yogis can travel to the Himalayas just by a thought?'

'I don't think he is that kind of Yogi,' said another.

'Who can say? Appearances are sometimes misleading,' said someone. They then moved off to their usual seat and sat there. For a long time Raju could hear them talking among themselves. After a while they left. Raju could hear them splashing the water with their feet. 'Let us go before it gets too dark. They say that there is an old crocodile in this part of the river.'

'A boy known to me was held up by his ankle once, at this very spot.'

'What happened, then?'

'He was dragged down, next day . . .'

Raju could hear their voices far off. He cautiously peeped out of his hiding. He could see their shadowy figures on the other bank. He waited till they vanished altogether from sight. He went in and lit a lamp. He was hungry. They had left his food wrapped in a banana leaf on the pedestal of the old stone image. Raju was filled with gratitude and prayed that Velan might never come to the stage of thinking that he was too good for food and that he subsisted on atoms from the air.

Next morning he rose early and went through his ablutions, washed his clothes in the river, lit the stove, made himself coffee, and felt completely at ease with the world. He had to decide on his future today. He should either go back to the town of his birth, bear the giggles and stares for a few days, or go somewhere else. Where could he go? He had not trained himself to make a living out of hard work. Food was coming to him unasked now. If he went away somewhere else certainly nobody was going to take the trouble to bring him food in return for just waiting for it. The only other place where it could happen was the prison. Where could he go now? Nowhere. Cows grazing on the slopes far off gave the place an air of sublime stillness. He realised that he had no alternative: he must play the role that Velan had given him.

With his mind made up he prepared himself to meet Velan and his friends in the evening. He sat as usual on the stone slab with beatitude and calm in his face. The thing that had really bothered him was that he might sound too brilliant in everything he said. He had observed silence as a precaution. But that fear was now gone. He decided to look as brilliant as he

[33]

could manage, let drop gems of thought from his lips, assume all the radiance available, and afford them all the guidance they required without stint. He decided to arrange the stage for the display with more thoroughness. With this view he transferred his seat to the inner hall of the temple. It gave one a better background. He sat there at about the time he expected Velan and others to arrive. He anticipated their arrival with a certain excitement. He composed his features and pose to receive them.

The sun was setting. Its tint touched the wall with pink. The tops of the coconut trees around were aflame. The bird-cries went up in a crescendo before dying down for the night. Darkness fell. Still there was no sign of Velan or anyone. They did not come that night. He was left foodless; that was not the main worry, he still had a few bananas. Suppose they never came again? What was to happen? He became panicky. All night he lay worrying. All his old fears came back. If he returned to the town he would have to get his house back from the man to whom he had mortgaged it. He would have to fight for a living space in his own home or find the cash to redeem it.

He debated whether to step across the river, walk into the village, and search for Velan. It didn't seem a dignified thing to do. It might make him look cheap, and they might ignore him altogether.

He saw a boy grazing his sheep on the opposite bank. He clapped his hands and cried, 'Come here.' He went down the steps and cried across the water, 'I am the new priest of this temple, boy, come here. I have a plantain for you. Come and take it.' He flourished it, feeling that this was perhaps a gamble; it was the last piece of fruit in his store and might presently be gone, as might the boy, and Velan might never know how badly he was wanted, while he, Raju, lay starving there until they found his bleached bones in the temple and added them to the ruins around. With these thoughts he flourished the banana. The boy was attracted by it and soon came across the water. He was short and was wet up to his ears. Raju said, 'Take off your turban and dry yourself, boy.'

'I am not afraid of water,' he said.

'You should not be so wet.'

The boy held out his hand for the plantain and said, 'I can swim. I always swim.'

'But I have never seen you here before,' Raju said.

'I don't come here. I go farther down and swim.'

'Why don't you come here?'

'This is a crocodile place,' he said.

'But I have never seen any crocodile.'

'You will sometime,' the boy said. 'My sheep generally graze over there. I came to see if a man was here.'

'Why?'

'My uncle asked me to watch. He said, "Drive your sheep before that temple and see if a man is there." That is why I came here today.'

Raju gave the boy the banana and said, 'Tell your uncle that the man is back here and tell him to come here this evening.'

He did not wait to ask who the uncle was. Whoever he might be, he was welcome. The boy peeled the plantain, swallowed it whole, and started munching the peel also. 'Why do you eat the peel? It will make you sick,' Raju said.

'No, it won't,' the boy replied. He seemed to be a resolute boy who knew his mind.

Raju vaguely advised, 'You must be a good boy. Now be off. Tell your uncle—'

The boy was off, after cautioning him, 'Keep an eye on those till I get back.' He indicated his flock on the opposite slope.

3

ONE fine day, beyond the tamarind tree, the station building was ready. The steel tracks gleamed in the sun; the signal posts stood with their red and green stripes and their colourful lamps; and our world was neatly divided into this side of the railway line and that side. Everything was ready. All our spare hours were spent in walking along the railway track up to the culvert half a mile away. We paced up and down our platform. A gold mohur sapling was planted in the railway yard. We passed through the corridor, peeping into the room meant for the stationmaster.

One day we were all given a holiday. 'The train comes to our town today,' people said excitedly. The station was decorated with festoons and bunting. A piper was playing, bands were banging away. Coconuts were broken on the railway track, and an engine steamed in, pulling a couple of cars. Many of the important folk of the town were there. The Collector and the Police Superintendent and the Municipal Chairman, and many of the local tradesmen, who flourished green invitation cards in their hands, were assembled at the station. The police guarded the platform and did not allow the crowds in. I felt cheated by this. I felt indignant that anyone should prohibit my entry to the platform. I squeezed myself through the railings at the farthest end, and by the time the engine arrived I was there to receive it. I was probably so small that no one noticed my presence.

Tables were laid and official gentlemen sat around refreshing themselves, and then several men got up and lectured. I was aware only of the word 'Malgudi' recurring in their speeches. There was a clapping of hands. The band struck up, the engine whistled, the bell rang, the guard blew his whistle, and the men who had been consuming refreshments climbed into the train. I was half inclined to follow their example, but there were many policemen to stop me. The train moved and was soon out of sight. A big crowd was now allowed to come on to the platform. My father's shop had record sales that day.

By the time a stationmaster and a porter were installed in their little stone house at the back of the station, facing our house, my father had become so prosperous that he acquired a *jutka* and a horse in order to go to the town and do his shopping.

My mother had been apathetic. 'Why should you have all this additional bother in this household, horse and horse-gram and all that, while the buffalo pair is a sufficient bother?'

He did not answer her in any detail, just swept off her objections with, 'You know nothing about these things, I have so much to do every day in the town. I have to visit the bank so often.' He uttered the word 'bank' with a proud emphasis, but it did not impress my mother.

And so there was an addition of a thatch-roofed shed to our yard, in which a brown pony was tied up, and my father had picked up a groom to look after it. We became the talk of the town with this horse and carriage, but my mother never reconciled herself to it. She viewed it as an extraordinary vanity on my father's part and no amount of explanation from him ever convinced her otherwise. Her view was that my father had overestimated his business, and she nagged him whenever he

[38]

was found at home and the horse and carriage were not put to proper use. She expected him to be always going round the streets in his vehicle. He had not more than an hour's job any day in the town and he always came back in time to attend to his shop, which he was now leaving in charge of a friend for a few hours in the day. My mother was developing into a successful nagger, I suppose, for my father was losing much of his aggressiveness and was becoming very apologetic about his return home whenever the horse and the carriage were left unused under the tamarind tree. 'You take it and go to the market, if you like,' he often said, but my mother spurned the offer, explaining, 'Where should I go every day? Some day it may be useful for going to the temple on a Friday. But ought you to maintain an extravagant turnout all through the year, just for a possible visit to the temple? Horse-gram and grass, do you know what they cost?' Fortunately, it did not prove such a liability after all. Worn out by Mother's persistent opposition, my father seriously considered disposing of the horse and (a fantastic proposal) converting the carriage into a single bullock-cart with a 'bow spring' mounted over the wheel, which a blacksmith of his acquaintance at the market gate had promised to do for him.

The groom who minded the horse laughed at the idea and said that it was an impossible proposition, convincing my father that the blacksmith would reduce the carriage to a piece of furniture fit for lounging under the tamarind tree. 'You could as well listen to a promise to turn the horse into a bullock!' he said, and then he made a proposal which appealed to my father's business instinct. 'Let me ply it for hire in the market. All gram and grass my charge—only let me use your shed. I will hand you two rupees a day and one rupee a month for the use of the shed, and anything I earn over two rupees should be mine.'

This was a delightful solution. My father had the use of the carriage whenever he wanted it, and earned a sum for it each day, and no liabilities. As the days passed, the driver came along and pleaded lack of engagements. A great deal of argument went on in the front part of my house, in semi-darkness, between my father and the driver as my father tried to exact his two rupees. Finally my mother too joined in, saying, 'Don't trust these fellows. Today with all that festival crowd, he says he has not made any money. How can we believe him?'

My mother was convinced that the cart-driver drank his earnings. My father retorted, 'What if he drinks? It is none of our business.'

Every day this went on. Every night the man stood under the tree and cringed and begged for remission. It was evident that he was misappropriating our funds. For within a few weeks the man came and said, 'This horse is growing bony and will not run properly, and is becoming wrong-headed. It is better we sell it off soon and take another, because all the passengers who get into this *jutka* complain and pay less at the end because of the discomfort suffered. And the springs over the wheels must also be changed.' The man was constantly suggesting that the turnout had better be sold off and a new one taken. Whenever he said it within my mother's hearing she lost her temper and shouted at him, saying that one horse and carriage were sufficient expense. This reduced my father to viewing the whole arrangement as a hopeless liability, until the man hinted that he had an offer of seventy rupees for both horse and carriage. My father managed to raise this to seventy-five and finally the man brought the cash and drove off the turnout himself. Evidently he had saved a lot of our own money for this enterprise. Anyway, we were glad to be rid of the thing. This was a nicely calculated transaction, for as soon as the trains began to arrive regularly at our station we found our *jutka* doing a brisk business carrying passengers to the town.

My father was given the privilege of running a shop at the railway station. What a shop it was! It was paved with cement, with shelves built in. It was so spacious that when my father had transferred all the articles from the hut-shop, the place was only one-quarter filled; there were so many blank spaces all along the wall that he felt depressed at the sight of it. For the first time he was beginning to feel that he had not been running a very big business after all.

My mother had come out to watch the operation and taunted him. 'With this stock you think of buying motor-cars and whatnot.' He had not at any time proposed buying a motor-car, but she liked to nag him.

Father said, rather weakly, 'Why drag in all that now?' He was ruminating. 'I shall need at least another five hundred rupees' worth of articles to fill up all this space.'

The stationmaster, an old man wearing a green turban round his head and silver-rimmed spectacles, came along to survey the shop. My father became extremely deferential at the sight of him. Behind him stood Karia the porter in his blue shirt and turban. My mother withdrew unobtrusively and went back home. The stationmaster viewed the shop from a distance with his head on one side as if he were an artist viewing a handiwork. The porter, ever faithful, followed his example, keeping himself in readiness to agree with whatever he might say. The stationmaster said, 'Fill up all that space, otherwise the ATS might come round and ask questions, poking his nose into all our affairs. It has not been easy to give you this shop.'

My father sat me in the shop and went over to the town to make the purchases. 'Don't display too much rice and other stuff—keep the other shop for such things,' advised the stationmaster. 'Railway passengers won't be asking for tamarind and lentils during the journey.' My father implicitly accepted his directions. The stationmaster was his palpable God now and he cheerfully obeyed all his commands. And so presently there hung down from nails in my father's other shop bigger bunches of bananas, stacks of Mempu oranges, huge troughs of fried stuff, and colourful peppermints and sweets in glass containers, loaves of bread, and buns. The display was most appetising, and he had loaded several racks with packets of cigarettes. He had to anticipate the demand of every kind of traveller and provide for it.

He left me in charge of his hut-shop. His old customers came down to gossip and shop, as had been their habit. But they found me unequal to it. I found it tedious to listen to their talk of litigation and irrigation. I was not old enough to appreciate all their problems and the subtleties of their transactions. I listened to them without response, and soon they discovered that I was no good companion for them. They left me in peace and wandered off to the other shop, seeking my father's company. But they found it untenable. They felt strange there. It was too sophisticated a surrounding for them. Very soon, unobtrusively, my father was back in his seat at the hut-shop, leaving me to handle the business in the new shop. As soon as a certain bridge off Malgudi was ready, regular service began on our rails; it was thrilling to watch the activities of the stationmaster and the blue-shirted porter as they 'received' and 'line-cleared' two whole trains each day, the noon train from Madras and the evening one from Trichy. I became very active indeed in the shop. As you might have guessed, all this business expansion in our family helped me achieve a very desirable end—the dropping off of my school unobtrusively.

4

THE banana worked a miracle. The boy went from house to house, announcing that the saint was back at his post. Men, women, and children arrived in a great mass. All that they wanted was to be allowed to look at him and watch the radiance on his face. The children stood around and gazed in awe. Raju tried to manage the situation by pinching a few cheeks and saying some inanities, or even indulging in baby-talk in order to soften the awkwardness of the situation. He went up to young boys and asked, 'What are you studying?' in the manner of big men he had seen in cities. But it was stupid to imitate that question here, because the boys giggled, looked at one another, and said, 'No school for us.'

'What do you do all day?' he asked, without any real interest in their problems.

One of the elders interposed to say, 'We cannot send our boys to the school as you do in towns; they have to take the cattle out for grazing.'

Raju clicked his tongue in disapproval. He shook his head. The gathering looked pained and anxious. Raju explained grandly, 'Boys must read, first. They must, of course, help their parents, but they must also find the time to study.' He added on an inspiration, 'If they cannot find the time to read during the day, why should they not gather in the evenings and learn?'

'Where?' asked someone.

'Maybe here.' Raju added, pointing at the vast hall, 'Maybe you could ask one of your masters. Is there no schoolmaster in your midst?'

'Yes, yes,' several voices cried in unison.

'Ask him to see me,' Raju commanded authoritatively, with the air of a president summoning a defaulting assistant master.

Next afternoon a timid man, who wore a short tuft with a turban over it, turned up at the temple hall. Raju had just finished his repast and was enjoying a siesta in the hall, stretching himself on its cool, granite floor. The timid man stood beside an ancient pillar and cleared his throat. Raju opened his eyes and looked at him blankly. It was not the custom there, in that society, to ask who or why, when so many came and went. Raju flourished an arm to indicate to the other to sit down and resumed his sleep. When he awoke later, he saw the man sitting close to him.

'I'm the teacher,' the man said, and in the muddled state of half-sleep Raju's old fears of schoolteachers returned: he forgot for a split second that he had left all those years behind. He sat up.

The master was rather surprised. He said, 'Don't disturb yourself. I can wait.'

'That's all right,' said Raju, recovering his composure and understanding his surroundings better. 'You are the schoolmaster?' he asked patronisingly. He brooded for a moment, then asked in a general way, 'How is everything?'

The other merely replied, 'No different from what it used to be.'

'How do you like it?'

'What does it matter?' the other said. 'I only try to do my best and do it sincerely.'

'Otherwise, what's the use of doing anything at all?' asked Raju. He was marking time. He was not very clear-headed yet after the deep sleep, and the problem of boys' education was not uppermost in his mind at the moment. He said tentatively, 'After all, one's duty—'

'I do my utmost,' said the other defensively, not wishing to give way. After these parleys, which lasted for half an hour, the village master himself clarified the position. 'It seems you suggested that the boys should be assembled here and taught at nights.'

'Oh! eh!' Raju said. 'Yes, I did, of course, but it's a matter in which the decision should be purely yours. After all, self-help is the best help; I may be here today and gone tomorrow. It's up to you to arrange it. I meant that if you want a place—you can have it.' He swept his arm about with the air of one conferring a gift on a whole community.

The teacher looked thoughtful for a moment and began, 'I'm not sure, however—'

But Raju suddenly became argumentative and definite. He said with a lot of authority, 'I like to see young boys become literate and intelligent.' He added with fervour because it sounded nice, 'It's our duty to make everyone happy and wise.'

This overwhelming altruism was too much for the teacher. 'I'll do anything,' he said, 'under your guidance.' Raju admitted the position with, 'I'm but an instrument accepting guidance myself.'

The result was that the teacher went back to the village a changed man. Next day he was back at the pillared hall with a dozen children of the village. They had their foreheads smeared with sacred ash, and their slates creaked in the silent night,

[46]

while the teacher lectured to them, and Raju, seated on his platform, looked on benignly. The teacher was apologetic about the numbers: he could muster only about a dozen boys. 'They are afraid of crossing the river in the dark; they have heard of a crocodile hereabouts.'

'What can a crocodile do to you if your mind is clear and your conscience is untroubled?' Raju said grandly. It was a wonderful sentiment to express. He was surprised at the amount of wisdom welling from the depths of his being. He said to the teacher, 'Don't be dispirited that there are only a dozen. If you do your work sincerely by a dozen, it'll be equivalent, really, to serving a hundred times that number.'

The teacher suggested, 'Do not mistake me, but will you speak to these boys whenever you can?' This gave Raju a chance to air his views on life and eternity before the boys. He spoke to them on godliness, cleanliness, spoke on Ramayana, the characters in the epics; he addressed them on all kinds of things. He was hypnotised by his own voice; he felt himself growing in stature as he saw the upturned faces of the children shining in the half-light when he spoke. No one was more impressed with the grandeur of the whole thing than Raju himself.

Now that I reflect upon it, I am convinced I was not such a dud after all. It seems to me that we generally do not have a correct measure of our own wisdom. I remember how I was equipping my mind all the time. I read a certain amount of good stuff in my railway-shopkeeping days. I sat in that shop, selling loaves of bread and aerated water. Sometimes schoolboys left their books with me for sale. Though my father thought very highly of our shop, I could not share his view. Selling bread and

[47]

biscuits and accepting money in exchange seemed to me a tame occupation. I always felt that I was too good for the task.

My father died during the rainy part of that year. His end was sudden. He had been selling and talking to his cronies in his hut-shop till late at night; then he counted the cash, came into the house, consumed his rice and buttermilk, laid himself down to sleep, and never woke again.

My mother adjusted herself to the status of a widow. My father left her enough to live on comfortably. I gave her as much of my time as possible. With her consent, I closed down my father's shop and set up at the railway station. It was then that I began to develop new lines. I stocked old magazines and newspapers, and bought and sold schoolbooks. Of course my customers were not many, but the train brought in more and more school-going population, and the 10.30 local was full of young men going off to Albert Mission College, which had just been started at Malgudi. I liked to talk to people. I liked to hear people talk. I liked customers who would not open their mouths merely to put a plantain in, and would say something on any subject except the state of crops, price of commodities, and litigation. I am afraid, after my father's death, his old friends wilted away and disappeared one by one, chiefly for want of an audience.

Students gathered at my shop while they waited for the trains. Gradually books appeared where there were coconuts before. People dumped old books and stolen books and all kinds of printed stuff on me. I bargained hard, showed indifference while buying and solicitude while selling. Strictly speaking, it was an irregular thing to do. But the stationmaster was a friendly man who not only obtained unlimited credit for anything he and his children took from my shop, but also enjoyed the privilege of drawing his reading material from the stack growing in front of my shop.

My bookselling business was an unexpected offshoot of my search for old wrapping-paper. When people bought something I hated to see them carry it off in their hands. I liked to wrap it up nicely, as well as I could, but as long as my father was in control he said, 'If anyone brings a piece of paper, he is welcome to wrap up anything; but I can't do it for him. Profit being what it is, we can't afford to spend it on wrapping-paper. If a man buys oil, let him bring a pot to carry it in. Do we provide him with that?' While he practised this philosophy it was impossible for anyone to find even a scrap of paper in our shop. After his death I adopted a new policy. I made it known far and wide that I was looking for old paper and books, and soon gathered a big dump. In my off-hours I sat sorting it out. During the interval between trains, when the platform became quiet, there was nothing more pleasing than picking up a bundle of assorted books and lounging in my seat and reading, occasionally breaking off to watch through the doorway the immense tamarind tree in the field. I read stuff that interested me, bored me, baffled me, and dozed off in my seat. I read stuff that pricked up a noble thought, a philosophy that appealed, I gazed on pictures of old temples and ruins and new buildings and battleships, and soldiers, and pretty girls around whom my thoughts lingered. I learned much from scrap.

The children were enchanted by the talk they had had in their class from Raju (even their master sat absorbed in open-mouthed wonder). They went home and described the wonders they had been told about. They were impatient to be back on the following evening and listen to more. Very soon the parents joined their children. They explained apologetically, 'Children come home rather late, you see, master, and are afraid to return home, especially crossing the river at night.'

'Excellent, excellent,' Raju said. 'I wanted to suggest it myself. I'm glad you have thought of it. There is no harm. In fact, you may also benefit by keeping your ears open. Keep your ears open and mouth shut, that'll take you far,' he said, hitting upon a brilliant aphorism.

A circle formed around him. They sat there looking on. The children sat there looking on. The master sat there looking on. The pillared hall was bright with the lanterns the villagers had brought with them. It looked like a place where a great assembly was about to begin. Raju felt like an actor who had come on the stage, and, while the audience waited, had no lines to utter or gestures to make. He said to the master, 'I think you may take the children away to their corner for their usual lessons; take one of the lamps with you.'

Even as he said it he could not help thinking how he was issuing an order about the boys who were not his, to the teacher who need not obey him, pointing to a lamp which again was not his. The teacher started to obey him, but the boys lingered on. He said, 'You must read your lessons first and then I will come and speak to you. Now I will first speak to your elders; what I say to them will not interest you.' And the children got up and went away with the teacher to a farther corner of the pillared hall.

Velan ventured to suggest, 'Give us a discourse, sir.' And as Raju listened without showing any emotion, but looking as if he were in deep contemplation, Velan added, 'So that we may have the benefit of your wisdom.' The others murmured a general approval.

Raju felt cornered. 'I have to play the part expected of me; there is no escape.' He racked his head secretly, wondering where to start. Could he speak about tourists' attractions in Malgudi, or should it be moral lessons? How once upon a time there was a so-and-so, so good or bad that when he came to do such-and-such a thing he felt so utterly lost that he prayed, and so on and so forth? He felt bored. The only subject on which he could speak with any authority now seemed to be jail life and its benefits, especially for one mistaken for a saint. They waited respectfully for his inspiration. 'Oh, fools,' he felt like crying out, 'why don't you leave me alone? If you bring me food, leave it there and leave me in peace, thank you.'

After a long, brooding silence, he brought out the following words: 'All things have to wait their hour.' Velan and his friends who were in the front row looked worried for a moment; they were deferential, no doubt, but they did not quite realise what he was driving at. After a further pause, he added grandiosely, 'I will speak to you when another day comes.'

Someone asked, 'Why another day, sir?'

'Because it is so,' said Raju mysteriously. 'While you wait for the children to finish their lessons, I'd advise you to pass the hour brooding over all your speech and actions from morning till now.'

'What speech and actions?' someone asked, genuinely puzzled by the advice.

'Your own,' said Raju. 'Recollect and reflect upon every word you have uttered since daybreak—'

'I don't remember exactly . . .'

'Well, that is why I say reflect, recollect. When you don't remember your own words properly, how are you going to remember other people's words?' This quip amused his audience. There were bursts of subdued laughter. When the laughter subsided Raju said, 'I want you all to think independently, of your own accord, and not allow yourselves to be led about by the nose as if you were cattle.'

There were murmurs of polite disagreement over this advice. Velan asked, 'How can we do that, sir? We dig the land and mind the cattle—so far so good, but how can we think philosophies? Not our line, master. It is not possible. It is wise persons like your good self who should think for us.'

'And why do you ask us to recollect all that we have said since daybreak?'

Raju himself was not certain why he had advised that, and so he added, 'If you do it you will know why.' The essence of sainthood seemed to lie in one's ability to utter mystifying statements. 'Until you try, how can you know what you can or cannot do?' he asked. He was dragging those innocent men deeper and deeper into the bog of unclear thoughts.

'I can't remember what I said a few moments ago; so many other things come into one's head,' wailed one of his victims.

'Precisely. That is what I wish to see you get over,' said Raju. 'Until you do it, you will not know the pleasure of it.' He picked out three men from the gathering. 'When you come to me tomorrow or another day, you must each repeat to me at least six words that you have been speaking since the morning. I am asking you to remember only six words,' he said pleadingly as a man who was making a great concession, 'not six hundred.'

'Six hundred! Is there anyone who can remember six hundred, sir?' asked someone with wonder.

'Well, I can,' said Raju. And he got the appreciative clicking of tongues which he expected as his legitimate due. Soon the

[52]

children were there, a great boon to Raju, who rose from his seat as if to say, 'That is all for the day,' and walked towards the river, the others following. 'These children must be feeling sleepy. Take them safely home, and come again.'

When the assembly met next, he provided it with a specific programme. He beat a soft rhythm with his hands and chanted a holy song with a refrain that could be repeated by his audience. The ancient ceiling echoed with the voices of men, women, and children repeating sacred texts in unison. Someone had brought in tall bronze lamps and lit them. Others fed them with oil; others had spent a whole day twisting bits of cotton into wicks for the lamps. People brought of their own accord little framed pictures of gods and hung them on the pillars. Very soon women started to come in batches during the day to wash the floor and decorate it with patterns in coloured flour; they hung up flowers and greenery and festoons everywhere. The pillared hall was transformed. Someone had also covered the platform in the middle of the hall with a soft, coloured carpet; mats were rolled out for the assembly to sit on.

Raju soon realised that his spiritual status would be enhanced if he grew a beard and long hair to fall on his nape. A clean-shaven, close-haired saint was an anomaly. He bore the various stages of his make-up with fortitude, not minding the prickly phase he had to pass through before a well-authenticated beard could cover his face and come down his chest. By the time he arrived at the stage of stroking his beard thoughtfully, his prestige had grown beyond his wildest dreams. His life had lost its personal limitations; his gatherings had become so large that they overflowed into the outer corridors and people sat right up to the river's edge.

With the exception of Velan and a few others, Raju never bothered to remember faces or names or even to know to whom he was talking. He seemed to belong to the world now. His influence was unlimited. He not only chanted holy verses and discoursed on philosophy, he even came to the stage of prescribing medicine; children who would not sleep peacefully at night were brought to him by their mothers; he pressed their bellies and prescribed a herb, adding, 'If he still gets no relief, bring him again to me.' It was believed that when he stroked the head of a child, the child improved in various ways. Of course, people brought him their disputes and quarrels over the division of ancestral property. He had to set apart several hours of his afternoon for these activities. He could hardly afford a private life now. There came a stage when he had to be up early and rush through all his own personal routine before his visitors should arrive. It was a strain. He sighed a deep sigh of relief and longed to be himself, eat like an ordinary human being, shout and sleep like a normal man, after the voices on the river had ceased for the night.

5

I CAME to be called Railway Raju. Perfect strangers, having heard of my name, began to ask for me when their train arrived at the Malgudi railway station. It is written on the brow of some that they shall not be left alone. I am one such, I think. Although I never looked for acquaintances, they somehow came looking for me. Men who had just arrived always stopped at my shop for a soda or cigarettes and to go through the book stack, and almost always they asked, 'How far is . . .?' or 'Are there many historical spots here?' or 'I heard that your River Sarayu has its source somewhere on those hills and that it is a beauty spot.' This sort of inquiry soon led me to think that I had not given sufficient thought to the subject. I never said, 'I don't know.' Not in my nature, I suppose. If I had had the inclination to say, 'I don't know what you are talking about,' my life would have taken a different turn. Instead, I said, 'Oh, yes, a fascinating place. Haven't you seen it? You must find the time to visit it, otherwise your whole trip here would be a waste.' I am sorry I said it, an utter piece of falsehood. It was not because I wanted to utter a falsehood, but only because I wanted to be pleasant.

Naturally, they asked me the way. I said, 'If you just go that way down to the Market Square and ask one of those taxi-drivers . . .' This was not a very satisfactory direction. Soon a man wanted me to show him the way to the Market Square and the taxi. There was a young son of the porter doing points-

[55]

signalling duty whenever a train was about to arrive, who had
no specified work to do at other times. I asked the young fellow
to mind the shop while I helped the traveller to find a taxi.

At the market fountain stood the old shark Gaffur, looking
for a victim. He made a speciality of collecting all the derelict
vehicles in the country and rigging them up; he breathed new
life into them and ran them on the mountain roads and into the
forests. His usual seat was on the parapet of the fountain,
while his car basked on the roadside beside the gutter. 'Gaffur,'
I called out. 'Here is a very good gentleman, a friend of mine.
He wants to see . . . You must take him out and bring him back
safely—that is why I have brought him to you personally,
although this is not an hour when I should be away from my
shop.' We haggled over the prices; I allowed the customer to
mention his figure and always tried to beat Gaffur down to it.
When he demurred at the sight of the vehicle, I took up
Gaffur's brief and explained, 'Gaffur is no fool to have this kind
of car. He searched far and wide to find this particular model;
this is the only car which can go up to all those places where in
some parts there are no roads at all, but Gaffur will take you
there and bring you back in time for dinner tonight. Can't you,
Gaffur?'

'Well,' he drawled, 'it is seventy miles each way; it is one
o'clock now. If we leave at once and if there are no punctures
on the way . . .' But I hustled him so much that Gaffur never
really completed his sentence. When they returned it could
not exactly be called dinner-time, unless you stretched it to
include midnight, but Gaffur did bring him back intact,
honked his car to wake me up, took his cash, and departed.
The next train for the man would be at eight on the following
morning. He had to stretch himself under the awning on the

platform of my shop and spend the night thus. If he felt hungry, I opened my store and sold him fruits and such things. Travellers are an enthusiastic lot. They do not mind any inconvenience as long as they have something to see. Why anyone should want to forgo food and comfort and jolt a hundred-odd miles to see some place, I could never understand, but it was not my business to ask for reasons; just as I did not mind what people ate or smoked in my shop, my business being only to provide the supply and nothing more. It seemed to me silly to go a hundred miles to see the source of Sarayu when it had taken the trouble to tumble down the mountain and come to our door. I had not even heard of its source till that moment; but the man who had gone was all praise for the spot. He said, 'I am only sorry I did not bring my wife and mother to see the place.' Later in life I found that everyone who saw an interesting spot always regretted that he hadn't come with his wife or daughter, and spoke as if he had cheated someone out of a nice thing in life. Later, when I had become a full-blown tourist guide, I often succeeded in inducing a sort of melancholia in my customer by remarking, 'This is something that should be enjoyed by the whole family,' and the man would swear that he would be back with his entire brood in the coming season.

The man who had gone to the source of the river spoke all night about it: how there was a small shrine on the peak right at the basin. 'It must be the source of Sarayu mentioned in the mythological stories of goddess Parvathi jumping into the fire; the carving on one of the pillars of the shrine actually shows the goddess plunging into the fire and water arising from the spot,' et cetera. Sometimes someone with a scholarly turn of mind would come and make a few additions to the facts, such as that the dome of the shrine must have been built in the third century before Christ or that the style of drapery indicated the third century after Christ. But it was all the same to me, and the age I ascribed to any particular place depended upon my mood at that hour and the type of person I was escorting. If he was the academic type I was careful to avoid all mention of facts and figures and to confine myself to general descriptions, letting the man himself do the talking. You may be sure he enjoyed the opportunity. On the other hand, if an innocent man happened to be at hand, I let myself go freely. I pointed out to him something as the greatest, the highest, the only one in the world. I gave statistics out of my head. I mentioned a relic as belonging to the thirteenth century before Christ or the thirteenth century after Christ, according to the mood of the hour. If I felt fatigued or bored with the person I was conducting, I sometimes knocked the whole glamour out by saying, 'Must be something built within the last twenty years and allowed to go to rack and ruin. There are scores of such spots all over the place.' But it was years before I could arrive at that stage of confidence and nonchalance.

The porter's son sat in the shop all day. I spent a little time each night to check the cash and stock. There was no definite arrangement about what he should be paid for his trouble. I gave him a little money now and then. Only my mother protested. 'Why do you want him to work for you, Raju? Either give him a definite commission or do it yourself instead of all this wandering in the country. What good does it do you, anyway?'

'You don't know, Mother,' I said, eating my late dinner. 'This is a far better job I am doing than the other one. I am seeing a lot of places and getting paid for it; I go with them in

their car or bus, talk to them, I am treated to their food sometimes, and I get paid for it. Do you know how well known I
am? People come asking for me from Bombay, Madras, and
other places, hundreds of miles away. They call me Railway
Raju and have told me that even in Lucknow there are persons
who are familiar with my name. It is something to become so
famous, isn't it, instead of handing out matches and tobacco?'
   'Well, wasn't it good enough for your father?'
   'I don't say anything against it. I will look after the shop
also.' This pleased the old lady. Occasionally she threw in a
word about her brother's daughter in the village before blowing
out the lamp. She was always hoping that some day I would
consent to marry the girl, though she never directly said so.
'Do you know Lalitha has got a prize in her school? I had a
letter from my brother today about it.'

Even as the train steamed in at the outer signal, I could scent a
customer. I had a kind of water-diviner's instinct. If I felt the
pull of good business I drifted in the direction of the coming
train; I could stand exactly where a prospective tourist would
alight and look for me: it was not only the camera or binoculars
slung on a shoulder that indicated to me the presence of a
customer; even without any of that I could spot him. If you
found me straying away in the direction of the barrier while
the engine was still running through the lines onto the platform
you might be sure that there was no customer for me on the
train. In a few months I was a seasoned guide. I had viewed
myself as an amateur guide and a professional shopman, but
now gradually I began to think of myself as a part-time shopkeeper and a full-time tourist guide. Even when I had no
tourist to guide I did not go back to my shop, but to Gaffur on

the fountain parapet, and listened to his talk about derelict automobiles.

I had classified all my patrons. They were very varied, I can tell you. Some were passionate photographers; these men could never look at any object except through their view-finders. The moment they got down from the train, even before lifting their baggage, they asked, 'Is there a place where they develop films?'

'Of course, Malgudi Photo Bureau. One of the biggest . . .'

'And if I want roll-films? I have, of course, enough stock with me, but if I run out . . . Do you think super-panchro three-colour something-or-other is available there?'

'Of course. That's his special line.'

'Will he develop and show me a print while I wait?'

'Of course, before you count twenty. He is a wizard.'

'That is nice. Now, where are you going to take me first?'

These were routine questions from a routine type. I had all the satisfactory answers ready. I generally took time to answer the latter question as to where I was going to take him first. It depended. I awaited the receipt of certain data before venturing to answer. The data were how much time and money he was going to spend. Malgudi and its surroundings were my special show. I could let a man have a peep at it or a whole panorama. It was adjustable. I could give them a glimpse of a few hours or soak them in mountain and river scenery or archaeology for a whole week. I could not really decide how much to give or withhold until I knew how much cash the man carried or, if he carried a cheque-book, how good it was. This was another delicate point. Sometimes a traveller offered to write a cheque for this man or that, and, of course, our Gaffur or the photo store or the keeper of the forest bungalow on top of the Mempi

Hills would not trust a stranger enough to accept his cheque. I had to put off such an offer with the utmost delicacy by saying, 'Oh, the banking system in our town is probably the worst you can think of. Sometimes they take twenty days to realise a cheque, but these poor fellows, how can they wait?'—rather a startling thing to say, but I didn't care if the banking reputation of our town suffered.

As soon as a tourist arrived, I observed how he dealt with his baggage, whether he engaged a porter at all or preferred to hook a finger to each piece. I had to note all this within a split second, and then, outside, whether he walked to the hotel or called a taxi or haggled with the one-horse *jutka*. Of course, I undertook all this on his behalf, but always with detachment. I did all this for him simply for the reason that he asked for Railway Raju the moment he stepped down on the platform and I knew he came with good references, whether he came from north or south or far or near. And at the hotel it was my business to provide him with the best room or the worst room, just as he might prefer. Those who took the cheapest dormitory said, 'After all, it's only for sleeping, I am going to be out the whole day. Why waste money on a room which is anyway going to be locked up all day? Don't you agree?'

'Surely, yes, yes.' I nodded, still without giving an answer to 'Where are you going to take me first?' I might still be said to be keeping the man under probation, under careful scrutiny. I never made any suggestion yet. No use expecting a man to be clear-headed who is fresh from a train journey. He must wash, change his clothes, refresh himself with *idli* and coffee, and only then can we expect anyone in South India to think clearly on all matters of this world and the next. If he offered me any refreshment, I understood that he was a comparatively liberal sort, but did not accept it until we were a little further gone in friendship. In due course, I asked him point-blank, 'How much time do you hope to spend in this town?'

'Three days at the most. Could we manage everything within the time?'

'Certainly, although it all depends upon what you most wish to see.' And then I put him in the confessional, so to speak. I tried to draw out his interests. Malgudi, I said, had many things to offer, historically, scenically, from the point of view of modern developments, and so on and so forth; or if one came as a pilgrim I could take him to a dozen temples all over the district within a radius of fifty miles; I could find holy waters for him to bathe in all along the course of the Sarayu, starting, of course, with its source on Mempi Peaks.

One thing I learned in my career as a tourist guide was that no two persons were interested in the same thing. Tastes, as in food, differ also in sightseeing. Some people want to be seeing a waterfall, some want a ruin (oh, they grow ecstatic when they see cracked plaster, broken idols, and crumbling bricks), some want a god to worship, some look for a hydro-electric plant, and some want just a nice place, such as the bungalow on top of Mempi with all-glass sides, from where you could see a hundred miles and observe wild game prowling around. Of those again there were two types, one the poet who was content to watch and return, and the other who wanted to admire nature and also get drunk there. I don't know why it is so: a fine poetic spot like the Mempi Peak House excites in certain natures unexpected reactions. I know some who brought women there; a quiet, wooded spot looking over a valley one would think fit for contemplation or poetry, but it only acted as an aphrodisiac. Well, it was not my business to comment. My

[62]

business stopped with taking them there, and to see that Gaffur went back to pick them up at the right time.

I was sort of scared of the man who acted as my examiner, who had a complete list of all the sights and insisted on his money's worth. 'What is the population of this town?' 'What is the area?' 'Don't bluff. I know when exactly that was built —it is not second-century but the twelfth.' Or he told me the correct pronunciation of words. 'R-o-u-t is not . . .' I was meek, self-effacing in his presence and accepted his corrections with gratitude, and he always ended up by asking, 'What is the use of your calling yourself a guide if you do not know . . .?' et cetera, et cetera.

You may well ask what I made out of all this? Well, there is no fixed answer to it. It depended upon the circumstances and the types of people I was escorting. I generally specified ten rupees as the minimum for the pleasure of my company, and a little more if I had to escort them far; over all this Gaffur, the photo store, the hotel manager, and whoever I introduced a customer to expressed their appreciation, according to a certain schedule. I learned while I taught and earned while I learned, and the whole thing was most enjoyable.

There were special occasions, such as the trapping of an elephant herd. During the winter months the men of the Forest Department put through an elaborate scheme for trapping elephants. They watched, encircled, and drove a whole herd into stockades, and people turned up in great numbers to watch the operation. On the day fixed for the drive, people poured in from all over the country and applied to me for a ringside seat in the spacious bamboo jungles of Mempi. I was supposed to have special influence with the men who were in charge of the drive: it meant several advance

[63]

trips to the forest camp, and doing little services for the officials by fetching whatever they required from the town, and when the time came to arrange for the viewing of the elephant-drive only those who came with me were allowed to pass through the gates of the special enclosures. It kept all of us happy and busy and well-paid. I escorted visitors in bunches and went hoarse repeating, 'You see, the wild herd is watched for months . . .' and so forth. Don't imagine that I cared for elephants personally; anything that interested my tourists was also my interest. The question of my own preferences was secondary. If someone wanted to see a tiger or shoot one, I knew where to arrange it: I arranged for the lamb to bait the tiger, and had high platforms built so that the brave hunters might pop off the poor beast when it came to eat the lamb, although I never liked to see either the lamb or the tiger die. If someone wanted to see a king cobra spread out its immense hood, I knew the man who could provide the show.

There was a girl who had come all the way from Madras and who asked the moment she set foot in Malgudi, 'Can you show me a cobra—a king cobra it must be—which can dance to the music of a flute?'

'Why?' I asked.

'I'd like to see one. That's all,' she said.

Her husband said, 'We have other things to think of, Rosie. This can wait.'

'I'm not asking this gentleman to produce it at once. I am not demanding it. I'm just mentioning it, that's all.'

'If it interests you, you can make your own arrangements. Don't expect me to go with you. I can't stand the sight of a snake; your interests are morbid.'

I disliked this man. He was taunting such a divine creature.

[64]

My sympathies were all for the girl; she was so lovely and elegant. After she arrived I discarded my khaki bush-coat and *dhoti* and took the trouble to make myself presentable. I wore a silk *jibba* and lace *dhoti* and groomed myself so well that my mother remarked when she saw me leave the house, 'Ah, like a bridegroom!' and Gaffur winked and said many an insinuating thing when I went to meet them at the hotel.

Her arrival had been a sort of surprise for me. The man was the first to appear. I had put him up at the Anand Bhavan Hotel. After a day of sightseeing he suddenly said one afternoon, 'I must meet the Madras train. Another person is coming.'

He didn't even stop to ask me what time the train would arrive. He seemed to know everything beforehand. He was a very strange man, who did not always care to explain what he was doing. If he had warned me that he was going to meet such an elegant creature at our station I should perhaps have decorated myself appropriately. As it was, I wore my usual khaki bush-coat and *dhoti*, a horrible unprepossessing combination at any time, but the most sensible and convenient for my type of work. The moment she got down from the train I wished I had hidden myself somewhere. She was not very glamorous, if that is what you expect, but she did have a figure, a slight and slender one, beautifully fashioned, eyes that sparkled, a complexion not white, but dusky, which made her only half visible—as if you saw her through a film of tender coconut juice. Forgive me if you find me waxing poetic. I gave some excuse and sent them off to the hotel, and stayed back to run home and tidy up my appearance.

I conducted a brief research with the help of Gaffur. He took me to a man in Ellaman Street, who had a cousin working in the

[65]

municipal office said to know a charmer with a king cobra. I carried on the investigation while I left the visitor to decipher episodes from Ramayan carved on the stone wall in Iswara Temple in North Extension—there were hundreds of minute carvings all along the wall. They kept the man fully occupied as he stooped and tried to study each bit. I knew all those panels and could repeat their order blindfolded, but he spared me the labour, he knew all about it.

When I returned from my brief investigation, I found the girl standing apart with every sign of boredom in her face. I suggested, 'If you can come out for an hour, I can show you a cobra.'

She looked delighted. She tapped the man on the shoulder as he was stooping over the frieze and asked, 'How long do you want to be here?'

'At least two hours,' he said without turning.

'I'll go out for a while,' she said.

'Please yourself,' he said. Then to me, 'Go to the hotel direct. I'll find my way back.'

We picked up our guide at the municipal office. The car rolled along the sand, crossed the stretch at Nallappa's grove, and climbed the opposite bank, the entire route carved by the wheels of wooden bullock-carts. Gaffur looked sourly at the man sitting by his side. 'Do you want me to reduce this to a bullock-cart, dragging us about these places? Where are we going? I see no other place than the cremation ground there,' he said, pointing at the smoke above a forlorn, walled area on the other side of the river. I didn't like such inauspicious words to be uttered before the angel in the back seat. I tried to cover them up hastily by saying something else aloud.

We arrived at a group of huts on the other side of the river.

[66]

Many heads peeped out of the huts as soon as our car stopped, and a few bare-bodied children came and stood around the car, gaping at the occupants. Our guide jumped out and went at a trot to the farthest end of the village street and returned with a man who had a red turban around his head, his only other piece of clothing being a pair of drawers.

'This man has a king cobra?' I looked him up and down and said hesitantly, 'Let me see it.'

At which the young boys said, 'He has a very big one in his house; it is true.' And I asked the lady, 'Shall we go and see it?'

We set off. Gaffur said, 'I'll stay here, otherwise these monkeys will make short work of this automobile.'

I let the other two go forward and whispered to Gaffur, 'Why are you in such a bad mood today, Gaffur? After all, you have gone over worse roads and never complained!'

'I have new springs and shock-absorbers. You know what they cost?'

'Oh, you will recover their cost soon; be cheerful.'

'What some of our passengers need is a tractor and not a motor-car. That fellow!' He was vaguely discontented. I knew his wrath was not against us, but against our guide, because he said, 'I think it will be good to make him walk back to the town. Why should anyone want to come so far to see a reptile?' I left him alone; it was no use trying to make him cheerful. Perhaps his wife had nagged him when he started out.

The girl stood under the shade of a tree while the man prodded a snake to make it come out of its basket. It was fairly large, and hissed and spread out its hood, while the boys screamed and ran off and returned. The man shouted at them, 'If you excite it, it will chase you all!'

I told the boys to keep quiet, and asked the man, 'You are sure you will not let it slip through?'

The girl suggested, 'You must play on the flute, make it rear its head and dance.' The man pulled out his gourd flute and played on it shrilly, and the cobra raised itself and darted hither and thither and swayed. The whole thing repelled me, but it seemed to fascinate the girl. She watched it swaying with the raptest attention. She stretched out her arm slightly and swayed it in imitation of the movement; she swayed her whole body to the rhythm—for just a second, but that was sufficient to tell me what she was, the greatest dancer of the century.

It was nearly seven in the evening when we got back to the hotel. As soon as she got down, she paused to murmur a 'Thanks' to no one in particular and went up the staircase. Her husband, waiting at the porch, said, 'That's all for the day. You could give me a consolidated account, I suppose, later. I shall want the car at ten o'clock tomorrow.' He turned and went back to his room.

I felt annoyed with him at this stage. What did he take me for? This fellow, telling me that he wanted the car at this hour or that hour. Did he think that I was a tout? It made me very angry, but the fact was that I really was a tout, having no better business than hanging around between Gaffur and a snake-charmer and a tourist and doing all kinds of things. The man did not even care to tell me anything about himself, or where he wanted to go on the following morning; an extraordinary fellow!

A hateful fellow. I had never hated any customer so much before. I told Gaffur as we were driving back, 'Tomorrow morning! He asks for the car as if it were his grandfather's property! Any idea where he wants to go?'

'Why should I bother about it? If he wants the car he can have it if he pays for it. That is all. I don't care who pays for a thing as long as they engage me . . .' He rambled on into a personal philosophy which I didn't care to follow.

My mother waited for me as usual. While serving me food she said, 'Where have you been today? What are the things you have done today?'

I told her about the visit to the snake-charmer. She said, 'They are probably from Burma, people who worship snakes.' She said, 'I had a cousin living in Burma once and he told me about the snake women there.'

'Don't talk nonsense, Mother. She is a good girl, not a snake-worshipper. She is a dancer, I think.'

'Oh, dancer! Maybe, but don't have anything to do with these dancing women. They are all a bad sort.' I ate my food in silence, trying to revive in my mind the girl's scent-filled presence.

At ten next day I was at the hotel. Gaffur's car was already at the porch; he cried, 'Aha! again,' at the sight of me. 'Big man! Hm, trying improvements!' His idiom was still as if he spoke of automobiles. He winked at me.

I ignored everything and asked in a businesslike manner, 'Are they in?'

'I suppose so. They have not come out yet, that's all I know,' said Gaffur. Twenty words where one would do. Something was wrong with him. He was becoming loquacious. And then I felt a sudden stab of jealousy as I realised that perhaps he too had been affected by the presence of the damsel and was desirous of showing off in her presence. I grew jealous and unhappy and said to myself, 'If this is how Gaffur is going to conduct himself in the future, I shall get rid of him and find someone else, that's all.' I had no use for a loquacious, nose-poking taxi-driver.

I went upstairs to Room 28 on the second floor of the hotel and knocked authoritatively. 'Wait,' said the voice from inside. It was the man's, not the girl's as I had hoped. I waited for a few minutes and fretted. I looked at my watch. Ten o'clock. And this man said, 'Wait.' Was he still in bed with her? It was a fit occasion, as it seemed to me, to tear the door down and go in. The door opened, and he came out, dressed and ready. He shut the door behind him. I was aghast. I was on the point of demanding, 'What about her?' But I checked my impulse. I went sheepishly down with him.

He gave me a look of approval, as if I had dressed to please *him*. Before getting into the car he said, 'Today I want to study those friezes again for a short while.'

'All right, all right,' I thought, 'study the friezes or whatever else you like. Why do you want me for that?'

As if in answer to my thoughts, he said, 'After that—' He took out of his pocket a piece of paper and read.

This man would go on wall-gazing all his life and leave her to languish in her hotel room. Strange man! Why did he not bring her along with him? Probably he was absent-minded. I asked, 'Is no one else coming?'

'No,' he replied curtly, as if understanding my mind. He looked at the paper in his hand and asked, 'Are you aware of the existence of cave-paintings in these parts?'

I laughed off the question. 'Of course, everyone does not have the taste to visit places like that, but there have been a few discriminating visitors who insisted on seeing them. But—but —it will take a whole day, and we may not be able to get back tonight.'

He went back to his room, returned after a few minutes with a downcast face. Meanwhile I, with Gaffur's help, calculated the expense involved in the trip. We knew that the path lay past the Peak House forest bungalow. One would have to halt there for the night and walk down a couple of miles. I knew where the caves were, but this was the first time I was going to set eyes on them. Malgudi seemed to unroll a new sightseeing place each time.

The man sat back in the car and said, 'You have probably no notion how to deal with women, have you?'

I was pleased that he was becoming more human in his approach. I said, 'I have no idea,' and laughed, thinking it might please him if I seemed to enjoy his joke. Then I made bold to ask, 'What is the trouble?' My new dress and deportment gave me a new courage. In my khaki bush-coat I would not have dared to take a seat beside him or talk to him in this way.

He looked at me with what seemed a friendly smile. He leaned over and said, 'If a man has to have peace of mind it is best that he forget the fair sex.' This was the first time in our association of three days that he had talked to me so freely. He had always been curt and taciturn. I judged that the situation must be pretty grave if it unloosened his tongue to this extent.

Gaffur sat in his seat with his chin in his hand. He was looking away from us. His whole attitude said, 'I am sorry to be wasting my morning with such time-killers as you two.' A courageous idea was developing in my head. If it succeeded it would lead to a triumphant end, if it failed the man might kick me out of his sight or call the police. I said, 'Shall I go and try on your behalf?'

'Would you?' he asked, brightening up. 'Go ahead, if you are bold enough.'

I didn't wait to hear further. I jumped out of the car and went up the steps four at a time. I paused at Number 28 to regain normal breath, and knocked.

'Don't trouble me, I don't want to come with you. Leave me alone,' came the girl's voice from within.

I hesitated, wondering how to speak. This was my first independent speech with the divine creature. I might either make a fool of myself or win the heavens. How should I announce myself? Would she know my famous name? I said, 'It's not he, but me.'

'What?' asked the sweet voice, puzzled and irritated.

I repeated, 'It is not him, but me. Don't you know my voice? Didn't I come with you yesterday to that cobra man? All night I didn't sleep,' I added, lowering my voice, and whispered through a chink in the door, 'The way you danced, your form and figure haunted me all night.'

Hardly had I finished my sentence when the door half opened and she looked at me. 'Oh, you!' she said, her eyes lighting up with understanding.

'My name is Raju,' I said.

She scrutinised me thoroughly. 'Of course, I know you.' I smiled affably, my best smile, as if I had been asked for it by a photographer. She said, 'Where is he?'

'Waiting in the car for you. Won't you get ready and come out?' She looked dishevelled, her eyes were red with recent tears, and she wore a faded cotton sari; no paint or perfume, but I was prepared to accept her as she was. I told her, 'You may come out as you are and no one will mind it.' And I added, 'Who would decorate a rainbow?'

[72]

She said, 'You think you can please me by all this? You think you can persuade me to change my mind?'

'Yes,' I said. 'Why not?'

'Why do you want me to go out with him? Leave me in peace,' she said, opening her eyes wide, which gave me another opportunity to whisper close to her face, 'Because life is so blank without your presence.'

She could have pushed my face back, crying 'How dare you talk like this!' and shut the door on me. But she didn't. She merely said, 'I never knew you would be such a troublesome man. Wait a minute, then.' She withdrew into her room. I wanted to cry with all my being, 'Let me in,' and bang on the door, but I had the good sense to restrain myself. I heard footsteps and saw that her husband had come to see the results.

'Well, is she coming or not? I am not prepared to waste all—'

'Hush,' I said. 'She will be out in a moment. Please go back to the car.'

'Really!' he muttered in amazement. 'You are a wizard!' He noiselessly turned and went back to his car. Presently the lady did come out like a vision, and said, 'Let us go. But for you I would have given you all a few surprises.'

'What?'

'I would have taken the next train home.'

'We are going to a wonderful spot. Please be your usual sweet self, for my sake.'

'All right,' she said and went down the steps; I followed. She opened the door of the car, went straight in, and took her seat, as her husband edged away to make space for her. I came over to the other side and sat down beside him. I was not prepared to go and sit down beside Gaffur at this stage.

[73]

Gaffur now turned his head to ask whether we might go. 'We cannot return tonight if we are going to the Peak House.'

'Let us try and come back,' the man pleaded.

'We will try, but there is no harm in being prepared to stay over if necessary. Take a change of clothing. No harm in it. I am asking Gaffur to stop at my house.'

The lady said, 'Just a minute, please.' She dashed upstairs and returned with a small suitcase. She said to the man, 'I have your clothes too in this.'

The man said, 'Very good,' and smiled, and she smiled and in the laughter the tension of the morning partly disappeared. Still, there was some uneasiness in the air.

I asked Gaffur to pull up at the railway station for a moment, the car facing away from my house. I didn't want them to see my house. 'Just a moment, please.' I dashed out. Directly the shop-boy sighted me he opened his mouth to say something. I ignored him, dashed up to my house, picked up a bag, and ran out, saying, 'I may stay out tonight. Don't wait,' to my mother in the kitchen.

We reached the Peak House at about four in the afternoon. The caretaker was delighted to see us. He was often rewarded by me unstintingly with my clients' money. I always made it a point to tell my clients beforehand, 'Keep that caretaker in good humour and he'll look after you and procure for you even the most impossible articles.' I repeated the formula now and the husband—he shall be referred to as Marco henceforth—said, 'Go ahead and do it. I look to you to help us through. You know I have only one principle in life. I don't want to be bothered with small things. I don't mind the expense.'

I told Joseph, the caretaker, to get us food and foodstuffs

from his village, two miles away. I asked Marco, 'Will you leave some cash with me? I'll render accounts later. I need not worry you again and again for small payments.'

One could not foresee how he would react to such a request. He was unsteady—sometimes he announced aloud his indifference to money, next minute he'd suddenly show every symptom of miserliness and behave like an auditor, but ultimately he'd pay for everything if, as I discovered, he got a voucher for payments. He would not yield an anna without a voucher, whereas if you gave him a slip of paper you could probably get him to write off his entire fortune.

Now I knew the trick. As I found him stumbling for words, I said, 'I'll see that you get proper receipts for every payment.' It pleased him; he opened his purse.

I had to dispose of the taxi. Gaffur would come back on the following afternoon. I made Gaffur sign a receipt, and gave some money to Joseph to fetch us food from a hotel in the village. Now that I was in charge of the arrangements, I had not much time to gaze on my beloved's face, although I was darting glances in her direction.

'The caves are a mile off, down that way,' Joseph said. 'We can't go there now. Tomorrow morning. If you leave after breakfast, you can come back for lunch.'

The Peak House was perched on the topmost cliff on Mempi Hills—the road ended with the house; there was a glass wall covering the north veranda, through which you could view the horizon a hundred miles away. Below us the jungle stretched away down to the valley, and on a clear day you might see also the Sarayu sparkling in the sun and pursuing its own course far away. This was like heaven to those who loved wild surroundings and to watch the game, which prowled outside

[75]

the glass wall at nights. The girl was in ecstasy. Our house was surrounded with rich vegetation. She ran like a child from plant to plant with cries of joy, while the man looked on with no emotion. Anything that interested her seemed to irritate him.

She suddenly halted, gazing on the sun-bathed plains thousands of feet below. I feared that when night came on she might get scared. We heard the jackals howling, and all kinds of grunts and roars. Joseph brought a hamper of food for us and left it on a table. He brought milk, coffee, and sugar, for the morning, and showed me where the coal stove was.

The lady cried, 'Nobody should get up till I call. I'll have coffee ready for everyone.'

Joseph said, 'Please lock the door inside,' and added, 'If you sit up on that veranda, you can watch tigers and other animals prowling about. But you must not make any noise; that's the secret of it.' We watched Joseph pick up a lantern and go down the steps; we could see his lantern faintly light the foliage on the way and disappear.

'Poor Joseph, how bold of him to go down alone!' the girl said, at which the husband replied casually, 'Nothing surprising. He has probably been born and bred here. Do you know him?' he asked, turning to me.

'Yes; he was born in that village and came to mind this place as a boy. He must be at least sixty years old.'

'How has he come to be a Christian?'

'There was a mission somewhere here; missionaries go and settle down in all sorts of places, you know,' I said.

Joseph had given us two lamps, brass ones filled with kerosene. One I kept on the kitchen table, and the other I gave the man for his room, leaving the rest of the building in darkness. Outside through the glass we could see the stars in the sky.

[76]

We sat around the table. I knew where the plates were. I set them on the table and served food—or, rather, attempted to serve food. It was about seven-thirty in the evening. We had seen a gorgeous sunset. We had seen the purple play of colour in the northern skies after that, and admired it; we saw the tops of the trees lit up by stray red rays even after the sun was out of view, and had found a common idiom to express our admiration.

The man just followed us about. I had become so lyrical that he suddenly said, 'Hey, Raju, so you are a poet too!' a compliment I accepted with becoming modesty.

At dinner, I picked up a dish and tried to serve. She said, 'No, no. Let me serve you both, and I will be the last to eat, like a good housewife.'

'Aha, that's a good idea,' the man said jocularly. She extended her hand for me to pass the dish to her. But I insisted on doing it myself. She suddenly darted forward and forcibly snatched it away from my hand. Oh, that touch made my head reel for a moment. I didn't see anything clearly. Everything disappeared into a sweet, dark haze, as under chloroform. My memory dwelt on the touch all through the dinner: I was not aware what we were eating or what they were saying. I sat with bowed head. I was nervous to see her face and meet her looks. I don't recollect when we finished eating and when she took away the dishes. I was only conscious of her soft movements. My thoughts dwelt on her golden touch. A part of my mind went on saying, 'No, no. It is not right. Marco is her husband, remember. It's not to be thought of.' But it was impossible to pull the thoughts back. 'He may shoot you,' said my wary conscience. 'Has he a gun?' commented another part of my mind.

[77]

After dinner she said, 'Let us go to the glass veranda. I must watch the game. Do you think they will come out at this hour?'

'Yes; if we are patient and lucky,' I said. 'But won't you be afraid? One has to wait in the dark.'

She laughed at my fears and invited Marco to go with her. But he said he wanted to be left alone. He pulled a chair to the lamp, took out his portfolio, and was soon lost in his papers. She said, 'Shield your lamp. I don't want my animals to be scared off.' She moved with light steps to the veranda, pulled up a chair, and sat down. On the way she had said to me, 'Have you documents to see to?'

'No, no,' I said, hesitating midway between my room and hers.

'Come along, then. Surely you aren't going to leave me to the mercy of prowling beasts?' I looked at the man to know what he would have to say, but he was absorbed in his papers. I asked, 'Do you want anything?'

'No.'

'I'll be on the veranda.'

'Go ahead,' he said without looking up from his papers.

She sat close to the glass pane, intently looking out. I softly placed a chair beside her, and sat down. After a while she said, 'Not a soul. Do animals come here at all, I wonder, or is it one of the usual stories?'

'No, lots of people have seen them—'

'What animals?'

'Lions . . .'

'Lions here?' she said and began laughing. 'I have read they were only in Africa. But this is really—'

'No; excuse me.' I had slipped. 'I meant tigers, and panthers, and bears, and sometimes elephants too are to be seen crossing the valley or coming for a drink of water at the pool.'

'I'm prepared to spend the whole night here,' she said. 'He will, of course, be glad to be left alone. Here at least we have silence and darkness, welcome things, and something to wait for out of that darkness.'

I couldn't find anything to say in reply. I was overwhelmed by her perfume. The stars beyond the glass shone in the sky.

'Can't an elephant break through the glass?' she asked, yawning.

'No; there is a moat on the other side. They can't approach us.'

Bright eyes shone amidst the foliage. She pulled my sleeve and whispered excitedly, 'Something—what can it be?'

'Probably a panther,' I said to keep up the conversation. Oh, the whispers, the stars, and the darkness—I began to breathe heavily with excitement.

'Have you caught a cold?' she asked.

I said, 'No.'

'Why are you breathing so noisily?'

I wanted to put my face close to her and whisper, 'Your dance was marvellous. You are gifted. Do it again sometime. God bless you. Won't you be my sweetheart?' But fortunately I restrained myself. Turning back, I saw that Marco had come with soft steps. 'What luck?' he asked in a whisper.

'Something came, but it's gone. Sit down, won't you?' I said, giving him the chair. He sat down, peering through the glass.

Next morning I found the atmosphere once again black and tense—all the vivacity of the previous evening was gone. When their room opened, only he came out, fully dressed and ready. I had made the coffee on the charcoal stove. He came over and mechanically held his hand out as if I were the man on the other side of a coffee bar. I poured him a cup of coffee. 'Joseph has brought tiffin. Will you not taste it?'

'No; let us be going. I'm keen on reaching the caves.'

'What about the lady?' I asked.

'Leave her alone,' he said petulantly. 'I can't afford to be fooling around, wasting my time.' In the same condition as yesterday! This seemed to be the spirit of their morning every day. How cordially he had come over and sat beside her last night on the veranda! How cordially they had gone into the hotel on that night! What exactly happened at night that made them want to tear at each other in the morning? Did they sit up in bed and fight, or did she fatigue him with a curtain lecture? I wanted to cry out, 'Oh, monster, what do you do to her that makes her sulk like this on rising? What a treasure you have in your hand, without realising its worth—like a monkey picking up a rose garland!' Then a thrilling thought occurred to me—probably she was feigning anger again, so that I might intercede.

He put down his cup and said, 'Now let us go.' I was afraid to ask him again about his wife. He was swinging a small cane impatiently. Could it be that he had been using it on her at night?

Even in my wild state, I did not make the mistake of asking again, 'Shall I call her?' as that might have led to a very serious situation. I only asked, 'Does she know about coffee?'

'Yes, yes,' he cried impatiently. 'Leave it there; she'll take it. She has enough sense to look after herself.' He waved the switch, and we started out. Only once did I turn my head to look back, in the hope that she might appear at the window and

[80]

call us back. 'Did I come all the way for this monster's company?' I asked myself as I followed him down the hill slope. How appropriate it would be if he should stumble and roll downhill! Bad thought, bad thought. He walked ahead of me. We were like a couple of African hunters—in fact, his dress, with his helmet and thick jacket, as I have already mentioned, was that of a wild African *shikari*.

Our path through grass and shrub led to the valley. The cave was half-way across it. I felt suddenly irritated at the speed of his walk, as if he knew the way, swinging his cane and hugging his portfolio. If he could show half the warmth of that hug elsewhere! I suddenly asked, 'Do you know the way?'

'Oh no,' he said.

'You are leading me!' I said, putting into it all the irony I was capable of.

He cried, 'Oh!' looked confused, and said, stepping aside, 'Well, lead us,' and through an irrelevant association added, 'kindly light.'

The entrance to the cave was beyond a thicket of lantana. A huge door on its rusty hinges stood open. And, of course, all the crumbling brick and plaster was there. It was a cave with a single rock covering its entire roof; why any man should have taken the trouble to build a thing like this in a remote spot was more than I could understand.

He stood outside and surveyed the entrance. 'You see, this entrance must have been a later improvisation; the cave itself, I know, must have been about first century A.D. The entrance and the door are of a later date. You see, that kind of tall entrance and the carved doorway became a current fashion in the seventh or eighth century, when the South Indian rulers became fond of . . .' He went on talking. Dead and decaying things seemed to unloosen his tongue and fire his imagination, rather than things that lived and moved and swung their limbs. I had little to do as a guide; he knew so much more of everything!

When he passed in, he completely forgot the world outside and its inhabitants. The roof was low, but every inch of the wall space was covered with painted figures. He flashed a torch on the walls. He took out of his pocket a mirror and placed it outside to catch the sunlight and throw a beam on the paintings. Bats were whirring about; the floor was broken and full of holes. But he minded nothing. He became busy measuring, writing down, photographing, all the time keeping up a chatter, not bothered in the least whether I listened or not.

I was bored with his ruin-collecting activities. The wall-painting represented episodes from the epics and mythology, and all kinds of patterns and motifs, with men, women, and kings and animals, in a curious perspective and proportion of their own, and ancient like the rocks. I had seen hundreds like them, and I saw no point in seeing more. I had no taste for them, just as he had no taste for other things.

'Be careful,' I said. 'There may be reptiles in those cracks.'

'Oh, no,' he said indifferently, 'reptiles don't generally come to such interesting places; moreover, I have this.' He flourished his stick. 'I can manage. I'm not afraid.'

I suddenly said, 'I seem to hear the sound of a car. If it's Gaffur, I'd like to be there at the bungalow, so do you mind if I go? I'll be back.'

He said, 'Keep him. Don't let him go away.'

'When you return, come the same way—so that we may not get lost.' He didn't answer, but resumed his studies.

I reached the house at a run and rested a while in the back-

[82]

yard to regain my breath. I went in, brushing back my hair with my hand and composing my features. As I entered, I heard her voice. 'Looking for me?' She was sitting on a boulder in the shade of a tree. She must have seen me come up. 'I saw you even half a mile away, but you couldn't see me,' she said like one who had discovered a fault.

'You were on the peak and I was in the valley,' I said. I went up to her and made some polite inquiries about her coffee. She looked both sad and profound. I sat down on a stone near her.

'You have returned alone. I suppose he is wall-gazing?' she said.

'Yes,' I replied briefly.

'He does that everywhere.'

'Well, I suppose he is interested, that's all.'

'What about me, interested in something else?'

'What is your interest?'

'Anything except cold, old stone walls,' she said.

I looked at my watch. I had already been away from him for nearly an hour. I was wasting time. Time was slipping through my fingers. If I were to make good, I should utilise this chance. 'Every night you generally sit up and quarrel, do you?' I asked boldly.

'When we are alone and start talking, we argue and quarrel over everything. We don't agree on most matters, and then he leaves me alone and comes back and we are all right, that's all.'

'Until it is night again,' I said.

'Yes, yes.'

'It's unthinkable that anyone should find it possible to quarrel or argue with you—being with you must be such bliss.'

She asked sharply, 'What do you mean?'

I explained myself plainly. I was prepared to ruin myself today if need be, but I was going to talk and tell her. If she wanted to kick me out, she could do it after listening to me. I spoke my mind. I praised her dancing. I spoke out my love, but sandwiched it conveniently between my appreciations of her art. I spoke of her as an artist in one breath, and continued in the next as a sweetheart. Something like, 'What a glorious snake dance! Oh, I keep thinking of you all night. World's artist number one! Don't you see how I am pining for you every hour!'

It worked. She said, 'You are a brother to me,' ('Oh, no,' I wanted to cry) 'and I'll tell you what happens.' She gave me an account of their daily quarrels.

'Why did you marry at all?' I asked recklessly.

She remained moody and said, 'I don't know. It just happened.'

'You married him because of his wealth,' I said, 'and you were advised by your uncle and the rest.'

'You see,' she began, plucking my sleeve. 'Can you guess to what class I belong?'

I looked her up and down and ventured, 'The finest, whatever it may be, and I don't believe in class or caste. You are an honour to your caste, whatever it may be.'

'I belong to a family traditionally dedicated to the temples as dancers; my mother, grandmother, and, before her, her mother. Even as a young girl I danced in our village temple. You know how our caste is viewed?'

'It's the noblest caste on earth,' I said.

'We are viewed as public women,' she said plainly, and I was thrilled to hear the words. 'We are not considered respectable; we are not considered civilised.'

[84]

'All that narrow notion may be true of old days, but it's different now. Things have changed. There is no caste or class today.'

'A different life was planned for me by my mother. She put me to school early in life; I studied well. I took my master's degree in economics. But after college, the question was whether I should become a dancer or do something else. One day I saw in our paper an advertisement—the usual kind you may have seen: "Wanted: an educated, good-looking girl to marry a rich bachelor of academic interests. *No caste restrictions*; good looks and university degree essential." I asked myself, "Have I looks?" '

'Oh, who could doubt it?'

'I had myself photographed clutching the scroll of the university citation in one hand, and sent it to the advertiser. Well, we met, he examined me and my certificate, we went to a registrar and got married.'

'Did you like him the moment you saw him?'

'Don't ask all that now,' she snubbed me. 'We had had many discussions before coming to a decision. The question was, whether it would be good to marry so much above our wealth and class. But all the women in my family were impressed, excited that a man like him was coming to marry one of our class, and it was decided that if it was necessary to give up our traditional art, it was worth the sacrifice. He had a big house, a motor-car, he was a man of high social standing; he had a house outside Madras, he was living in it all alone, no family at all; he lived with his books and papers.'

'So you have no mother-in-law!' I said.

'I'd have preferred any kind of mother-in-law, if it had meant one real, live husband,' she said. I looked up at her to divine

[85]

her meaning, but she lowered her eyes. I could only guess. She said, 'He is interested in painting and old art and things like that.'

'But not one which can move its limbs, I suppose,' I said.

I sighed deeply, overcome with the sadness of her life. I placed my hand on her shoulder and gently stroked it. 'I am really very unhappy to think of you, such a gem lost to the world. In his place I would have made you a queen of the world.' She didn't push away my hand. I let it travel and felt the softness of her ear and pushed my fingers through the locks of her hair.

Gaffur's car did not turn up. A passing truck-driver brought the message that it had had a breakdown and would be coming on the following day. No one in the party minded really. Joseph looked after us quite well. Marco said it gave him more time to study the walls. I did not mind. It gave me an occasion to watch the game beyond the sheet glass every night, holding her hand, while Marco sat in his room, poring over his notes.

When Gaffur's car did turn up Marco said, 'I want to stay on here; it is going to take more time than I thought. Could you fetch from my room in the hotel my black trunk? I have some papers in it. I'd prefer to have you here also, if it is all the same to you.'

I seemed to hesitate, and then looked up at the girl for a moment. There was a mute appeal in her eyes. I said yes.

'You may treat it as a part of your professional work,' he said, 'unless you feel it's going to hurt your general business.'

'All right,' I said, hesitantly. 'It's true, but I'd also like to be of service to you. Once I take charge of anyone, I always feel that they are my responsibility till I see them off again safely.'

As I was getting into the car she said to her husband, 'I'll also go back to the town; I want a few things from my box.'

I added, 'We may not be able to return tonight.'

He asked his wife, 'Can you manage?'

'Yes,' she said.

As we were going down the mountain road I often caught Gaffur looking at us through the mirror, and we moved away from the range of his vision. We reached our hotel in the evening. I followed her to her room. 'Should we go back this evening?' I asked her.

'Why?' she asked. 'Suppose Gaffur's car stops on the way? Better not risk it on that road. I'll stay here tonight.'

I went home to change. My mother was full of information the moment she saw me, and full of inquiries. I brushed everything aside. I rushed through my washing and grooming and took out another set of special clothes. I gave my old clothes in a bundle to my mother. 'Will you tell that shop-boy to take them to the *dhobi* and have them washed and ironed neatly? I may want them tomorrow.'

'Becoming a dandy?' she said, surveying me. 'Why are you always on the run now?' I gave her some excuse and started out again.

I engaged Gaffur for my own rounds that day. I was a true guide. Never had I shown anyone the town with greater zest. I took Rosie all over the place, showed her the town hall tower; showed her Sarayu, and we sat on the sands and munched a large packet of salted nuts. She behaved like a baby—excited, thrilled, appreciative of everything. I took her through the Suburban Stores and told her to buy anything she liked. This was probably the first time that she was seeing the world. She was in ecstasies. Gaffur warned me when he got me alone for a

[87]

moment outside the store, 'She is a married woman, remember.'

'What of it?' I said. 'Why do you tell me this?'

'Don't be angry, sir,' he said. 'Go slow; that is all I can say.'

'You are unhealthy-minded, Gaffur. She is like a sister to me,' I said, and tried to shut him up.

All he said was, 'You are right. What is it to me? After all, that man is here, who has really married her. And I've my own wife to bother about.'

I left him and went back to the store. She had picked up a silver brooch, painted over and patterned like a peacock. I paid for it and pinned it on her sari. We dined on the terrace of the Taj, from where she could have a view of the River Sarayu winding away. When I pointed it out to her she said, 'It's good. But I have had views of valleys, trees, and brooks to last me a lifetime.' We laughed. We were getting into a state of perpetual giggling.

She liked to loaf in the market, eat in a crowded hotel, wander about, see a cinema—these common pleasures seemed to have been beyond her reach all these days. I had dismissed the car at the cinema. I did not want Gaffur to watch my movements. We walked to the hotel after the picture. We had hardly noticed what it was. I had taken a box. She wore a light-yellow crêpe sari which made her so attractive that people kept looking at her.

Her eyes sparkled with vivacity and gratitude. I knew I had placed her in my debt.

It was nearing midnight. The man at the hotel desk watched us pass without showing any interest. Desk-men at hotels learn not to be inquisitive. At the door of Number 28 I hesitated. She opened the door, passed in, and hesitated, leaving the door half open. She stood looking at me for a moment, as on the first day.

'Shall I go away?' I asked in a whisper.

'Yes. Good night,' she said feebly.

'May I not come in?' I asked, trying to look my saddest.

'No, no. Go away,' she said. But on an impulse I gently pushed her out of the way, and stepped in and locked the door on the world.

6

RAJU lost count of the time that passed in these activities, one day being like another and always crowded. Several months (or perhaps years) had passed. He counted the seasons by the special points that jutted out, such as the harvest in January, when his disciples brought him sugar-cane and jaggery cooked with rice; when they brought him sweets and fruits, he knew that the Tamil New Year was on; when *Dasara* came they brought in extra lamps and lit them, and the women were busy all through the nine days, decorating the pillared hall with coloured paper and tinsel; and for *Deepavali* they brought him new clothes and crackers and he invited the children to a special session and fired the crackers. He kept a rough count of time thus, from the beginning of the year to its end, through its seasons of sun, rain, and mist. He kept count of three cycles and then lost count. He realised that it was unnecessary to maintain a calendar.

His beard now caressed his chest, his hair covered his back, and around his neck he wore a necklace of prayer-beads. His eyes shone with softness and compassion, the light of wisdom emanated from them. The villagers kept bringing in so many things for him that he lost interest in accumulation. He distributed whatever he had to the gathering at the end of the day. They brought him huge chrysanthemum garlands, jasmine and rose petals in baskets. He gave them all back to the women and children.

He protested to Velan one day, 'I'm a poor man and you are poor men; why do you give me all this? You must stop it.' But it was not possible to stop the practice; they loved to bring him gifts. He came to be called Swami by his congregation, and where he lived was called the Temple. It was passing into common parlance. 'The Swami said this or that,' or 'I am on my way to the Temple.' People loved this place so much that they lime-washed its walls and drew red bands on them.

In the first half of the year they had evening rains, which poured down fussily for a couple of hours to the tune of tremendous thunder; later in the year they had a quieter sort of rain, steadily pattering down. But no rain affected the assembly. People came shielding themselves with huge bamboo mats or umbrellas or coconut thatch. The hall became more packed during the wet season, since the people could not overflow into the outer courtyard. But it made the gathering cosy, interesting, and cool; and the swish of rain and wind in the trees and the swelling river (which made them carry their children aloft on their shoulders and cross the river only at certain shallow points) lent a peculiar charm to the proceedings. Raju loved this season, for its greenness everywhere, for the variety of cloud-play in the sky, which he could watch through the columned halls.

But he suddenly noticed at the end of the year that the skies never dimmed with cloud. The summer seemed to continue. Raju inquired, 'Where are the rains?'

Velan pulled a long face. 'The first rains have totally kept off, Swamiji, and the millet crop, which we should have harvested by now, is all scorched on the stalks. It's a big worry.'

'A thousand banana seedlings are dead,' said another. 'If it continues, who knows?' They looked anxious.

Raju, ever a soothsayer, said consolingly, 'Such things are common; don't worry too much about them. Let us hope for the best.'

They became argumentative. 'Do you know, Swamiji, our cattle which go out to graze nose about the mud and dirt and come back, having no grass to eat?'

Raju had some soothing remark for every complaint. They went home satisfied. 'You know best, master,' they said and left. Raju recollected that for his bath nowadays he had to go down three more steps to reach the water. He went down and stood looking along the river course. He looked away to his left, where the river seemed to wind back to the mountain ranges of the Mempi, to its source, where he had often conducted tourists. Such a small basin, hardly a hundred square feet with its little shrine—what had happened there to make this river shrink so much here? He noticed that the borders were wide, more rocks were showing, and the slope on the other side seemed to have become higher.

Other signs too were presently to be noticed. At the Harvest Festival, the usual jubilation was absent. 'Sugar-canes have completely wilted; with difficulty we have brought in this bit. Please accept it.'

'Give it to the children,' Raju said. Their gifts were shrinking in size and volume.

'The astrologer says that we shall have very early rains in the coming year,' someone said. The talk was always about the rains. People listened to discourses and philosophy with only half-interest. They sat around, expressing their fears and hopes. 'Is it true, Swami, that the movement of aeroplanes disturbs the clouds and so the rains don't fall? Too many aeroplanes in the sky.' 'Is it true, Swami, that the atom bombs are responsible for the drying up of the clouds?' Science, mythology, weather reports, good and evil, and all kinds of possibilities were connected with the rain. Raju gave an explanation for each in the best manner he could manage, but he found his answers never diverted their minds.

He decreed, 'You must not think too much of it. The rain-god sometimes teases those who are obsessed with thoughts of him. How would you feel if someone went on mentioning and repeating your name all hours of the day and night for days and days on end?' They enjoyed the humour of the analogy, and went their ways. But a situation was developing which no comforting word or discipline of thinking could help. Something was happening on a different plane over which one had no control or choice, and where a philosophical attitude made no difference. Cattle were unable to yield milk; they lacked the energy to drag the plough through the furrows; flocks of sheep were beginning to look scurvy and piebald, with their pelvic bones sticking out.

The wells in the villages were drying up. Huge concourses of women with pitchers arrived at the river, which was fast narrowing. From morning to night they came in waves and took the water. Raju watched their arrival and departure as they passed in files on the high ground opposite, looking picturesque, but without the tranquillity inherent in a picture. They quarrelled at the water-hole for priorities, and there were fear, desperation, and lamentation in their voices.

The earth was fast drying up. A buffalo was found dead on a foot-track. The news was brought to the Swami early one morning by Velan. He stood above him as he slept and said, 'Swami, I want you to come with us.'

'Why?'

'Cattle have begun to die,' he said with quiet resignation.

'What can I do about it?' Raju felt like asking, sitting up in his bed. But he could not say such a thing. He said soothingly, 'Oh, no; it can't be.'

'A buffalo was found dead on the forest path beyond our village.'

'Did you see it yourself?'

'Yes, Swami, I come from there.'

'Can't be as bad as that, Velan. It must have died of some other disease.'

'Please come along and see it, and if you can tell us why it is dead, it will relieve our minds. A learned man like you should see and tell.'

They were clearly losing their heads. They were entering a nightmare phase. The Swami knew so little of cattle, dead or alive, that it was of no practical use his going to see this one, but since they wanted it, he asked Velan to be seated for a few moments, and went down with him. The village street looked deserted. Children played about in the road dust, because the master had gone to town with a petition for relief addressed to the revenue authorities, and so the day-school was closed. Women were moving about with water-pots on their heads. In passing, 'Could hardly get half a pot today,' said some. 'What's the world coming to? You must show us the way, Swami.'

Raju merely raised a hand and waved it as if to say, 'Be peaceful; everything will be all right; I will fix it with the gods.' A small crowd followed him and Velan to the forest path, saying the same thing over and over again. Someone reported worse happenings in the next village; cholera was breaking out and thousands were dying, and so forth; he was snubbed by the rest as a scaremonger. Raju paid little attention to the jabber around him.

There it was outside the village, on a rough foot-track that led into the forest, a buffalo with bones sticking out. Crows and kites, already hovering about, flew off at the approach of men. There was a sickening odour, and henceforth Raju began to associate the season with it. It could not be mitigated with soothsaying. He held his upper cloth to his nostrils and gazed at the carcass for a while. 'Whose was this?' he asked.

They looked at one another. 'Not ours,' someone said. 'It belonged to the next village.' There was some relief at this thought. If it was one from the next village, it was far removed. Anything, any explanation, any excuse served to console people now.

'It belonged to no one,' said another. 'It looks like a wild buffalo.'

This was even better. Raju felt relieved at the possibility of there being other solutions and explanations. He added, peering at it again, 'It must have been bitten by a poisonous insect.' This was a comforting explanation, and he turned back without letting his eye dwell on the barren branches of trees, and the ground covered with bleached mud without a sign of green.

The piece of interpretation by the Swamiji pleased the public. It brought them untold comfort. The air of tension suddenly relaxed. When the cattle were penned for the night, they looked on them without anxiety. 'There is enough about for the cattle to feed on,' they said. 'Swami says that the buffalo died of a poisonous bite. He knows.' In support of it, many anecdotes were told of the death of animals from

[95]

mysterious causes. 'There are snakes which bite into their hoofs.' 'There are certain kinds of ants whose bite is fatal to animals.'

More cattle were found dead here and there. When the earth was scratched it produced only a cloud of fine dust. The granary of the previous year, in most of the houses, remained unreplenished and the level was going down. The village shopman was holding out for bigger prices. When people asked for a measure of rice he demanded fourteen annas for it. The man who wanted the rice lost his temper and slapped his face. The shopman came out with a chopper and attacked the customer; and those who sympathised with the man gathered in front of the shop and invaded it. The shopman's relatives and sympathisers came at night with crowbars and knives and started attacking the other group.

Velan and his men also picked up axes and knives and started out for the battle. Shrieks and cries and imprecations filled the air. The little hay that was left was set on fire, and the dark night was ablaze. Raju heard the cries, coming on the night air, and then he saw the blaze lighting up the landscape beyond the mound. Only a few hours before, everything had seemed peaceful and quiet. He shook his head, saying to himself, 'The village people do not know how to remain peaceful. They are becoming more and more agitated. At this rate, I think I'll look for a new place.' He went back to sleep, unable to take any further interest in their activities.

But news was brought to him early in the morning. Velan's brother told him while he was still half asleep that Velan was down with an injured skull and burns, and he gave a list of women and children hurt in the fight. They were mustering themselves to attack the other group tonight.

Raju was amazed at the way things were moving. He did not know what he was expected to do now, whether to bless their expedition or prevent it. Personally, he felt that the best thing for them would be to blow one another's brains out. That'd keep them from bothering too much about the drought. He felt a pity for Velan's condition. 'Is he seriously hurt?' he asked.

Velan's brother said, 'Oh, no. Just cut up here and there,' as though he wasn't satisfied with the marks.

Raju wondered for a while whether he should visit Velan, but he felt a tremendous reluctance to move. If Velan was hurt, he'd get healed; that was all. And now the brother's description of the injuries, whether false or true, suited his programme. There was no urgency to go and see Velan. He feared that if he made it a habit he would not be left in peace, as the villagers would always have a reason to call him out. He asked Velan's brother, 'How did you yourself manage to remain intact?'

'Oh, I was also there, but they didn't hit me. If they had I would have laid ten of them low. But my brother, he was careless.'

'Thin as a broomstick, but talks like a giant,' thought Raju, and advised, 'Tell your brother to apply turmeric to his wounds.' From the casual tone with which this man was speaking, Raju wondered if it was possible that he himself had dealt a blow to Velan from behind; anything seemed possible in this village. All the brothers in the place were involved in litigation against one another; and anyone might do anything in the present sensational developments. Velan's brother rose to go. Raju said, 'Tell Velan to rest in bed completely.'

'Oh, no, master. How can he rest? He is joining the

[97]

party tonight and he will not rest till he burns their houses.'

'It is not right,' Raju said, somewhat irritated by all this pugnacity.

Velan's brother was one of the lesser intelligences of the village. He was about twenty-one, a semi-moron who had grown up as a dependent in Velan's house, yet another of Velan's trials in life. He spent his days taking the village cattle out to the mountains for grazing: he collected them from various houses early in the day, and drove them to the mountainside, watched over them, and brought them back in the evening. All day he lounged under a tree's shade, eating a ball of boiled millet when the sun came overhead, and watching for the sun to slant westward to drive the cattle homeward. He had hardly anyone to speak to except his cattle the whole day and he spoke to them on equal terms and abused them and their genealogy unreservedly. Any afternoon in the stillness of the forest, if one had the occasion to observe, one could hear the hills echoing to the choice, abusive words that he hurled at the animals as he followed them with his stick. He was considered well-equipped for this single task, and from each house was given four annas a month. They did not trust him with any more responsible tasks. He was one of those rare men in the village who never visited the Swamiji, but preferred to sleep at home at the end of the day. But now he had come, almost for the first time. The others were preoccupied and busy with their preparations for the coming fight, and he was one of those whose employment was affected by the drought; no one saw any sense in sending the cattle out to nose about the dry sand and paying the idiot four annas a month.

He had come here this morning, not because anyone had sent him to carry a message for the Swamiji, but because he was at a loose end and had suddenly felt that he might as well pay a visit to the temple and receive the Swami's blessing. The fight was the last thing the villagers would have liked to bring to the Swami's attention, although after finishing it they might have given him a mild version. But this boy brought the news on his own initiative and defended their action. 'But, Swami, why did they cut my brother's face?' He added sullenly, 'Should they be left free to do all this?'

Raju argued with him patiently. 'You beat the shopman first, didn't you?'

The boy took it literally and said, 'I didn't beat the shopman. The man who beat him was . . .' He gave a number of local names.

Raju felt too weary to correct him and improve his understanding. He simply said, 'It is no good; nobody should fight.' He felt it impossible to lecture him on the ethics of peace, and so merely said, 'No one should fight.'

'But they fight!' the boy argued. 'They come and beat us.' He paused, ruminating upon the words, and added, 'And they will kill us soon.'

Raju felt bothered. He did not like the idea of so much commotion. It might affect the isolation of the place and bring the police on the scene. He did not want anyone to come to the village. Raju suddenly began to think positively on these matters. He gripped the other's arm above his elbow and said, 'Go and tell Velan and the rest that I don't want them to fight like this. I'll tell them what to do later.' The boy prepared himself to repeat his usual arguments. But Raju said impatiently, 'Don't talk. Listen to what I say.'

'Yes, master,' the boy said, rather frightened at this sudden vehemence.

'Tell your brother, immediately, wherever he may be, that unless they are good I'll never eat.'

'Eat what?' asked the boy, rather puzzled.

'Say that I'll not eat. Don't ask what. I'll not eat till they are good.'

'Good? Where?'

This was frankly beyond the comprehension of the boy. He wanted to ask again, 'Eat what?' but refrained out of fear. His eyes opened wide. He could not connect the fight and this man's food. He wanted only to be released from the terrific grip over his left elbow. He felt he had made a mistake in coming to this man all alone—the bearded face, pushed so close to him, frightened him. This man might perhaps eat him up. He became desperately anxious to get out of the place. He said, 'All right, sir. I'll do it,' and the moment Raju let his hold go he shot out of the place, was across the sands and out of sight in a moment.

He was panting when he ran into the assembly of his village elders. They were sitting solemnly around a platform in the centre of the village, discussing the rains. There was a brick platform built around an ancient peepul-tree, at whose root a number of stone figures were embedded, which were often anointed with oil and worshipped. This was a sort of town hall platform for Mangala. It was shady and cool and spacious; there was always a gathering of men on one side conferring on local problems, and on the other women who carried loaded baskets on their heads and rested; children chased each other; and the village dogs slumbered.

Here were sitting the elders of the village, discussing the rain, the fight tonight, and all the strategies connected with it. They had still many misgivings about the expedition. How the

Swami would view the whole thing was a thing that could be understood only later. He might not approve. It would be best not to go to him until they themselves were clear in their heads about what to do. That the other group deserved punishment was beyond question. Among those talking were quite a number with bruises and cuts. But they had a fear of the police; they remembered a former occasion when there had been a faction fight, and the government posted a police force almost permanently and made the villagers feed them and pay for their keep.

Into this council of war burst Velan's brother. The atmosphere became tense. 'What is it, brother?' asked Velan.

The boy stopped to recover breath before speaking. They took him by the shoulder and shook him, at which he became more confused and blabbered and finally said, 'The Swami, the Swami, doesn't want food any more. Don't take any food to him.'

'Why? Why?'

'Because, because—it doesn't rain.' He added also, suddenly, recollecting the fight, 'No fight, he says.'

'Who asked you to go there?' asked his brother authoritatively.

'I—I didn't, but when I—found myself there he asked me and I told him—'

'What did you tell him?'

The boy became suddenly wary. He knew he would be thrashed if he said he had mentioned the fight. He didn't like to be gripped by the shoulder—in fact, he was averse to being gripped in any manner at all; but there the Swami squeezed his elbow and brushed his beard on his face, and there these men were tearing at his shoulder. He felt sorry he had ever got involved. It was best not to have anything to do with them.

They would wrench his shoulder off if they knew he'd been telling the master about the fight. So he covered up the entire business in the best manner he could think of. He blinked. They demanded of him again, 'What did you tell him?'

'That there is no rain,' he said, mentioning the easiest subject that occurred to him.

They patted him on the head and said contemptuously, 'Big prophet to carry the news! He didn't know about it till then, I suppose.' A laugh followed. The boy also simpered and tried to get over it.

Then he remembered the message he had been entrusted with, and thought it safer to say something about it, otherwise the great man might come to know of it and lay a curse on him. And so he said, coming back to the original starting point, 'He wants no food until it is all right.'

He uttered it with such solemnity and emphasis that they asked, 'What did he say? Tell us exactly.'

The boy deliberated for a moment and said, 'Tell your brother not to bring me any more food. I won't eat. If I don't eat, it'll be all right; and then everything will be all right.' They stared at him, puzzled. He smiled, rather pleased at the importance he was receiving. They remained in thought for a moment.

And then one of them said, 'This Mangala is a blessed country to have a man like the Swami in our midst. No bad thing will come to us as long as he is with us. He is like Mahatma. When Mahatma Gandhi went without food, how many things happened in India! This is a man like that. If he fasts there will be rain. Out of his love for us he is under-taking it. This will surely bring rain and help us. Once upon a time a man fasted for twenty-one days and brought down

[102]

the deluge. Only great souls that take upon themselves tasks such as this—' The atmosphere became electrified. They forgot the fight and all their troubles and bickerings.

The village was astir. Everything else seemed inconsequential now. Someone brought the news that upstream a crocodile had been found dead on the sand, having no watery shelter and being scorched by the sun. Someone else came with the news that the fast-drying lake bed in a nearby village was showing up an old temple which had been submerged a century ago, when the lake was formed. The image of God was still intact in the inner shrine, none the worse for having lain under water so long; the four coconut trees around the temple were still there . . . And so on and so forth. More and more details were coming in every hour. Hundreds of people were now walking across the lake bed to visit the temple, and some careless ones lost their lives, sucked in by loose mud. All this now produced a lot of public interest, but no fear. They were now even able to take a more lenient view of the shopman who had assaulted his customer. 'After all, so and so should not have called him a whoreson; not a proper word.'

'Of course, one's kith and kin are bound to support one. What are they worth otherwise?' Velan brooded over the cut on his forehead, and a few others suddenly recollected their various injuries. They could not decide how far this could be forgiven. They consoled themselves with the thought that a good number in the other group must also be nursing injuries at that moment; it was a very satisfying thought. They suddenly decided that they should have a third party to come and arbitrate, so that the fight could be forgotten, provided the other group paid for the burned-down haystacks and entertained the chief men of this group at a feast. And they spent their time discussing the conditions of peace and rose in a body, declaring, 'Let us all go and pay our respects to Swami, our saviour.'

Raju was waiting for his usual gifts and food. He had, no doubt, fruits and other edible stuff left in his hamper, but he hoped they would bring him other fare. He had suggested to them that they should try to get him wheat flour, and rice flour, and spices. He wanted to try some new recipes, for a change. He had a subtle way of mentioning his special requirements. He generally began by taking Velan aside and saying, 'You see, if a little rice flour and chili powder could be got, along with some other things, I can do something new. On Wednesdays . . .' He enunciated some principle of living such as that on a special Wednesday he always liked to make his food with rice flour and such-and-such spice, and he mentioned it with an air of seriousness so that his listeners took it as a spiritual need, something of the man's inner discipline to keep his soul in shape and his understanding with the Heavens in order. He had a craving for *bonda*, which he used to eat in the railway station stall when a man came there to vend his edibles on a wooden tray to the travellers. It was composed of flour, potato, a slice of onion, a coriander leaf, and a green chili—and oh! how it tasted—although he probably fried it in anything; he was the sort of vendor who would not hesitate to fry a thing in kerosene, if it worked out cheaper. With all that, he made delicious stuff, and when Raju used to ask the vendor how he made it, he gave him a recipe starting with, 'Just a small piece of ginger,' and then it went on to this and that. While discoursing on *Bhagavad-Gita* to his audience the other evening, Raju had had a sudden craving to try this out himself—he was now equipped with a charcoal stove and frying pan, and what could be more musical than well-kneaded dough dropping into boiling oil? He had enumerated his wants to Velan as delicately as possible.

When he heard voices beyond the mound, he felt relieved. He composed his features for his professional role and smoothed out his beard and hair, and sat down in his seat with a book in his hand. As the voices approached, he looked up and found that a bigger crowd than usual was crossing the sands. He was puzzled for a second, but felt that perhaps they were jubilant over the fact that he had prevented a fight. He felt happy that he had after all achieved something, and saved the village. That idiot brother of Velan did not seem so bad after all. He hoped that they had the flour in a bag. It'd be improper to ask for it at once; they were bound to leave it in the kitchen.

They softened their steps and voices as they came nearer the pillared hall. Even the children hushed their voices when they approached the august presence.

They sat around in a silent semicircle as before, each in his place. The women got busy at once sweeping the floor and filling the mud lamps with oil. For ten minutes Raju neither looked at them nor spoke, but turned the leaves of his book. He felt curious to see how much of Velan's person was intact. He stole a glance across, and saw the scars on his forehead, and threw a swift look around and found that actually there was less damage than he had pictured in his mind. He resumed his studies, and only after he had gone through ten minutes of reading did he look up as usual and survey the gathering. He looked at his flock, fixed his eyes on Velan in particular, and said, 'Lord Krishna says here—' He adjusted his page to the light and read a passage. 'Do you know what it means?' He entered into a semi-philosophical discourse on a set of rambling themes, starting with the eating of good food and going on to absolute trust in God's goodness.

They listened to him without interrupting him, and only when he paused for breath at the end of nearly an hour did Velan say, 'Your prayers will surely be answered and save our village. Every one of us in the village prays night and day that you come through it safely.'

Raju was puzzled by what he heard. But he thought that such high and bombastic well-wishing was their habit and idiom and that they were only thanking him for putting enough sense into their heads not to go on with their fight. The assembly grew very loquacious and showered praise on him from all directions. A woman came up and touched his feet. Another followed. Raju cried, 'Have I not told you that I'll never permit this? No human being should ever prostrate before another human being.'

Two or three men came up, one of them saying, 'You are not another human being. You are a Mahatma. We should consider ourselves blessed indeed to be able to touch the dust of your feet.'

'Oh, no. Don't say that—' Raju tried to withdraw his feet. But they crowded round him. He tried to cover his feet. He felt ridiculous playing this hide-and-seek with his feet. He could find no place to put them. They tugged at him from various sides and they seemed ready to tickle his sides, if it would only give them his feet. He realised that there was really no escape from this demonstration and that it would be best to let them do what they liked. Almost everyone in the crowd had touched his feet and withdrawn, but not too far away; they surrounded him and showed no signs of moving. They gazed on his face and kept looking up in a new manner; there was a greater solemnity in the air than he had ever known before. Velan said, 'Your penance is similar to Mahatma Gandhi's. He has left us a disciple in you to save us.' In their own rugged idiom, in the best words they could muster, they were thanking him. Sometimes they all spoke together and made a confused noise. Sometimes they began a sentence and could not get through with it. He understood that they spoke with feeling. They spoke gratefully, although their speech sounded bombastic. The babble was confusing. But their devotion to him was unquestionable. There was so much warmth in their approach that he began to feel it was but right they should touch his feet; as a matter of fact, it seemed possible that he himself might bow low, take the dust of his own feet, and press it to his eyes. He began to think that his personality radiated a glory . . . The crowd did not leave at the usual hour, but lingered on.

Velan had assumed that he was on a fast today and for the first time these months had failed to bring in any food. Just as well. When they attached so much value to his fasting he could not very well ask, 'Where is the stuff for my *bonda*?' It would be unseemly. No harm in attending to it later. They had assumed that he was fasting in order to stop their fight, and he was not going to announce to them that he had already had two meals during the day. He would just leave it at that, and even if his eyes should droop a little out of seeming fatigue, it would be quite in order. Now that it was all over, why couldn't they go away? He signalled to Velan to come nearer, 'Why not send away the women and children? Isn't it getting late?'

The crowd left at nearly midnight, but Velan remained where he had sat all the evening, leaning against a pillar. 'Don't you feel sleepy?' Raju asked.

'No, sir. Keeping awake is no big sacrifice, considering what you are doing for us.'

'Don't attach too much value to it. It's just a duty, that is all, and I'm not doing anything more than I ought to do. You can go home if you like.'

'No, sir. I'll go home tomorrow when the Headman comes to relieve me. He will come here at five o'clock and stay on till the afternoon. I'll go home, attend to my work, and come back, sir.'

'Oh, it's not at all necessary that someone should always be here. I can manage quite well.'

'You will graciously leave that to us, sir. We are only doing our duty. You are undertaking a great sacrifice, sir, and the least we can do is to be at your side. We derive merit from watching your face, sir.'

Raju felt really touched by this attitude. But he decided that the time had come to get to the bottom of it. So he said, 'You are right. "One who serves the performer of a sacrifice derives the same merit", says our scripture, and you are not wrong. I thank God that my effort has succeeded, and you are all at peace with one another; that's my main concern. Now that's over, things are all right. You may go home. Tomorrow I'll take my usual food, and then I shall be all right. You will remember to fetch me rice flour, green chili, and—'

Velan was too respectful to express his surprise loudly. But he couldn't check himself any more. 'Do you expect it to rain tomorrow, sir?'

'Well . . .' Raju thought for a moment. What was this new subject that had crept into the agenda? 'Who can say? It's God's will. It may.' It was then that Velan moved nearer and gave an account of what his brother had told them, and its

[108]

effect on the population around. Velan gave a very clear account of what the saviour was expected to do—stand in knee-deep water, look to the skies, and utter the prayer lines for two weeks, completely fasting during the period—and lo, the rains would come down, provided the man who performed it was a pure soul, was a great soul. The whole countryside was now in a happy ferment, because a great soul had agreed to go through the trial.

The earnestness with which he spoke brought the tears to Raju's eyes. He remembered that not long ago he had spoken to them of such a penance, its value and technique. He had described it partly out of his head and partly out of traditional accounts he had heard his mother narrate. It had filled an evening's programme and helped him divert his audience's mind from the drought. He had told them, 'When the time comes, everything will be all right. Even the man who would bring you the rain will appear, all of a sudden.' They interpreted his words and applied them now to the present situation. He felt that he had worked himself into a position from which he could not get out. He could not betray his surprise. He felt that after all the time had come for him to be serious—to attach value to his own words. He needed time—and solitude to think over the whole matter. He got down from his pedestal; that was the first step to take. That seat had acquired a glamour, and as long as he occupied it people would not listen to him as to an ordinary mortal. He now saw the enormity of his own creation. He had created a giant with his puny self, a throne of authority with that slab of stone. He left his seat abruptly, as if he had been stung by a wasp, and approached Velan. His tone hushed with real humility and fear; his manner was earnest. Velan sat still as if he were a petrified sentry.

'Listen to me, Velan; it is essential that I should be alone tonight. It is essential that I should be alone through the day tomorrow too. And then come and see me tomorrow night. I'll speak to you tomorrow night. Until then neither you nor anyone else should see me.'

This sounded so mysterious and important that Velan got up without a word. 'I'll see you tomorrow night, sir. Alone?'

'Yes, yes; absolutely alone.'

'Very well, master; you have your own reasons. It is not for us to ask why or what. Big crowds will be arriving. I'll have men along the river to turn them back. It'll be difficult, but if it is your order it must be carried out.' He made a deep obeisance and went away. Raju stood looking after him for a while. He went into an inner room which he was using as a bedroom, and laid himself down. His body was aching from too much sitting up the whole day; and he felt exhausted by the numerous encounters. In that dark chamber, as the bats whirred about and the far-off sounds of the village ceased, a great silence descended. His mind was filled with tormenting problems. He tried to sleep. He had a fitful, nightmare-ridden, thought-choked three hours.

Did they expect him to starve for fifteen days and stand in knee-deep water eight hours? He sat up. He regretted having given them the idea. It had sounded picturesque. But if he had known that it would be applied to him, he might probably have given a different formula: that all villages should combine to help him eat *bonda* for fifteen days without a break. Up to them to see that the supply was kept up. And then the saintly man would stand in the river for two minutes a day, and it should bring down the rain sooner or later. His mother used to say, 'If there is one good man anywhere, the rains would

[110]

descend for his sake and benefit the whole world,' quoting from a Tamil poem. It occurred to him that the best course for him would be to run away from the whole thing. He could walk across, catch a bus somewhere, and be off to the city, where they would not bother too much about him—just another bearded *sadhu* about, that was all. Velan and the rest would look for him and conclude that he had vanished to the Himalayas. But how to do it? How far could he go? Anyone might spot him within half an hour. It was not a practical solution. They might drag him back to the spot and punish him for fooling them. It was not even this fear; he was perhaps ready to take the risk, if there was half a chance of getting away. But he felt moved by the recollection of the big crowd of women and children touching his feet. He felt moved by the thought of their gratitude. He lit a fire and cooked his food, bathed in the river (at a spot where he had to scoop the sand and wait five minutes for the spring to fill his vessel), and gulped down a meal before anyone should arrive even accidentally. He kept a reserve of food, concealed in an inner sanctum, for a second meal at night. He thought suddenly that if they would at least leave him alone at night, he could make some arrangement and survive the ordeal. The ordeal then would be only standing knee-deep in water (if they could find it), muttering the litany for eight hours. (This he could suitably modify in actual practice.) It might give him cramps, but he'd have to bear it for a few days, and then be believed the rains would descend in their natural course sooner or later. He would not like to cheat them altogether about the fast if he could help it.

When Velan arrived at night, he took him into his confidence. He said, 'Velan, you have been a friend to me. You must listen to me now. What makes you think that I can bring the rain?'

'That boy told us so. Did you not tell him so?'

Raju hesitated without giving a direct reply. Perhaps even at this point he might have rectified the whole thing with a frank statement. Raju hesitated for a moment. By habit, his nature avoided the direct and bald truth even now. He replied dodgingly, 'It's not that that I am asking. I want to know what has made you think so about me.'

Velan blinked helplessly. He did not quite understand what the great man was implying. He felt that it must mean something very noble, of course, but he was unable to answer the question. He said, 'What else should we do?'

'Come nearer. Sit down and listen to me. You may sleep here. I'm prepared to fast for the sake of your people and do anything if I can help this country—but it is to be done only by a saint. I am no saint.' Velan uttered many sounds of protest. Raju felt really sorry to be shattering his faith; but it was the only way in which he could hope to escape the ordeal. It was a cool night. Raju asked Velan to go up with him to the river step. He took his seat on it, and Velan sat on a step below. Raju moved down to his side. 'You have to listen to me, and so don't go so far away, Velan. I must speak into your ears. You must pay attention to what I am going to say. I am not a saint, Velan, I'm just an ordinary human being like anyone else. Listen to my story. You will know it yourself.' The river trickling away in minute driblets made no noise. The dry leaves of the peepul-tree rustled. Somewhere a jackal howled. And Raju's voice filled the night. Velan listened to him without uttering a word of surprise or interjection, in all humility. Only he looked a little more serious than usual, and there were lines of care on his face.

7

I WAS accepted by Marco as a member of the family. From guiding tourists I seemed to have come to a sort of concentrated guiding of a single family. Marco was just impractical, an absolutely helpless man. All that he could do was to copy ancient things and write about them. His mind was completely in it. All practical affairs of life seemed impossible to him; such a simple matter as finding food or shelter or buying a railway ticket seemed to him a monumental job. Perhaps he married out of a desire to have someone care for his practical life, but unfortunately his choice was wrong—this girl herself was a dreamer if ever there was one. She would have greatly benefited by a husband who could care for her career; it was here that a handy man like me proved invaluable. I nearly gave up all my routine jobs in order to be of service to them.

He stayed for over a month at Peak House and I was in entire charge of all his affairs. He never stinted any expense as long as a voucher was available. They still kept their room in the hotel. Gaffur's car was permanently engaged, almost as if Marco owned it. The car did at least one trip a day between the Peak House and the town. Joseph looked after Marco so well that it was unnecessary for anyone else to bother about him. It was understood that I should devote a lot of time to looking after him and his wife, without sacrificing any other job I might have. He paid me my daily rate and also let me look after my 'routine jobs'. My so-called routine jobs now sounded big, but actually reduced themselves to keeping Rosie company and amusing her. Once in two days she went up to see her husband. She was showing extra solicitude for him nowadays. She fussed a great deal over him. It was all the same to him. His table was littered with notes and dates, and he said, 'Rosie, don't go near it. I don't want you to mess it up. It is just coming to a little order.' I never cared to know what exactly he was doing. It was not my business. Nor did his wife seem to care for the task he was undertaking. She asked, 'How is your food?' She was trying a new technique on him, after the inauguration of our own intimacy. She arranged his room. She spoke to Joseph about his food. Sometimes she said, 'I'll stay on here and keep you company.' And Marco acknowledged it in an absent-minded, casual manner. 'All right. If you like. Well, Raju, are you staying on or going back?'

I resisted my impulse to stay on, because I knew I was having her company fully downhill. It would be polite to leave her alone with him. So I said, without looking at him, 'I must go back. I have some others coming in today. You don't mind, I hope.'

'Not at all. You are a man of business. I should not monopolise you so much.'

'What time will you need the car tomorrow?'

He looked at his wife and she just said, 'Tomorrow, as early as you can.' He generally said, 'Bring me a few sheets of carbon, will you?'

As the car sped downhill, Gaffur kept throwing glances at me through the looking-glass. I was cultivating a lot of reserve with him nowadays. I didn't like him to gossip too much about anything. I was afraid of gossip. I was still sensitive to such things and I was nervous at being alone with Gaffur and felt relieved as long as his remarks were confined to automobiles; but it was not in his nature to stick to this subject. He would begin with automobiles but soon get mixed up. 'You must give me an hour for brake adjustments tomorrow. After all, mechanical brakes, you know; I still maintain they are better than hydraulic. Just as an old, uneducated wife is better than the new type of girl. Oh, modern girls are very bold. I wouldn't let my wife live in a hotel room all by herself if I had to remain on duty on a hilltop.'

It made me uncomfortable and I turned the topic deftly. 'Do you think car designers have less experience than you?'

'Oh, you think these engineers know more? A man like me who has to kick and prod a car to keep it on the road has, you may be sure . . .' I was safe; I had turned his mind from Rosie. I sat in suspense. I was in an abnormal state of mind. Even this did not escape Gaffur's attention. He mumbled often as he was driving me downhill, 'You are becoming rather stuck-up nowadays, Raju. You are not the old friend you used to be.' It was a fact. I was losing a great deal of my mental relaxation. I was obsessed with thoughts of Rosie. I revelled in memories of the hours I had spent with her last or in anticipation of what I'd be doing next. I had several problems to contend with. Her husband was the least of them. He was a good man, completely preoccupied, probably a man with an abnormal capacity for trust. But I was becoming nervous and sensitive and full of anxieties in various ways. Suppose, suppose—suppose? What? I myself could not specify. I was becoming fear-ridden. I couldn't even sort out my worries properly. I was in a jumble. I was suddenly seized with fears, sometimes with a feeling that I didn't look well enough for my sweetheart. I was obsessed with the thought that I hadn't perhaps shaved my chin smoothly enough, and that she would run her fingers over my upper lip and throw me out. Sometimes I felt I was in rags. The silk *jibba* and the lace-edged *dhoti* were being overdone or were old-fashioned. She was about to shut the door on me because I was not modern enough for her. This made me run to the tailor to have him make a few dashing bush-shirts and corduroys, and invest in hair- and face-lotions and perfumes of all kinds. My expenses were mounting. The shop was my main source of income, together with what Marco gave me as my daily wage. I knew that I ought to look into the accounts of the shop a little more closely. I was leaving it too much to the boy to manage. My mother often told me, whenever she was able to get at me, 'You will have to keep an eye on that boy. I see a lot of hangers-on there. Have you any idea what cash he is collecting and what is happening generally?'

I usually told her, 'I should certainly know how to manage these things. Don't think I'm so careless.' And she left me alone. And then I went over to the shop, assumed a tone of great aggressiveness, and checked the accounts. The boy produced some accounts, some cash, a statement of stock, something else that he needed for running the show, and some of his problems. I was in no mood to listen to his problems. I was busy and preoccupied, so I told him not to bother me with petty details and gave an impression (just an impression and nothing more) of being a devil for accounts.

He always said, 'Two passengers came asking for you, sir.'

Oh, bores, who wanted them, anyway? 'What did they want?' I asked with semi-interest.

'Three days' sightseeing, sir. They went away disappointed.'

They were always there. My reputation had survived my interest in the job. Railway Raju was an established name, and still pilgrims and travellers sought his help. The boy persisted. 'They wanted to know where you were.' This gave me food for thought. I didn't want this fool of a fellow to send them up to my Room 28 at the hotel. Fortunately, he did not know. Otherwise he might have done so. 'What shall I tell them, Raju-sir?' He always called me 'Raju-sir'. It was his idea of combining deference with familiarity.

I merely replied, 'Tell them I'm busy; that is all. I have no time. I'm very busy.'

'May I act as their guide, sir?' he asked eagerly. This fellow was acting as a successor in my jobs one by one. Next, probably, he would ask permission to keep the girl company! I felt annoyed with his question and asked him, 'Who will look after the shop?'

'I have a cousin. He can watch the shop for an hour or two, while I am away.'

I could not think of a reply. I could not decide. The whole thing was too bothersome. My old life, in which I was not in the least interested, was dogging my steps; my mother facing me with numerous problems; municipal tax, the kitchen-tiles needing attention, the shop, accounts, letters from the village, my health, and so on and so forth; to me she was a figure out of a dream, mumbling vague sounds; and this boy had his own way of cornering and attacking me. Then Gaffur with his sly remarks and looks, ever on the brink of gossip—Oh, I was tired of it all. I was in no mood for anything. My mind was on other matters. Even my finances were unreal to me, although if I cared to look at my savings-book I could know at a glance how the level of the reservoir was going down. But I did not want to examine it too closely as long as the man at the counter was able to give me the cash I wanted. Thanks to my father's parsimonious habits, I had a bank account. The only reality in my life and consciousness was Rosie. All my mental powers were now turned to keep her within my reach, and keep her smiling all the time, neither of which was at all easy. I would willingly have kept at her side all the time, as a sort of parasite; but in that hotel it was not easy. I was always racked with the thought that the man at the desk and the boys at the hotel were keeping an eye on me and were commenting behind my back.

I did not want to be observed going to Room 28. I was becoming self-conscious about it. I very much wished that the architecture of the place could be altered so that I might go up without having the desk-man watch me. I was sure he was noting down the hour of my arrival with Rosie, and of my departure. His morbid, inquisitive mind, I was sure, must have been working on all the details of my life behind the closed doors of Room 28. I didn't like the way he looked at me whenever I passed: I didn't like the curve of his lip—I knew he was smiling at an inward joke at my expense. I wished I could ignore him, but he was an early associate of mine, and I owed him a general remark or two. While passing him, I tried to look casual, and stopped to say, 'Did you see that Nehru is going to London?' or 'The new taxes will kill all initiative,' and he agreed with me and explained something, and that was enough. Or we discussed the Government of India's tourist plans or hotel arrangements, and I had to let him talk— the poor fellow never suspected how little I cared for tourism or taxes or anything now. I sometimes toyed with the thought of changing the hotel. But it was not easy. Both Rosie and her husband seemed to be deeply devoted to this hotel. He was somehow averse to changing, although he never came down from his heights, and the girl seemed to have got used to this room with its view of a coconut grove outside, and people irrigating it from a well. It was a fascination that I could not easily understand or explain.

In other ways too I found it difficult to understand the girl. I found as I went on that she was gradually losing the free and easy manner of her former days. She allowed me to make love to her, of course, but she was also beginning to show excessive consideration for her husband on the hill. In the midst of my caresses, she would suddenly free herself and say, 'Tell Gaffur to bring the car. I want to go and see him.'

I had not yet reached the stage of losing my temper or speaking sharply to her. So I calmly answered, 'Gaffur will not come till this time tomorrow. You were up only yesterday. Why do you want to go again? He expects you there only tomorrow.'

'Yes,' she would say and remain thoughtful. I didn't like to see her sit up like that on her bed and brood, her hair unattended, her dress all crinkled. She clasped her knees with her hands.

'What is troubling you?' I had to ask her. 'Won't you tell me? I will always help you.'

She would shake her head and say, 'After all, he is my husband. I have to respect him. I cannot leave him there.'

My knowledge of women being poor and restricted to one, I could not decide how to view her statements. I could not understand whether she was pretending, whether her present pose was pretence or whether her account of all her husband's shortcomings was false, just to entice me. It was complex and obscure. I had to tell her, 'Rosie, you know very well that even if Gaffur came, he couldn't drive uphill at this hour.'

[119]

'Yes, yes, I understand,' she would reply and lapse into a mysterious silence again.

'What is troubling you?'

She started crying. 'After all ... After all ... Is this right what I am doing? After all, he has been so good to me, given me comfort and freedom. What husband in the world would let his wife go and live in a hotel room by herself, a hundred miles away?'

'It is not a hundred miles, but fifty-eight only,' I corrected. 'Shall I order you coffee or anything to eat?'

'No,' she would say point-blank, but continue the train of her own thoughts. 'As a good man he may not mind, but is it not a wife's duty to guard and help her husband, whatever the way in which he deals with her?' This last phrase was to offset in advance any reminder I might make about his indifference to her.

It was a confusing situation. Naturally, I could take no part in this subject: there was nothing I could add to or subtract from what she was saying. Distance seemed to lend enchantment to her view now. But I knew that she would have to spend only a few hours with him to come downhill raging against him, saying the worst possible things. Sometimes I heartily wished that the man would descend from his heights, take her, and clear out of the place. That would at least end this whole uncertain business once for all and help me to return to my platform duties. I could possibly try to do that even now. What prevented me from leaving the girl alone? The longer Marco went on with his work, the longer this agony was stretched. But he seemed to flourish in his solitude; that's probably what he had looked for all his life. But why could he not do something about his wife? A blind fellow. Sometimes I felt angry at the

[120]

thought of him. He had placed me in a hopeless predicament. I was compelled to ask her, 'Why don't you stay up with him, then?'

She merely replied, 'He sits up all night writing, and—'

'If he sits up all night writing, during the day you should talk to him,' I would say with a look of innocence.

'But all day he is in the cave!'

'Well, you may go and see it too. Why not? It ought to interest you.'

'While he is copying, no one may talk to him.'

'Don't talk to him, but study the objects yourself. A good wife ought to be interested in all her husband's activities.'

'True,' she said, and merely sighed. This was a thoroughly inexperienced and wrong line for me to take; it led us nowhere, but only made her morose.

Her eyes lit up with a new hope when I spoke about the dance. It was after all her art that I first admired; of late, in our effort to live the lovers' life, that all-important question was pushed to the background. Her joy at finding shops, cinemas, and caresses made her forget for a while her primary obsession. But not for long. She asked me one evening, point-blank, 'Are you also like him?'

'In what way?'

'Do you also hate to see me dance?'

'Not at all. What makes you think so?'

'At one time you spoke like a big lover of art, but now you never give it a thought.'

It was true. I said something in excuse, clasped her hands in mine, and swore earnestly, 'I will do anything for you. I will give my life to see you dance. Tell me what to do. I will do it for you.'

She brightened up. Her eyes lit up with a new fervour at the mention of dancing. So I sat up with her, helping her to day-dream. I found out the clue to her affection and utilised it to the utmost. Her art and her husband could not find a place in her thoughts at the same time; one drove the other out.

She was full of plans. At five in the morning she'd start her practice and continue for three hours. She would have a separate hall, long enough and wide enough for her to move in. It must have a heavy carpet, which would be neither too smooth under the feet nor too rough, and which would not fold while she practised her steps on it. At one corner of the room she'd have a bronze figure of Nataraja, the god of dancers, the god whose primal dance created the vibrations that set the worlds in motion. She would have incense sticks burning. After her morning practice, she would call up the chauffeur.

'Are you going to have a car?' I asked.

'Naturally, otherwise how can I move about? When I have so many engagements, it will be necessary for me to have a car. It'll be indispensable, don't you think?'

'Surely. I'll remember it.'

She would then spend an hour or two in the forenoon studying the ancient works of the art, *Natya Shastra of Bharat Muni*, a thousand years old, and various other books, because without a proper study of the ancient methods it would be impossible to keep the purity of the classical forms. All the books were in her uncle's house, and she would write to him to send them on to her by and by. She would also want a *pundit* to come to her to help her to understand the texts, as they were all written in an old, terse style. 'Can you get me a Sanskrit *pundit*?' she asked.

'Of course I can. There are dozens of them.'

'I shall also want him to read for me episodes from *Ramayana* and *Mahabarata*, because they are a treasure house, and we can pick up so many ideas for new compositions from them.'

A little rest after lunch; and at three o'clock she would go out and do shopping, and a drive and return home in the evening or see a picture, unless, of course, there was a performance in the evening. If there was a performance, she would like to rest till three in the afternoon and reach the hall only half an hour before the show. 'That would be enough, because I shall do all the make-up and dressing before I leave the house.'

She thought of every detail, and dreamed of it night and day. Her immediate need would be a party of drummers and musicians to assist her morning practice. When she was ready to appear before the public, she would tell me and then I could fix her public engagements. I felt rather baffled by her fervour. I wished I could keep pace at least with her idiom. I felt that I ought immediately to pick up and cultivate the necessary jargon. I felt silly to be watching her and listening to her, absolutely tongue-tied. There were, of course, two ways open: to bluff one's way through and trust to luck, or to make a clean breast of it all. I listened to her talk for two days and finally confessed to her, 'I am a layman, not knowing much of the technicalities of the dance; I'd like you to teach me something of it.'

I didn't want her to interpret it as an aversion on my part to the art. That might drive her back into the arms of her husband, and so I took care to maintain the emphasis on my passion for the art. It gave us a fresh intimacy. This common interest brought us close together. Wherever we were she kept talking to me on the various subleties of the art, its technicalities, and explaining as to a child its idioms. She seemed to notice our surroundings less and less. In Gaffur's car as we sat she said, 'You know what a *pallavi* is? The time-scheme is all-important in it. It does not always run in the simple style of one-two, one-two; it gets various odds thrown in, and at a different tempo.' She uttered its syllables, 'Ta-ka-ta-ki-ta, Ta-ka.' It amused me. 'You know, to get the footwork right within those five or seven beats requires real practice, and when the tempo is varied . . .' This was something that Gaffur could safely overhear, as we went up the hill, as we came out of a shop, as we sat in a cinema. While seeing a picture, she would suddenly exclaim, 'My uncle has with him a very old song written on a palm leaf. No one has seen it. My mother was the only person in the whole country who knew the song and could dance to it. I'll get that song too from my uncle. I'll show you how it goes. Shall we go back to our room? I don't want to see more of this picture. It looks silly.'

We immediately adjourned to Room 28, where she asked me to remain seated, and went into the ante-room and came back with her dress tucked in and tightened up for the performance. She said, 'I'll show you how it goes. Of course, I'm not doing it under the best of conditions. I need at least a drummer . . . Move off that chair, and sit on the bed. I want some space here.'

She stood at one end of the hall and sang the song lightly, in a soft undertone, a song from an ancient Sanskrit composition of a lover and lass on the banks of Jamuna; and it began with such a verve, when she lightly raised her foot and let it down, allowing her anklets to jingle, I felt thrilled. Though I was an ignoramus, I felt moved by the movements, rhythm, and time, although I did not quite follow the meaning of the words. She stopped now and then to explain: '*Nari* means girl—and *mani* is a jewel. . . . The whole line means: "It is impossible for me to bear this burden of love you have cast on me." ' She panted while she explained. There were beads of perspiration on her forehead and lip. She danced a few steps, paused for a moment, and explained, 'Lover means always God,' and she took the trouble to explain further to me the intricacies of its rhythm. The floor resounded with the stamping of her feet. I felt nervous that those on the floor below might ask us to stop, but she never cared, never bothered about anything. I could see, through her effort, the magnificence of the composition, its symbolism, the boyhood of a very young god, and his fulfilment in marriage, the passage of years from youth to decay, but the heart remaining ever fresh like a lotus on a pond. When she indicated the lotus with her fingers, you could almost hear the ripple of water around it. She held the performance for nearly an hour; it filled me with the greatest pleasure on earth. I could honestly declare that, while I watched her perform, my mind was free, for once, from all carnal thoughts; I viewed her as a pure abstraction. She could make me forget my surroundings. I sat with open-mouthed wonder watching her. Suddenly she stopped and flung her whole weight on me with 'What a darling. You are giving me a new lease of life.'

Next time we went up the hill our strategy was ready. I would drop her there and come back to town. She would stay behind for two days, bearing all the possible loneliness and irritation, and speak to her husband. It was imperative that before we proceeded any further we should clear up the entire matter with her husband. She would do the talking for two days. And then I would go up and meet them, and then we would plan further stages of work for her career. She had suddenly become very optimistic about her husband, and often leaned over to whisper, 'I think he will agree to our proposal,' so that Gaffur should not know, or revelled in further wishful thoughts. 'He is not bad. It's all a show, you know. He is merely posing to be uninterested. You don't talk to him at all. I'll do all the talking. I know how to tackle him. Leave him to me.' And so she spoke until we reached the top. 'Oh, see those birds! What colours! You know, there is a small piece about a parrot on a maiden's arm. I'll dance it for you sometime.'

He was in an unbelievably cheerful mood. He greeted his wife with greater warmth than ever before. 'Do you know there is a third cave; a sort of vault leads into it. I scraped the lime, and there you have a complete fresco of musical notations, in symbolic figures. The style is of the fifth century. I am puzzled how such a wide period-difference has come about,' he said, greeting us on the veranda itself. He had pulled up a chair and was watching the valley, with papers on his lap. He held up his latest discovery. His wife looked at it with due ecstasy and cried, 'Musical notations! What wonderful things! Do take me to see them, will you?'

'Yes; come with me tomorrow morning. I'll explain it to you.'

'Oh, wonderful!' And she cried, in a highly affected voice, 'I'll try and sing them to you.'

'I doubt if you can. It's more difficult than you imagine.'

She looked fevered and anxious about pleasing him. It seemed to bode no good. This all-round cheeriness somehow did not please me. He turned and asked, 'What about you, Raju? Would you like to see my discovery?'

'Of course, but I have to get back to town as soon as possible. I just came to leave the lady here, because she was so anxious; and to know if you want anything and if things are quite satisfactory.'

'Oh, perfect, perfect!' he cried. 'That Joseph is a wonderful man. I don't see him, I don't hear him, but he does everything for me at the right time. That's how I want things to be, you know. He moves on ball-bearings, I think.'

That's what I thought when I saw Rosie demonstrate to me in her hotel room, her whole movement being so much against the fixed factors of bone and muscle, walls and floor.

Marco continued his rhapsody on Joseph. 'I can never thank you enough for finding me a place like this and a man like Joseph. He's really a wonder. What a pity he should be wasting his talent on this hilltop!'

'You are very appreciative,' I said. 'I'm sure he'll be elated to know your opinion.'

'Oh, I have told him that without any reserve. I have also invited him to join my household any time he wished to come and settle in the plains.'

He was unusually loquacious and warm. His nature flourished on solitude, and cave-frescoes. How happy he'd have been, I thought, to have had Joseph for a wife! My mind was busy with these thoughts as he was talking. Rosie went on like a good wife, saying, 'I hope there is food to eat, and everything is okay. If there is milk may I give you all coffee?' She ran in and returned to say, 'Yes, there is milk. I'll make coffee for all of you. I won't take more than five minutes.'

I was somehow feeling not quite at ease today. There was a

lot of suspense and anxiety at the back of my mind. I was nervous of what he would say to Rosie and really anxious that he should not hurt her. Also, at the same time, a fear that if he became too nice to her, she might not care for me. I wanted him to be good to her, listen to her proposals, and yet leave her to my care! What an impossible, fantastic combination of circumstances to expect!

While Rosie was fussing with the coffee inside, he brought out another chair for me. 'I always do my work here,' he said. I felt that he honoured the valley with his patronage. He took out a bundle of sheets in an album, and a few photographs. He had made voluminous notes on all the cave-paintings. He had filled sheet after sheet with their description, transcription, and what not. They were obscure, but still I went through them with a show of interest. I wished I could ask questions on their value, but again I found myself tongue-tied, because I lacked the idiom. I wished I had been schooled in a jargon-picking institution; that would have enabled me to move with various persons on equal terms. No one would listen to my plea of ignorance and take the trouble to teach me as Rosie did. I listened to him. He was flinging at me dates, evidence, generalisations, and descriptions of a variety of paintings and carvings. I dared not ask what was the earthly use of all that he was doing. When coffee arrived, brought on a tray by Rosie (she had glided in softly, as if to show that she could rival Joseph's steps; I was startled when she held the cups under my nose), he said to me, 'When this is published, it'll change all our present ideas of the history of civilisation. I shall surely mention in the book my debt to you in discovering this place.'

Two days later I was back there. I went there at noon, at a time when I was sure that Marco would have gone down to the cave so that I might possibly get Rosie alone for a few moments. They were not in the bungalow. Joseph was there, arranging their midday meal in the back room. He said, 'They have gone down and are not back yet.'

I looked up at Joseph's face as if to get a sign of how things were. But he seemed evasive. I asked cheerily, 'How is everything, Joseph?'

'Very well, sir.'

'That man thinks so well of you!' I said to flatter him.

But he took it indifferently. 'What if he does! I only do my duty. In my profession, some may curse, and some may bless, but I don't care who says what. Last month there was a group who wanted to assault me because I said I could not procure girls for them, but was I afraid? I ordered them to quit next morning. This is a spot for people to live in. I give them all the comforts ungrudgingly. It costs eight annas sometimes to get a pot of water, and I have to send cans and pots with any bus or truck going downhill, and wait for its return—but the guests will never know the difficulty. They are not expected to. It's my business to provide, and it's their business to pay the bill. Let there be no confusion about it. I do my duty and others must do theirs. But if they think I'm a procurer, I get very angry.'

'Naturally, no one would like it,' I said just to cut his monologue. 'I hope this man does not bother you in any way?'

'Oh, no, he is a gem. A good man; would be even better if his wife left him alone. He was so happy without her. Why did you bring her back? She seems to be a horrible nagger.'

'Very well, I'll take her downhill and leave the man in peace,'

I said, starting for the cave. The pathway on the grass had become smooth and white with Marco's tread. I passed through the thicket and was crossing the sandy stretch when I found him coming in the opposite direction. He was dressed heavily as usual, the portfolio swung in his grip. A few yards behind him followed Rosie. I could not read anything from their faces.

'Hello!' I cried cheerily, facing him. He looked up, paused, opened his mouth to say something, swallowed his words, stepped aside to avoid encountering me, and resumed his forward march. Rosie followed as if she were walking in her sleep. She never even turned to give me a look. A few yards behind Rosie I brought up the rear, and we entered the bungalow gate as a sort of caravan. I felt it would be best to follow their example of silence, and to look just as moody and morose as they. It matched the company very well.

From the top of the veranda he turned to address us. He said, 'It'll not be necessary for either of you to come in.' He went straight into his room and shut the door.

Joseph emerged from the kitchen door, wiping a plate. 'I'm waiting to take instructions for dinner.'

Rosie without a word passed up the steps, moved down the veranda, opened the door of his room, passed in, and shut the door. This utter quietness was getting on my nerves. It was entirely unexpected and I did not know how to respond to it. I thought he would either fight us or argue or do something. But this behaviour completely baffled me.

Gaffur came round, biting a straw between his teeth, to ask, 'What time are we going down?'

I knew this was not his real intention in coming, but to see the drama. He must have whiled away his time gossiping with Joseph; and they must have pooled their information about the girl. I said, 'Why are you in a hurry, Gaffur?' and added with bitterness, 'when you can stay on and see a nice show.'

He came close to me and said, 'Raju, this is not at all good. Let us get away. Leave them alone. After all, they are husband and wife; they'll know how to make it up. Come on. Go back to your normal work. You were so interested and carefree and happy then.'

I had nothing to say to this. It was very reasonable advice he was giving me. Even at that moment, it would have been all different if God had given me the sense to follow Gaffur's advice. I should have gone quietly back, leaving Rosie to solve her problems with her husband. That would have saved many sharp turns and twists in my life's course. I told Gaffur, 'Wait near the car, I'll tell you,' keeping irritation out of my voice.

Gaffur went away, grumbling. Presently I heard him sounding the horn—as irate bus-drivers do when their passengers get down at a wayside teashop. I decided to ignore it. I saw the door on the other side open. Marco showed himself outside the front veranda, and said, 'Driver, are you ready to go?'

'Yes, sir,' said Gaffur.

'Very well then,' said the man. He picked up his bundle and started walking to the car. I saw him through the glass shutters of the hall window. It puzzled me. I tried to cross the hall and go out through the door, but it was bolted. I quickly turned, ran down the steps, and went round to Gaffur's car. Marco had already taken his seat. Gaffur had not started the engine yet. He was afraid to ask about the others, but marked time by fumbling with the switch-key. He must have been surprised at the effect of sounding the horn. God knows why he did it;

perhaps he was testing it or idling or wanted to remind everyone concerned that time was passing.

'Where are you going?' I asked Marco, taking courage and putting my head into the car.

'I'm going down to the hotel to close my account there.'

'What do you mean?' I asked.

He looked me up and down with a fierce glance. 'I do not have to explain. I took the room and I am closing the account; that is all. Driver, you may present me your bill direct. Have a receipt ready when you want payment.'

'Is no one else coming?' ventured Gaffur, looking in the direction of the bungalow.

The man merely said, 'No,' and added, 'If anyone else is coming, I'll get out.'

'Driver,' I said with a sudden tone of authority. Gaffur was startled at being called 'driver' by me. 'Take that man wherever he may want to go and bring me back the car tomorrow—and you will make complete settlement of all your bills with him. Keep a separate account for my own trips.' I could have made a further demonstration of arrogance by saying I had brought the car for my own business and so forth, but I saw no point in all that. As I stood watching Marco, a sudden impulse moved me even without my knowledge. I opened the door of the car and pulled him out of it.

For all the heavy helmet and glasses that he wore, he was frail—too much frieze-gazing and cave-visiting had emaciated him. 'What? Are you attempting to manhandle me?' he shouted.

'I want to talk to you. I want you to talk. You can't just go away like this.' I found his breath coming and going sharply. I calmed down and said, softening my style, 'Come in and

[132]

have your food and speak out. Let us talk, discuss things, and
then do what you like. You can't abandon a wife in this place
and go away.' I looked at Gaffur and said, 'You are not in a
hurry, are you?'

'No, no. Have your food and come, sir. Plenty of time still.'

'I'll ask Joseph to give you food,' I added. I felt sorry that
I had not taken charge of the situation earlier.

'Who are you?' Marco asked suddenly. 'What is your
business with me?'

'A great deal. I have helped you. I have given a lot of time
to your business. I undertook a lot of responsibility for you,
these several weeks.'

'And I dispense with your service from this minute,' he
cried. 'Give me your bill and be done with it.' Even in his most
excited, emotional state, he would not forget his vouchers.

I said, 'Had we better not go into it calmly, sitting down and
calculating? I have with me some money that you left with me
before.'

'Very well,' he grunted. 'Let us be done with everything,
and then you get out of my sight.'

'Easily done,' I said. 'But look here, this bungalow has two
suites of rooms, and I can engage one perfectly legitimately.'

Joseph appeared on the steps. 'Will you be wanting a dinner
tonight?'

'No,' he said.

'Yes; I may,' I said. 'You may leave, Joseph, if you are in a
hurry. If I am staying, I'll send for you. Open the other suite
and account it to me.'

'Yes, sir.' He unlocked another door and I strode into it
with the air of a proprietor. I left the door open. It was my
room and I was free to leave the door ajar if I chose.

[133]

I looked out of the window. The sun's rays from the west were touching the tops of trees with gold. It was a breathtaking sight. I wished Rosie could see it. She was inside. I had lost the privilege of walking into their room. I sat down in the wooden chair in my suite and wondered what to do. What was it that I had done now? I had no clear programme. I had no doubt successfully pulled him out of the car. But that took us nowhere. He had gone and bolted himself in his room, and I was in mine. If I had let him go, I might at least have had a chance to bring Rosie round and get her to talk about herself. Now I had made a mess. Could I go out and ask Gaffur to sound the horn again so that the man might emerge from his room?

Half an hour passed thus. There was absolutely no sign of any speech or movement. I tiptoed out of my room. I went to the kitchen. Joseph was gone. I lifted the lids of the vessels. Food was there. No one seemed to have touched it. Heaven knew they were both starving. I felt a sudden pity for the man. Rosie must have completely faded out. It was her habit to ask for something to eat every two hours. At the hotel I constantly ordered a tray for her; if we were out I would stop all along the way to buy fruit or refreshment. Now the poor girl must be exhausted—and add to it the walk up and down to the cave. I felt suddenly angry at the thought of her. Why couldn't she eat or tell me what was what instead of behaving like a deaf-mute? Had the monster cut off her tongue? I wondered in genuine horror. I put the food on plates, put them on a tray, walked to their door. I hesitated for a second—only for a second; if I hesitated longer, I knew I would never go in. I pushed the door with my feet. Rosie was lying on her bed with eyes shut. (Was she in a faint? I wondered for a second.) I had never seen her in such a miserable condition before. He was sitting in his chair, elbow on the table, his chin on his fist. I had never seen him so vacant before. I felt pity for him. I held myself responsible for it. Why couldn't I have kept out of all this? I placed the tray before him.

'People have evidently forgotten their food today. If you have a burden on your mind it's no reason why you should waste your food.'

Rosie opened her eyes. They were swollen. She had large, vivacious eyes, but they looked as if they had grown one round larger now, and were bulging and fearsome, dull and red. She was a sorry sight in every way. She sat up and told me, 'Don't waste any more of your time with us. You go back. That's all I have to say,' in a thick, gruff, crackling voice. Her voice shook a little as she spoke. 'I mean it. Leave us now.'

What had come over this woman? Was she in league with her husband? She had every authority to ask me to get out. Probably she repented her folly in encouraging me all along. All I could say in reply was, 'First, you must have your food. For what reason are you fasting?'

She merely repeated, 'I want you to go.'

'Aren't you coming down?' I persisted to Marco. The man behaved as if he were a deaf-mute. He never showed any sign of hearing us.

She merely repeated, 'I am asking you to leave us. Do you hear?'

I grew weak and cowardly at her tone. I muttered, 'I mean, you are—or he may want to go down, if it is so—'

She clicked her tongue in disgust. 'Do you not understand? We want you to leave.'

I grew angry. This woman who had been in my arms forty-

[135]

eight hours ago was showing off. Many insulting and incrim-
inating remarks welled up in my throat. But even in that stress
I had the sense to swallow back my words, and, feeling that it
would be dangerous to let myself stand there any longer,
turned on my heel and went in a stride to the car. 'Gaffur, let
us go.'

'Only one passenger?'

'Yes.' I banged the door and took my seat.

'What about them?'

'I don't know. You had better settle with them later.'

'If I have to come again to talk to them, who pays the fare
for the trip?'

I beat my brow. 'Begone, man. You can settle all that later.'

Gaffur sat in his seat with the look of a philosopher, started
the car, and was off. I had a hope, as I turned to look, that she
might watch me from the window. But no such luck. The car
sped downward. Gaffur said, 'It's time your elders found a
bride for you.' I said nothing in reply, and he said, through the
gathering darkness, 'Raju, I'm senior in years. I think this is
the best thing you have done. You will be more happy hereafter.'

Gaffur's prophecy was not fulfilled in the coming days. I
cannot remember a more miserable period of my life. The
usual symptoms were present, of course: no taste for food, no
sound sleep, no stability (I couldn't stay put in any one place),
no peace of mind, no sweetness of temper or speech—no, no, no,
a number of no's. With all seriousness I returned to my normal
avocation. But everything looked so unreal. I relieved the boy
at the shop, sat there and handed out things and received cash,
but always with a feeling that it was a silly occupation. I

[136]

walked up and down the platform when the train arrived. Sure as anything, I could always get someone to take round.

'Are you Railway Raju?'

'Yes,' and then the fat paterfamilias, wife, and two children.

'You see, we are coming from . . . and So-and-so mentioned your name to us as a man who would surely help us . . . You see, my wife is keen on a holy bath at the source of Sarayu, and then I'd like to see an elephant camp, and anything else you suggest will be most welcome. But remember, only three days. I couldn't get even an hour of extra leave; I'll have to be in my office on . . .'

I hardly paid attention to what they said. I knew all their lines in advance; all that I paid attention to was the time at their disposal, and the extent of their financial outlay. Even the latter did not really interest me. It was more mechanical than intentional. I called up Gaffur, sat in the front seat, took the party about. While passing the New Extension, I pointed without even turning my head, 'Sir Frederick Lawley . . .' When we passed the statue, I knew exactly when the question would come, 'Whose is this statue?' and I knew when the next question was coming and had my answer ready, 'The man left behind by Robert Clive to administer the district. He built all the tanks and dams and developed this district. Good man. Hence the statue.' At the tenth-century Iswara temple at Vinayak Street, I reeled off the description of the frieze along the wall: 'If you look closely, you will see the entire epic *Ramayana* carved along the wall,' and so forth. I took them to the source of Sarayu on the misty heights of Mempi Peak, watched the lady first plunge in the basin, the man avowing that he did not care and then following her example. I then took them into the inner shrine, showed them the ancient stone

[137]

image on the pillar, with Shiva absorbing the Ganges river in his matted locks . . .

I collected my fee, and my commission from Gaffur and the rest, and saw them off next day. I did it all mechanically, without zest. I was, of course, thinking of Rosie all the time. 'That man has probably starved her to death, driven her mad, or left her in the open to be eaten by tigers,' I told myself. I looked forlorn and uninterested and my mother tried to find out why. She asked, 'What has gone wrong with you?'

'Nothing,' I replied. My mother had been so little used to seeing me about the house that she felt surprised and uneasy. But she left me alone. I ate, slept, hung about the railway platform, conducted visitors about, but I was never at peace with myself. My mind was all the while troubled. It was a natural obsession. I didn't even know what had happened, what all the silence and unnatural calm meant. This was a most unexpected development. As I had visualised, I had thought in my dreamy-happy way that he'd present me with his wife and say, 'I'm happy you are going to look after her and her art; I'd like to be left alone to pursue my cave studies; you are such a fine fellow to do this for us.' Or, on the other hand, he might have rolled up his sleeve to throw me out— one or the other, but I never bargained for this kind of inexplicable stalemate. And what was more, for the girl to support him with such ferocity. I was appalled at the duplicity of her heart. I agonised over and over again, piecing together the data and reading their meaning. I deliberately refrained from opening the subject with Gaffur. He respected my sentiment and never mentioned it again, although I was hoping desperately each day that he would say something about them. On certain days when I wanted him, he was not available. I knew then that he must have gone to the Peak House. I refrained from going near the Anand Bhavan. If any of my customers wanted a hotel I sent them nowadays to the Taj. I did not have to bother myself about them unduly. Marco had said he'd settle their accounts direct—well, you could depend upon him to do it. I came into the picture only to collect a commission from them, as from Gaffur himself. But I was prepared to forgo it all. I was in no mood to make money. In the world of gloom in which I was plunged there was no place for money. There must have been some money, I suppose, somewhere. My mother was able to carry on the household as before, and the shop continued to exist. I knew Gaffur's account must also have been settled. But he never said a word about it. So much the better. I didn't want to be reminded of the life that was gone.

I felt bored and terrified by the boredom of normal life, so much had I got used to a glamorous, romantic existence. Gradually I found taking tourists around a big nuisance. I began to avoid the railway station. I let the porter's son meet the tourists. He had already attempted his hand at it before. Of course, the tourists might miss my own speeches and descriptions, but lately I had become dull-witted, and they probably preferred the boy, as he was at least as curious and interested as they in seeing places. Perhaps he was beginning to answer to the name of Railway Raju too.

How many days passed thus? Only thirty, though they looked to me like years. I was lying asleep on the floor of my house one afternoon. I was half awake and had noted the departure of the Madras Mail at four-thirty. When the chug-chug of the train died away, I tried to sleep again, having been disturbed by its noisy arrival. My mother came and said,

'Someone is asking for you.' She didn't wait for questions, but went into the kitchen.

I got up and went to the door. There stood Rosie on the threshold, with a trunk at her feet and a bag under her arm. 'Rosie, why didn't you say you were coming? Come in, come in. Why stand there? That was only my mother.' I carried her trunk in. I could guess a great many things about her. I didn't want to ask her any questions. I didn't feel like knowing anything. I fussed about her, lost my head completely. 'Mother!' I cried. 'Here is Rosie! She is going to be a guest in our house.'

My mother came out of the kitchen formally, smiled a welcome, and said, 'Be seated on that mat. What's your name?' she asked kindly, and was rather taken aback to hear the name 'Rosie'. She expected a more orthodox name. She looked anguished for a moment, wondering how she was going to accommodate a 'Rosie' in her home.

I stood about awkwardly. I had not shaved since the morning; I had not combed my hair; my *dhoti* was discoloured and rumpled; the vest I wore had several holes on the back and chest. I folded my arms across my chest to cover the holes. I could not have made a worse impression if I had tried hard. I was ashamed of the torn mat—it had been there since we built the house—the dark hall with the smoky walls and tiles. All the trouble I used to take to create an impression on her was gone in a moment. If she realised that this was my normal setting, God knew how she would react. I was glad at least I was wearing my torn vest instead of being bare-bodied as was my habit at home. My mother hardly ever noticed the hairiness of my chest, but Rosie, oh—

My mother was busy in the kitchen, but she managed to

[140]

come out for a moment to observe the formality of receiving a
guest. A guest was a guest, even though she might be a Rosie.
So my mother came up and sat down on the mat with an air of
settling down to a chat. The very first question she asked was,
'Who has come with you, Rosie?' Rosie blushed, hesitated, and
looked at me. I moved a couple of steps backward in order that
she might see me only dimly, and not in all my raggedness.

I replied, 'I think she has come alone, Mother.'

My mother was amazed. 'Girls today! How courageous
you are! In our day we wouldn't go to the street corner without
an escort. And I have been to the market only once in my life,
when Raju's father was alive.'

Rosie blinked and listened in silence, not knowing how to
react to these statements. She simply opened her eyes wide
and raised her brows. I watched her. She looked a little paler
and slightly careworn—not the swollen-eyed, gruff-toned
monster she had seemed the other day. Her tone was sweet
as ever. She looked slightly weak, but as if she hadn't a care
in the world. My mother said, 'Water is boiling; I'll give you
coffee. Do you like coffee?' I was relieved that the conversation
was coming down to this level. I hoped my mother would
continue to talk about herself rather than ask questions. But
it was not to be. She asked next, 'Where do you come from?'

'From Madras,' I answered promptly.

'What brings you here?'

'She has come to see some friends.'

'Are you married?'

'No,' I answered promptly.

My mother shot a look at me. It seemed to be meaningful.
She withdrew her glance swiftly from me, and, looking at her
guest kindly, asked, 'Don't you understand Tamil?'

I knew I should shut up now. I let Rosie answer in Tamil, 'Yes. It's what we speak at home.'

'Who else have you in your house?'

'My uncle, my aunt, and—' She was trailing away, and my mother shot at her the next terrible question. 'What is your father's name?'

It was a dreadful question for the girl. She knew only her mother and always spoke of her. I had never questioned her about it. The girl remained silent for a moment and, said, 'I have . . . no father.'

My mother was at once filled with the greatest sympathy and cried, 'Poor one, without father or mother. I am sure your uncle must be looking after you well. Are you a B.A.?'

'Yes.' I corrected. 'She is an M.A.'

'Good, good, brave girl. Then you lack nothing in the world. You are not like us uneducated women. You will get on anywhere. You can ask for your railway ticket, call a policeman if somebody worries you, and keep your money. What are you going to do? Are you going to join government service and earn? Brave girl.' My mother was full of admiration for her. She got up, went in, and brought her a tumbler of coffee. The girl drank it off gratefully. I was wondering how best I could sneak out and groom myself properly. But there was no chance. My father's architectural sense had not gone beyond building a single large hall and a kitchen. Of course, there was the front *pyol* on which visitors and menfolk generally sat. But how could I ask Rosie to move there? It was too public—the shop-boy and all his visitors would come round, gaze at her and ask if she was married. This was a slightly difficult situation for me. We had got used to common living in that hall. It had never occurred to us to be otherwise. We never wanted anything more than this. My father lived in his shop, I played under the tree, and we received male visitors on the outside *pyol* and left the inner room for mother or any lady that might come. When we slept we went in. If it was warm, we slept on the *pyol*. The hall was a passage, a dressing-room, drawing-room, study, everything combined. My shaving mirror was on a nail; my finest clothes hung on a peg; for a bath I dashed to a chamber in the back-yard, half open to the sky, and poured over my head water drawn straight from the well. I ran up and down and conducted my toilet while my mother came into or out of the kitchen or slept or sat moping in the hall. We had got used to each other's presence and did not mind it in the least. But now with Rosie there?

My mother, as if understanding my predicament, said to the girl, 'I'm going to the well. Will you come with me? You are a city girl. You must know something of our village life too.' The girl quietly rose and followed her; I hoped she'd not be subjected to an inquisition at the well. The minute their backs were turned I got busy, ran hither and thither, scraped my chin in a hurry, cut myself a little, bathed, groomed myself, and changed into better clothes, and by the time they were back from the well I was in a condition to be viewed by the Princess of the Earth. I went over to the shop and sent the boy to fetch Gaffur.

'Rosie, if you would like to wash and dress, go ahead. I'll wait outside. We'll go out after that.'

It was perhaps an unwarranted luxury to engage Gaffur for an outing. But I saw no other way. I could not talk to her in our home, and I could not make her walk through the streets. Although I had done it before, today it seemed different. I felt a little abashed to be seen with her.

[143]

I told Gaffur, 'She is back.'

He said, 'I know it. They were here at the hotel, and he went by the Madras train.'

'You never told me anything.'

'Why should I? You were going to know anyway.'

'What, what has happened?'

'Ask the lady herself, now that you have her in your pocket.' He sounded resentful.

I told him placatingly, 'Oh, don't be sour, Gaffur . . . I want the car for the evening.'

'I'm at your service, sir. What do I have the taxi for unless it is to drive you where you command?' He winked and I was relieved to see him back in his old cheerful mood. When Rosie appeared at the door I went and told my mother, 'We will come back, Mother, after a little outing.'

'Where?' asked Gaffur, looking at us through the glass. As we hesitated he asked puckishly, 'Shall I drive to the Peak House?'

'No, no,' Rosie cried, becoming very alert at the mention of it. 'I have had enough of it.' I didn't pursue the subject.

As we passed the Taj I asked, 'Would you like to eat there?'

'Your mother gave me coffee; that is enough. What a fine mother you have!'

'The only trouble is she asks you about marriage!' We laughed nervously at this joke.

'Gaffur, drive on to the river,' I said. He drove through the market road, honking his horn impatiently through the crowd. It was a crowded hour. Lots of people were moving around. The lights were up. Shop lights sparkled and lit up the thoroughfare. He took a sharp turn at Ellaman Street—that narrow street in which oil-merchants lived, the oldest street in the city, with children playing in it, cows lounging, and donkeys and dogs blocking the passage so narrow that any passing car almost touched the walls of the houses. Gaffur always chose this way to the river, although there was a better approach. It gave him some sort of thrill to honk his car and scatter the creatures in the road in a fright. Ellaman Street ended with the last lamp on the road, and the road imperceptibly merged into the sand. He applied the brake under the last lamp, with a jerk sufficient to shake us out of the car. He was in an unusually jovial mood today; he was given to his own temperaments and moods, and no one could predict how he would behave at a given moment. We left him under the lamp. I said, 'We want to walk about.' He winked at me mischievously in reply.

The evening had darkened. There were still a few groups sitting here and there on the sand. Some students were promenading. Children were playing and running in circles and shouting. On the river step, some men were having their evening dip. Far off at Nallappa's grove cattle were crossing the river with their bells tinkling. The stars were out. The Taluk office gong sounded seven. A perfect evening—as it had been for years and years. I had seen the same scene at the same hour for years and years. Did those children never grow up? I became a little sentimental and poetic, probably because of the companion at my side. My feelings and understanding seemed to have become suddenly heightened. I said, 'It's a beautiful evening,' to start a conversation. She briefly said, 'Yes.' We sought a secluded place, away from the route of promenading students.

I spread out my handkerchief, and said, 'Sit down, Rosie.' She picked away the kerchief and sat down. The gathering

[145]

darkness was congenial. I sat close to her and said, 'Now tell me everything from beginning to end.'

She remained in thought for a while and said, 'He left by the train this evening, and that is all.'

'Why did you not go with him?'

'I don't know. It is what I came for. But it didn't happen that way. Well, it is just as well. We were not meant to be in each other's company.'

'Tell me what happened. Why were you so rude to me that day?'

'I thought it best that we forgot each other, and that I went back to him.'

I did not know how to pursue this inquiry. I had no method of eliciting information—of all that had gone before. I fumbled and hummed and ha'd in questioning, till I suddenly felt that I was getting nowhere at all. I wanted a chronological narration, but she seemed unable to provide it. She was swinging forwards and backwards and talking in scraps. I was getting it all in a knot. I felt exasperated. I said, 'Answer me now, step by step. Give an answer to each question. I left you with him to speak about the proposal we had discussed. What did you tell him?'

'What we had agreed—that he should permit me to dance. He was quite happy till I mentioned it. I never spoke about it that whole day or till late next day. I led him on to tell me about his own activity. He showed me the pictures he had copied, the notes he had made, and spoke far into the night about their significance. He was going to be responsible for the rewriting of history, he said. He was talking about his plans for publishing his work. He said later he would go to Mexico, and to some of the Far Eastern countries to study similar subjects and add them on to his work. I was full of enthusiasm although I did not follow everything he said. I felt after all an understanding was coming between us—there in that lonely house, with trees rustling and foxes and animals prowling around, some light glimmering in the far-off valley. Next morning I went with him to the cave to have a look at the musical notations he had discovered. We had to pass through the main cave and beyond it into a vault by a crumbling ladder. A fierce, terrifying place. Nothing on earth would have induced me to go to a spot like that, stuffy, fierce, and dark. "There may be cobras here," I said. He ignored my fears. "You should feel at home, then," he said and we laughed. And then he lit up a lantern and showed me the wall on which he had scraped off the lime and discovered new pictures. They were the usual grotesque, ancient paintings of various figures, but he managed to spell out the letters around them, and take them down as musical notations. It was nothing I could make out or make use of. They were abstract verse about some theories of an ancient musical system or some such thing. I said, "If these were about dancing, I could perhaps have tried—" He looked up sharply. The word "dance" always stung him. I was afraid to go on with the subject. But there, squatting on the ancient floor, amidst cobwebs and bats, in that dim lantern light, I felt courage coming back. "Will you permit me to dance?"

'Promptly. came his reply, with a scowl, the old face was coming back. "Why?"

' "I think I'd be very happy if I could do that. I have so many ideas. I'd like to try. Just as you are trying to—"

' "Oh, you want to rival me, is that it? This is a branch of learning, not street-acrobatics."

' "You think dancing is street-acrobatics?"

' "I'm not prepared to discuss all that with you. An acrobat on a trapeze goes on doing the same thing all his life; well, your dance is like that. What is there intelligent or creative in it? You repeat your tricks all your life. We watch a monkey perform, not because it is artistic but because it is a monkey that is doing it." I swallowed all the insults; I still had hopes of converting him. I lapsed into silence and let him do his work. I turned the subject to other things, and he was normal again. After dinner that night he went back to his studies and I to my game-watching on the veranda. As usual, there was nothing to watch, but I sat there turning over in my head all that he had said and all that I had said, and wondering how to get through the business. I ignored all insults and troubles in the hope that if we reached agreement in the end, it'd all be forgotten. As I sat there, he came behind me, and, putting his hand on my shoulder, said, "I thought we had come to a final understanding about that subject. Did you or did you not promise that you'd never mention it again?" '

The Taluk office gong sounded eight and all the crowd had vanished. We were alone on the sand. Still I'd not learned anything about Rosie. Gaffur sounded the horn. It was no doubt late, but if I went home she would not be able to speak. I said, 'Shall we spend the night at the hotel?'

'No. I'd like to go back to your house. I have told your mother that I'll be back.'

'All right,' I said, remembering my cash position. 'Let us stay here for half an hour more. Now tell me.'

'His tone', she resumed, 'was now so kind that I felt I need not bother even if I had to abandon my own plans once and for all: if he was going to be so nice, I wanted nothing more—I'd almost made up my mind that I would ask nothing of him.

Yet as a last trick I said, encouraged by his tone, "I want you to see just one small bit, which I generally do as a memento of my mother. It was her piece, you know." I got up and pulled him by his hand to our room. I pushed aside the chair and other things. I adjusted my dress. I pushed him down to sit on the bed, as I had done with you. I sang that song about the lover and his girl on the banks of Jamuna and danced the piece for him. He sat watching me coldly. I had not completed the fifth line when he said, "Stop, I have seen enough."

'I stopped, abashed. I'd been certain that he was going to be captivated by it and tell me to go ahead and dance all my life. But he said, "Rosie, you must understand, this is not art. You have not sufficient training. Leave the thing alone."

'But here I committed a blunder. I said haughtily, "Every-one except you likes it."

' "For instance?"

' "Well, Raju saw me do it, and he was transported. Do you know what he said?"

' "Raju! Where did you do it for him?"

' "At the hotel." And then he said, "Come and sit here," pointing at the chair, like an examining doctor. He subjected me to a close questioning. I think it went on all night. He asked details of our various movements ever since we came here, what time you came to the hotel each day, when you left, where you kept yourself in the room, and how long, and so on, all of which I had to answer. I broke down and cried. He got from my answers enough indication of what we had been doing. Finally he said, "I didn't know that that hotel catered to such fervid art-lovers! I was a fool to have taken too much decency for granted." Till dawn we sat there. He on the bed, and I on the chair. I was overcome with sleep and put my

[149]

head on the table, and when I awoke he was gone to the caves.

'Joseph had left some coffee for me. I tidied myself up and went down in search of him. I felt I had made the capital blunder of my life. I had been indiscreet in talking to him as I had been indiscreet and wrong in all my actions. I realised I had committed an enormous sin. I walked as in a dream down to the cave. My mind was greatly troubled. I didn't want anything more in life than to make my peace with him. I did not want to dance. I felt lost . . . I was in terror. I was filled with some sort of pity for him too, as I remembered how he had sat up unmoving on the bed all night while I sat in the chair. The look of despair and shock in his face haunted me. I walked down the valley, hardly noticing my surroundings. If a tiger had crossed my path I'd hardly have noticed it . . . I found him sitting in his cave on his usual folding stool, sketching out his copies. His back was turned to the entrance when I went in. But as I got into the narrower entrance the light was blocked and he turned. He looked at me coldly. I stood like a prisoner at the bar. "I have come to apologise sincerely. I want to say I will do whatever you ask me to do. I committed a blunder . . ."

'He returned to his work without a word. He went on as if he had been alone. I waited there. Finally, when he had finished his day's work, he picked up his portfolio and papers and started out. He put on his helmet and spectacles and went past me as if I had not existed. I had stood there for nearly three hours, I think. He had measured, copied, noted down, and examined with a torch, but without paying the slightest attention to me. When he went back to the bungalow, I followed him. That's where you saw us. I went to his room. He sat in

[150]

his chair and I on the bed. No word or speech. You came into the room again. I sincerely hoped you would leave us and go away, and that we could be peaceful between ourselves . . . Day after day it went on. I stayed on hopefully. I found that he would not eat the food I touched. So I let Joseph serve him. I ate my food alone in the kitchen. If I lay on the bed, he slept on the floor. So I took to sleeping on the floor, and he went and lay on the bed. He never looked at me or spoke. He arranged with Joseph and went down a couple of times, leaving me alone in the bungalow. He returned and went about his business without worrying about me. But I followed him, day after day, like a dog—waiting on his grace. He ignored me totally. I could never have imagined that one human being could ignore the presence of another human being so completely. I followed him like a shadow, leaving aside all my own pride and self-respect; I hoped that ultimately he'd come round. I never left his side even for a moment, whether in his room or in the cave. It was a strain to remain speechless in that vast lonely place. I thought I had gone dumb. Joseph was the only one to whom I could say a word whenever he appeared, but he was a reserved man and did not encourage me. I had spent three weeks thus, in a vow of silence. I could not stand it any more. So one night as he sat at his table I said, "Have you not punished me enough?" My voice sounded strange, and like someone else's to me after so many weeks. It had a booming quality in that silent place that startled me. He started at the sound, turned, looked at me, and said, "This is my last word to you. Don't talk to me. You can go where you please or do what you please."

' "I want to be with you. I want you to forget everything. I want you to forgive me—" I said. Somehow I began to like

[151]

him very much. It seemed enough if he forgave me and took me back.

'But he said, "Yes, I'm trying to forget—even the earlier fact that I ever took a wife. I want to get out of here too—but I have to complete my work; and I'm here for that. You are free to get out and do what you please."

' "I'm your wife and I'm with you."

' "You are here because I'm not a ruffian. But you are not my wife. You are a woman who will go to bed with anyone that flatters your antics. That's all. I don't, don't want you here, but if you are going to be here, don't talk. That is all."

'I felt too hurt. I thought that Othello was kindlier to Desdemona. But I bore everything. I had a wild hope that in the end he'd relent, that when we left this place he might change. Once we were back in our home, everything would be all right.

'One day he started packing up. I tried to help him, but he would not let me; and then I packed up my things too, and followed him. Gaffur's car arrived. Both of us came down to the hotel. Back in Twenty-eight. The room looked poisonous to me now. He stayed for a day settling accounts; and at train time he went with the baggage to the railway station. I followed him mutely. I waited patiently. I knew he was going back to our home at Madras. I wanted very much to go back home. The porter carried our trunks. He pointed at my portion of the baggage and told the porter, "I don't know about these—not mine." So the porter looked at me for a second and separated my box. When the train arrived the porter carried only his baggage, and he took his seat in a compartment. I didn't know what to do. I picked up my trunk and followed. When I tried to step into the compartment he said, "I have no ticket for you," and he flourished a single ticket and shut the door on me. The train moved. I came to your home.'

She sat sobbing for a while. I comforted her. 'You are in the right place. Forget all your past. We will teach that cad a lesson by and by.' I made a grandiose announcement, 'First, I'll make the world recognise you as the greatest artist of the time.'

Within a short time my mother understood everything. When Rosie had gone in for a bath, she said, cornering me, 'This cannot go on long, Raju—you must put an end to it.'

'Don't interfere, Mother. I am an adult. I know what I am doing.'

'You can't have a dancing-girl in your house. Every morning with all that dancing and everything going on! What is the home coming to?'

Encouraged by me, Rosie had begun to practise. She got up at five in the morning, bathed, and prayed before the picture of a god in my mother's niche, and began a practice session which went on for nearly three hours. The house rang with the jingling of her anklets. She ignored her surroundings completely, her attention being concentrated upon her movements and steps. After that she helped my mother, scrubbed, washed, swept, and tidied up everything in the house. My mother was pleased with her and seemed kind to her. I never thought that my mother would create a problem for me now, but here she was. I said, 'What has come over you all of a sudden?'

My mother paused. 'I was hoping you would have the sense to do something about it. It can't go on like this for ever. What will people say?'

'Who are "people"?' I asked.

[153]

'Well, my brother and your cousins and others known to us.'

'I don't care for their opinion. Just don't bother about such things.'

'Oh! That's a strange order you are giving me, my boy. I can't accept it.'

The gentle singing in the bathroom ceased; my mother dropped the subject and went away as Rosie emerged from her bath fresh and blooming. Looking at her, one would have thought that she had not a care in the world. She was quite happy to be doing what she was doing at the moment, was not in the least bothered about the past, and looked forward tremendously to the future. She was completely devoted to my mother.

But unfortunately my mother, for all her show of tenderness, was beginning to stiffen inside. She had been listening to gossip, and she could not accommodate the idea of living with a tainted woman. I was afraid to be cornered by her, and took care not to face her alone. But whenever she could get at me, she hissed a whisper into my ear. 'She is a real snake-woman, I tell you. I never liked her from the first day you mentioned her.'

I was getting annoyed with my mother's judgement and duplicity. The girl, in all innocence, looked happy and carefree and felt completely devoted to my mother. I grew anxious lest my mother should suddenly turn round and openly tell her to quit. I changed my tactics and said, 'You are right, Mother. But you see, she is a refugee, and we can't do anything. We have to be hospitable.'

'Why can't she go to her husband and fall at his feet? You know, living with a husband is no joke, as these modern girls imagine. No husband worth the name was ever conquered by

[154]

powder and lipstick alone. You know, your father more than once . . .' She narrated an anecdote about the trouble created by my father's unreasonable, obstinate attitude in some family matter and how she met it. I listened to her anecdote patiently and with admiration, and that diverted her for a while. After a few days she began to allude to the problems of husband and wife whenever she spoke to Rosie, and filled the time with anecdotes about husbands: good husbands, mad husbands, reasonable husbands, unreasonable ones, savage ones, slightly deranged ones, moody ones, and so on and so forth; but it was always the wife, by her doggedness, perseverance, and patience, that brought him round. She quoted numerous mythological stories of Savitri Seetha, and all the well-known heroines. Apparently it was a general talk, apropos of nothing, but my mother's motives were naïvely clear. She was so clumsily roundabout that anyone could see what she was driving at. She was still supposed to be ignorant of Rosie's affairs, but she talked pointedly. I knew how Rosie smarted under these lessons, but I was helpless. I was afraid of my mother. I could have kept Rosie in a hotel, perhaps, but I was forced to take a more realistic view of my finances now. I was helpless as I saw Rosie suffer, and my only solace was that I suffered with her.

My worries were increasing. The boy at the shop was becoming more clamorous. My sales were poor, as the railways were admitting more pedlars on the platforms. My cash receipts were going down and my credit sales alone flourished. The wholesale merchants who supplied me with goods stopped credit to me. The boy's method of account-keeping was so chaotic that I did not know whether I was moving forward or backward. He produced cash from the counter in a haphazard

[155]

manner, and there were immense gaps on the shelves all over the shop. The boy was probably pocketing money and eating off the stuff. With my credit at the wholesalers' gone, the public complained that nothing one wanted was ever available. Suddenly the railways gave me notice to quit. I pleaded with the old stationmaster and porter, but they could do nothing; the order had come from high up. The shop was given to a new contractor.

I could not contemplate the prospect of being cut off from the railways. I grew desperate and angry. I shed tears at seeing a new man in the place where I and my father had sat. I slapped the boy on the cheek and he cried, and his father, the porter, came down on me and said, 'This is what he gets for helping you! I'd always told the boy— He was not your paid servant, anyway.'

'Payment for him? He has swallowed all the cash, credit, and every consumable article in the shop. Fattened himself on it! He must pay me for all his gluttony, which has ruined my business.'

'It's not he who has ruined you, but the *saithan* inside, which makes you talk like this.' He meant Rosie, I'm sure; she was peeping out of the doorway of our house. My mother watched from the *pyol* in great pain. It was a most unedifying spectacle.

I did not like the porter's reference, and so said something violent and tried to attack him. The stationmaster appeared on the scene and said, 'If you create a disturbance here, I'll have to prohibit your entry.'

The new shopman watched the scene with detachment. A whiskered fellow—I did not like his leering look. I turned on him fiercely, leaving the porter, and cried, 'Well, you'll also face the same situation, remember, some day. Don't be too sure.'

He twirled his whiskers and said, 'How can everyone hope for the same luck as yours?' He winked mischievously, at which I completely lost my temper and flew at him. He repelled me me with a back-stroke of his left hand as if swatting a fly, and I fell back, and knocked against my mother, who had come running onto the platform, a thing she had never done in her life. Luckily, I didn't knock her down.

She clung to my arm and screamed, 'Come away. Are you coming or not?' And the porter, the whiskered man, and everyone swore, 'You are saved today, because of that venerable old lady.' She dragged me back to the house; a few batches of paper, a register, and one or two odd personal belongings which I had kept in the shop were under my arm; with these I entered my house, and I knew my railway association was now definitely ended. It made my heart heavy. I felt so gloomy that I did not turn to see Rosie standing aside, staring at me. I flung myself in a corner of the hall and shut my eyes.

8

MY creditor was the Sait, a wholesale merchant in Market Road. He called on me the next day. There was a knock on the door, and there he was. I was watching Rosie at her practice, leaning against the wall and lounging on the mat. I felt abashed at the sight of the Sait at my door. I knew why he had come. He had brought a fat ledger wrapped up in a blue cloth. He seemed pleased at the sight of me, as if he had feared that I had run away from my post. I was at a loss to say anything for a moment. I didn't want to show confusion. After the railway station episode, I was recovering my sense of perspective again. While watching Rosie do her practice I seemed to get a clearer notion of what I should be doing. The sound of her anklets, and the whispered music she sang, her rhythm and movement, helped. I felt that I was once again becoming a man of importance. My mother, fortunately for me, had not spoken a word to me since the previous evening, and that saved me a great deal of embarrassment and strain. My mother could not help speaking to Rosie; in spite of all her prejudice, she liked the girl really and could not help treating her kindly. She had not the heart to starve her or offend her in any way. She attended on her enough to give her food and shelter, and left her alone. Only she could not trust herself to speak to me after the scene at the railway station. I am sure she felt that I had ruined, by my erratic ways, what her husband had so laboriously built up. But fortunately she did not take it out on the poor girl, but let her alone—after her usual dose of homilies and parables, all of which Rosie took in good humour.

The Sait was a thin man with a multi-coloured turban on his head. He was a prosperous businessman, very helpful with credit, but, of course, expected proper settlement of debts. He was at my door. I knew why. I fussed over him, and said, 'Come on, come on. Be seated. What a rare pleasure!' I dragged him and seated him on the *pyol*.

He was a good friend of mine, and he hesitated to talk about the dues. There was an awkward silence for a moment. Only Rosie's anklet-jingles could be heard for a while. He listened to it and asked, 'What is it?'

'Oh!' I said casually. 'A dance practice is going on.'

'Dance practice!' He was astounded. It was the last thing he expected in a home like mine. He sat thinking for a while, as if putting two and two together. He shook his head lightly. The story of the '*saithan* inside' had evidently reached him. He suppressed any inquiry regarding it as not his business, and said, 'What has come over you, Raju? You have not paid my dues for months and months, and you used to be so regular!'

'Business conditions have not been good, old man,' I said with a sort of affected resignation and cheer.

'No, it's not that. One must—'

'Oh, and that boy whom I trusted cheated completely.'

'What is the use of blaming others?' he asked. He seemed to be a ruthless man, who was bent upon harassing me. He took out his notebook, opened it out, and pointed at the bottom of a column. 'Eight thousand rupees! I can't let this go on very long. You will have to do something about it.'

I was tired of being told to do 'something about something'. My mother started it with regard to the girl, someone

[159]

else about something else. The girl had started to say, 'We must do something,' and now this man; I felt irritated by his advice and said curtly, 'I know it.'

'What do you propose to do about it?'

'Of course you are going to be paid—'

'When?'

'How can I say? . . . You must wait.'

'All right. You want another week?' he asked.

'Week!' I laughed at the joke. He looked hurt. Everyone seemed hurt by me at this time.

He became very serious and said, 'Do you think it is a laughing matter? Do you think I have come to amuse you?'

'Why do you raise your voice, Sait? Let us be friends.'

'Friendship has nothing to do with this,' he said, lowering his voice. When he raised it the jingling inside could not be heard. But when he lowered it we could hear Rosie's steps in the background. A smile, perhaps, played over my lips as I visualised her figure on the other side of the wall. He felt irritated at this again. 'What, sir, you laugh when I say I want money, you smile as if you were dreaming. Are you in this world or in paradise? I came to talk to you in a businesslike manner today, but it is not possible. All right, don't blame me.' He bundled up his account book and rose to go.

'Don't go, Sait. Why are you upset?' I asked. Everything I said unfortunately seemed to have a ring of levity about it. He stiffened and grew more serious. The more he scowled, the more I found it impossible to restrain myself. I don't know what devil was provoking so much mirth in me at this most inappropriate moment. I was bubbling with laughter. I suppressed a tremendous urge to giggle. Somehow his seriousness

[160]

affected me in this way. Finally, when he turned away from me in utter wrath, the profound solemnity of this puny man with his ledger clutched under his arm and his multi-coloured turban struck me as so absurd that I was convulsed with laughter. He turned his head, threw a brief glance at me, and was off.

With a smiling face, I re-entered the house and took up my position on the mat. Rosie paused for a second to ask, 'Something very amusing? I heard your laughter.'

'Yes, yes, something that made me laugh.'

'Who was he?' she asked.

'A friend,' I said. I did not want her to know these troubles. I didn't want anyone to be bothered with these things. I did not like to be bothered by anything. Living with Rosie under the same roof was enough for me. I wanted nothing more in life. I was slipping into a fool's paradise. By not talking about money, I felt I had dismissed the subject—a stupid assumption. The world outside Rosie seemed so unreal that it was possible for me to live on such an assumption. But not for long.

Within a week or ten days I found myself involved in court affairs. My sense of humour had completely ruined my relations with the Sait, and he had proceeded directly to get satisfaction through a court. My mother was distraught. I had not a friend in the world except Gaffur. I sought him out one day at the fountain parapet and told him where I stood. I was returning from the court. He was all sympathy, and said, 'Have you a lawyer?'

'Yes. The one there over the cotton godown.'

'Oh—he is the adjournment expert. He can keep the case going for years. So don't worry. Is it a civil suit or criminal suit?'

'Criminal! They have made out a case against me that, when he came to ask for his dues, I threatened to beat him. I wish I had done so!'

'What a pity! If it were a civil case, it could go on for years, and you would be none the worse for it while it lasted. Have you got *that* in your house?' he asked slyly. I gave him a fierce look. And he said, 'How can I blame a woman for what you are?. . . . Why don't you look after tourists again?'

'I can't go near the railway station now. The railway staff are going to depose against me, to prove that I beat people up.'

'Is it true?'

'Hm. If I catch the porter's son, I'm going to wring his neck.'

'Don't do such things, Raju; you will not help yourself. You have brought sufficient confusion on yourself. Do pull yourself together. Why don't you do sensible things?'

I thought this over. I said, 'If I had five hundred rupees, I could start a new life.' I outlined to him a plan to utilise Rosie's services and make money. The thought of her warmed me up. 'She is a gold-mine,' I cried. 'If I had money to start her with—oh!' My visions soared. I said to him, 'You know *Bharat Natyam* is really the greatest art business today. There is such a craze for it that people will pay anything to see the best. I cannot do anything about it because I have no money. Can't you help me, Gaffur?' He was amused at my request. It was now my turn to feel upset at laughter. I said, 'I have done so much for your business.'

He was essentially a man of heart. He appealed to my reason. 'I'm not a rich man, Raju. You know how I borrow money for even the upkeep of the car. If I had five hundred, I'd let my passengers ride on better tyres. No, no, Raju . . .

[162]

Listen to my advice. Send her away and try to get back to ordinary, real life. Don't talk all this art business. It's not for us.'

On hearing this, I grew so upset that I said something to hurt him. He got back into his driving seat with a serious face. 'If you like a drive any time, call me; that's all I can do to help you. And, remember, I'm not asking for the old dues from you—'

'Set it off against the commission due to me for all your Peak House trips,' I said haughtily.

'Very well,' he said, and started his car. 'Call me any time you want the car; it's always there. I pray that God may give you better sense.' He was off. I knew here was another friend passing out of my life.

Unfortunately, he was not the last. My mother's turn came soon. I was rapt, watching Rosie do a piece called 'The Dancing Feet'. Rosie said she had introduced a couple of variations, and wanted me to give my opinion. I was becoming a sort of expert on these matters nowadays. I watched her critically, but what I watched were the curves that tempted me to hug her on the spot. But my mother was passing in and out, and nowadays we had to seize our romantic moments and get through with it at odd times—for instance, when my mother went to fetch water. We knew exactly how long she would be away and utilised it. It was all irksome, but very novel, and made me forget my troubles. Whenever I watched her sway her figure, if there was no one about I constantly interrupted her performance, although I was supposed to watch her from an art critic's point of view. She pushed me away with, 'What has come over you?' She was a devoted artist; her passion for physical love was falling into place and had ceased to be a primary obsession with her.

I had a little money still left in the savings, although I gave no hint of it to anyone. A couple of days after the Sait's coming, I drew the entire amount from the bank. I did not want it to be seized. This was keeping us. I had a small lawyer handling my case in the court. I had to give him part of my money for court fees and such things. He had his office in the attic of a cotton shop in Market Road—a choking place with one shelf of books, one table, one chair, and one bench for clients. He had 'spotted me on the very first day while I was loitering with terror in my eyes, obeying the first summons. He had ingratiated himself into my favour while I waited in the corridor. He asked, 'Did you hit the Sait, really? Speak the truth to me.'

'No, sir. It's a lie.'

'Evidently they want to bring in a criminal motive to quicken the procedure. We will dispute that first, and then the civil; we've a lot of time. Don't worry. I'll deal with all that. How much money have you in your pocket?'

'Only five rupees.'

'Give it here.' If I had said 'two' he'd probably have been content to take that. He pocketed it, held up a sheet of paper for my signature, and said, 'That's right. It fixes all your affairs up nicely.'

At the court I was asked to go behind an enclosure while the judge looked at me. The Sait was there with his notebook, and he had his lawyer, of course; we glared at each other. His lawyer said something; my five-rupee lawyer said something, gesticulating in my direction; and the court-servant patted my back and told me to go. My lawyer nodded to me. It was all over before I could understand anything. My lawyer met me outside. 'Managed to get an adjournment. I'll tell you the next date later. Meet me at my office, over the cotton godown—come by the staircase on the side lane.' He was off. If this was all the bother there was, I felt I could get through it easily. I was in excellent hands.

I told my mother on returning from the court, 'There is nothing to worry about, Mother; it's going nicely.'

'He may throw us out of this house. Where will you go after that?'

'Oh, all that will take a long time. Don't unduly burden your mind,' I cried.

She gave me up in despair. 'I don't know what is coming over you. You don't take anything seriously nowadays.'

'It's because I know what to worry about; that's all,' I said grandly.

Nowadays our domestic discussions were carried on in the presence of Rosie. No privacy was needed; we had got used to her. Rosie behaved as if she did not hear these domestic matters. She looked fixedly at the floor or at the pages of a book (the only things I managed to salvage from our shop), and moved off to a corner of the hall, as if to be out of earshot. She did not, even when she was alone with me, embarrass me by asking any questions about our affairs.

My mother had adjusted herself to my ways as an unmitigated loafer, and I thought she had resigned herself to them. But she had her own scheme of tackling me. One morning as I was watching Rosie's footwork with the greatest concentration, my uncle dropped in like a bolt from the blue. He was my mother's elder brother, an energetic landowner in my mother's village who had inherited her parents' home and was a sort of general adviser and director of all our family matters.

Marriages, finances, funerals, litigation, for everything he was consulted by all the members of the family—my mother and her three sisters, scattered in various parts of the district. He seldom left his village, as he conducted most of his leadership by correspondence. I knew my mother was in touch with him— a postcard a month from him, closely written, would fill her with peace and happiness for weeks and she would ceaselessly talk about it. It was his daughter that she wanted me to marry— a proposal which she fortunately pushed into the background, in view of recent developments.

Here entered the man himself, standing at the door and calling in his booming voice, 'Sister!' I scrambled to my feet and ran to the door. My mother came hurrying from the kitchen. Rosie stopped her practice. The man was six feet, darkened by the sun from working in the fields, and had a small knotted tuft on his skull; he wore a shirt with an upper cloth, his *dhoti* was brown, not white like a townsman's. He carried a bag of jute material in his hand (with a green print of Mahatma Gandhi on it), and a small trunk. He went straight to the kitchen, took out of the bag a cucumber, a few limes, and plantains and greens, saying, 'These are for my sister, grown in our gardens.' He placed them on the floor of the kitchen for his sister. He gave a few instructions as to how to cook them.

My mother became very happy at the sight of him. She said, 'Wait, I'll give you coffee.'

He stood there explaining how he came by a bus, what he had been doing when he received my mother's letter, and so on and so forth. It was a surprise to me to know that she had written to him to come. She had not told me. 'You never told me you wrote to Uncle!' I said.

'Why should she tell you?' snapped my uncle. 'As if you

[166]

were her master!' I knew he was trying to pick a quarrel with me. He lowered his voice to a whisper, pulled me down by the collar of my shirt, and asked, 'What is all this one hears about you? Very creditable development you are showing, my boy. Anybody would be proud of you!' I wriggled myself free and frowned. He said, 'What has come over you? You think yourself a big man? I can't be frightened of scapegraces like you. Do you know what we do when we get an intractable bull calf? We castrate it. We will do that to you, if you don't behave.' .

My mother went on minding the boiling water as if she didn't notice what went on between us. I had thought she would come to my support, but she seemed to enjoy my predicament, having designed it herself. I felt confused and angry. As I moved out I could overhear my mother speaking to him in whispers. I could guess what she was saying. I went back to my mat, rather shaken.

Rosie was standing where I had left her with her hip slightly out, her arm akimbo. She was like one of those pillar-carvings in the temples. The sight of her filled me with a sudden nostalgia for the days when I took people to see the old temples and I sighed for the variety of life and contacts and experiences I used to have. Rosie looked a little scared. 'Who is he?' she asked in a low tone.

'Don't bother about him. He must be crazy. You don't have to worry.'

That was enough for her. My guidance was enough. She accepted it in absolutely unquestioning faith and ignored everything else completely. It gave me a tremendous confidence in myself and seemed to enhance my own dimensions. I told her, 'You need not stop your dance. You may go on with it.'

[167]

'But, but—' She indicated my uncle.

'Forget his existence completely,' I said. I was in a very challenging mood, but inside me I trembled still to think what my uncle might have to say. 'You don't have to bother about anyone except me,' I said with sudden authority. (My uncle used to be called in to frighten me when I was a boy.) 'This is my house. I do as I please here. If people don't like me, they need not visit me; that is all.' I laughed weakly.

What was the use of pouring out all these challenging statements to this girl? She resumed her song and dance, and I sat observing her, with extra attention as if I were her teacher. I observed my uncle peep out of the kitchen, and so I made myself more deliberately teacher-like. I issued commands and directions to Rosie. My uncle watched my antics from the kitchen. Rosie went on with her practice as if she were in her private room. My uncle presently came over to watch, his eyes bulging with contempt and cynicism. I ignored him completely. He watched for a moment, and let out a loud 'Hm! So this is what is keeping you busy! Hm! Hm! Never dreamed that anyone in our family would turn out to be a dancer's backstage-boy!'

I remained silent for a while before mustering courage and resolution to attack him. He mistook my silence for fear and brought out another of his broadsides. 'Your father's spirit will be happy to see you now, literally grovelling at the feet of a dancing-girl.'

He was out to provoke me. I turned round and said, 'If you have come to see your sister, you had better go in and stay with her. Why do you come where I am?'

'Aha!' he cried, delighted. 'Good to see some spirit in you. There is still hope for you, although you need not try it on

[168]

your uncle first. Did I not mention a moment ago what we do to recalcitrant bull calves?' He was squatting on the floor now, sipping his coffee.

'Don't be vulgar,' I said. 'At your age too!'

'Hey, wench!' he cried to Rosie, addressing her in the singular, or something even lower than singular. 'Now stop your music and all those gesticulations and listen to me. Are you of our family?' He waited for an answer. She stopped her dance and simply stared at him. He said, 'You are not of our family? Are you of our clan?' He again waited for her to answer and answered himself. 'No. Are you of our caste? No. Our class? No. Do we know you? No. Do you belong to this house? No. In that case, why are you here? After all, you are a dancing-girl. We do not admit them in our families. Understand? You seem to be a good, sensible girl. You should not walk into a house like this and stay on. Did anyone invite you? No. Even if you are invited you should go on staying where you belong, and not too long here. You cannot stay like this in our house. It is very inconvenient. You should not be seducing young fools, deserting your husband. Do you follow?' She sank down at this onslaught, covering her face with her hands. My uncle was evidently gratified at the success of his efforts, and proceeded to drive home his point. 'You see, you should not pretend to cry at these things. You must understand why we say such things. You must clear out by the next train. You must promise to go. We will give you money for your railway ticket.'

At this a big sob burst from her. I was completely maddened by it. I flew at my uncle and knocked the cup out of his hand, shouting, 'Get out of this house.'

He picked himself up, saying, 'You tell me to get out. Has it come to this? Who are you, puppy, to ask me to get out? I'll

[169]

make you get out. This is my sister's house. You go out if you want enjoyment with dancing-girls—'

My mother came running out of the kitchen with tears in her eyes. She flew straight at the sobbing Rosie, crying, 'Are you now satisfied with your handiwork, you she-devil, you demon. Where have you dropped on us from? Everything was so good and quiet—until you came; you came in like a viper. Bah! I have never seen anyone work such havoc on a young fool! What a fine boy he used to be! The moment he set his eyes on you, he was gone. On the very day I heard him mention the "serpent girl" my heart sank. I knew nothing good could come out of it.' I didn't interrupt my mother; I allowed her all the speech she wanted to work off feelings she had bottled up all these weeks. She then catalogued all my misdeeds down to my latest appearance in the court, and how I was going to lose even this house, so laboriously built by my father.

The girl looked up with her tear-drenched face and said amidst sobs, 'I will go away, Mother. Don't speak so harshly. You were so good to me all these days.'

My uncle now interrupted to tell his sister, 'This is your mistake, Sister. That wench is right in a way. Why should you have been so good to her? You should have told her at the beginning what was what.'

I seemed powerless to suppress this man or send him away. He said what he liked and stayed where he liked. Unless I physically pushed him out, there was no way of saving poor Rosie; but he could knock me flat if I laid hands on him. I was appalled at the somersault in my mother's nature the moment she got support in the shape of a brother. I went over to Rosie, put my arm around her to the shock of the two (my uncle cried, 'The fellow has lost all shame!'), and whispered to her, 'Shut your ears to all that they say. Let them say what they like. Let them exhaust themselves. But you are not leaving. I'm going to be here, and you are going to be here. Others who don't like the arrangement are welcome to leave.'

Thus they went on a little longer, and when they could say nothing more they retired to the kitchen. I never spoke a word more. I learned a great secret, that of shutting my ears, and I felt happy that Rosie too could put herself through this hardening process, absolutely relying on my support. She lifted her head and sat up, watching the household coldly. My mother called me in to eat when food was ready. I took care to see that Rosie was also fed. My mother didn't call us until she had fed my uncle on the vegetables he had brought and had cooked them according to his specifications. After food he went over to the *pyol*, spread out his upper cloth, sat on it munching *pan*, and then lay down on the cool floor to sleep. I felt relieved to hear his snores. The calm after the storm was absolute. My mother served us food without looking at us. A great silence reigned in the house. It continued until three-thirty in the afternoon.

My uncle renewed the fight by coming in to announce to all whom it might concern, 'An hour more for the train. Is the passenger ready?' He looked at Rosie sitting below a window and reading. She looked up, disturbed. I never left her side that whole afternoon. Whatever people might say, I wanted to be near at hand to support her. As long as my uncle remained in town there could be no relaxation of the vigil. I'd have given anything to know when my uncle would be leaving. But he was a man of independent notions and was not affected by my genuine desire to have him go.

Rosie looked up, slightly scared. I held a hand up to give her

[171]

courage. My mother came out of her corner and, looking kindly at Rosie, said, 'Well, young woman, it has been nice having you, but you know, it is time for you to go.' She was trying new tactics now, of kindliness and a make-believe that Rosie had agreed to leave. 'Rosie, girl, you know the train is at four-thirty. Have you packed up all your things? I found your clothes scattered here and there.'

Rosie blinked unhappily. She did not know how to answer. I intervened to say, 'Mother, she is not going anywhere.'

My mother appealed to me. 'Have some sense, Raju. She is another man's wife. She must go back to him.'

There was such calm logic in what she said, I had nothing more to do but repeat blindly, 'She can't go anywhere, Mother. She has got to stay here.'

And then my mother brought out her trump card. 'If she is not going, I have to leave the house,' she said.

My uncle said, 'Did you think she was helpless, and only a dependant on you?' He thumped his chest and cried, 'As long as I am breathing, I will never let down a sister.'

I appealed to my mother, 'You don't have to go, Mother.'

'Then throw that wench's trunk out and give her a push towards the railway, and your mother will stay. What do you take her for? You think she is the sort that can keep company with all kinds of dancing—'

'Shut up, Uncle,' I said, and I was taken aback by my own temerity. I feared he might repeat his threat to recalcitrant bulls. Fortunately, he said, 'Who are you, puppy, to say if I am to shut up or speak? You think I notice you? Are you sending that . . . that . . . out or not? That's all we want to know.'

'No; she is not going,' I said very calmly.

He heaved a sigh, glared at the girl, looked at my mother.

'Well, Sister, you must start packing, then. We will go by the evening bus.'

My mother said, 'All right. I can pack in a minute.'

'Don't go, Mother,' I pleaded.

'See that girl's obstinacy. She watches it all so calmly,' said my uncle.

Rosie pleaded, 'Mother, don't go.'

'Oho!' said my uncle. 'She has reached the stage of addressing you as Mother. Next she will be calling me Uncle-in-law, I suppose.' He turned to me with a horrible grin and said, 'Your mother needn't quit really. This house is hers for her lifetime. If I had had her co-operation, I'd have shown you a few nice tricks today. She would have stayed on till the end. My brother-in-law was no fool. He made you master of only one half of the home . . .' All of a sudden he entered into legal complexities, arising from my father's will, and described how he would have tackled the whole situation if he had been in my mother's position, and how he would have disputed every inch of the ground and taken the matter to the Supreme Court, and how he would have shown the world what to do with scape-graces who had no respect for family traditions but yet tried to enjoy their ancestors' hard-earned wealth. I was relieved as long as he waxed eloquent over legalities, as it helped him forget Rosie for the time being. True to the tradition of the landed gentry, he found litigation an engrossing subject. But the spell was broken when my mother came in to say, 'I'm ready.' She had picked up a few clothes here and there. Her large steel trunk, which had never been moved from its place in a corner for decades and decades, was packed and ready to be lifted out. She had a basket with a handle into which she had thrown a few copper and brass vessels. My uncle announced, 'These belong

[173]

to our house, given by my father when this girl, my dear sister, married and was going to set up her own family. It's our gift to her, and so don't gaze on it with such a look.'

I looked away and said, 'She certainly can take what she likes. Nobody will say anything.'

'Aha, you are proud of that, are you?' he said. 'You are showing a lot of liberality to your mother, aren't you?'

I had never in my life seen him so unpleasant. We had always been in terror of him when we were children, but this was the first occasion I had seen so much of him as an adult. My mother looked saddened rather than angry, and seemed almost ready to come to my rescue. She interrupted him sharply to say with extraordinary consideration in her voice, 'I need nothing more. This will do.' She picked up several small prayer-books, which she read every day of her life before her midday meal, sitting before the pictures of the god, in meditation. I had seen her for years at the same time sitting with closed eyes in front of the niche in the wall, and it now filled me with sadness that I would not see her there any more. I followed her about the house as she picked out her articles and packed. My uncle, as if to keep an eye on me, followed my steps. Apparently he feared I might induce my mother to stay on.

In spite of his supervision, I asked, 'Mother, when will you be back?'

She hesitated to answer, and said finally, 'I'll—I'll—let us see.'

'The moment she gets a telegram that the line is clear,' said Uncle and added, 'We are not the sort to let down our sisters, remember. That house in the village is always hers to return to; so that she has not got to be at anybody's mercy.

[174]

Our house belongs to our sister as much as to us,' he added boastfully.

'Don't fail to light the lamps in the god's niche,' said my mother, going down the steps. 'Be careful with your health.' Uncle carried the trunks and she carried the basket. Soon they were at the end of the street and turned the corner. I stood on the step watching. At the threshold stood Rosie. I was afraid to turn round and face her, because I was crying.

We were a married couple to all appearances. Rosie cooked the food, and kept the house. I seldom went out except to do a little shopping. All day long she danced and sang. I made love to her constantly and was steeped in an all-absorbing romanticism, until I woke up to the fact that she was really getting tired of it all. Some months passed before she asked me, 'What are your plans?'

'Plans!' said the sleeper, awakening. 'What plans?'

She smiled at this and said, 'There you are, always lying on the mat watching me or holding me in your arms. I have now had good practice—I can manage a show of four hours, although with accompaniments it would have been much more helpful—'

'I'm here, accompanying and marking time for you. What other accompaniment do you want?'

'I need a full orchestra. We have stayed indoors long enough,' she said. I found her so earnest that I had not the courage to joke any more.

I said, 'I'm also thinking. Very soon we must do something.'

' "Rosie" is a silly name,' I said as a first step after two days of hard thinking. 'The trouble with you is that although your people are a traditional dance family, they didn't know how to

[175]

call you. For our public purposes, your name must be changed. What about Meena Kumari?'

She shook her head. 'It's no better. I see no reason to change my name.'

'You don't understand, my dear girl. It's not a sober or sensible name. If you are going to appear before the public with that name, they will think it's someone with cheap tricks, such as those we see in gambling side-shows. For a classical dancer, you should call yourself something that is poetic and appealing.'

She realised that there was a point in what I said, and she picked up a pad and pencil and noted down all the names that came into her head. I added my own. We wanted to see how they sounded and also how they looked on paper. Sheet after sheet was filled up and discarded. It became a sort of joke. We seemed to be forgetting our main job in enjoying the fun. Each name had something ridiculous about it, comic-sounding or an impossible association. At dead of night she sat up to ask, 'What about ......?'

'The name of the wife of a demon-king—people will be frightened,' I said. Eventually, after four days of hard thinking and elimination (a labour which gave us the satisfaction of being engaged in professional duties), we arrived at 'Nalini', a name that could have significance, poetry, and universality, and yet be short and easily remembered.

With the attainment of a new name, Rosie entered a new phase of life. Under the new name, Rosie and all she had suffered in her earlier life were buried from public view. I was the only one who knew her as Rosie and called her so. The rest of the world knew her as Nalini. I bestirred myself, began to go out

[176]

and meet people in the town. I attended meetings of various groups—at the University, the town hall, and the Club, and watched for a chance. When the Albert Mission boys had their annual social, I mixed in their affairs through the slender link of the clerk in the Union, who had once read with me at the old *pyol* school, and I suggested, 'Why not a dance recital instead of the usual Shakespeare tragedy?' I held forth on the revival of art in India so vehemently that they could not easily brush me aside, but had to listen. Heaven knew where I had found all this eloquence. I delivered such a lecture on the importance of our culture and the place of the dance in it that they simply had to accept what I said. Someone doubted if a classical dance would be suitable for a student assembly. I proved that the classical dance could be viewed as the lightest of entertainments, considering its versatility. I was a man with a mission. I dressed myself soberly for the part in a sort of rough-spun silk shirt and an upper cloth and a hand-spun and hand-woven *dhoti*, and I wore rimless glasses—a present from Marco at one of our first meetings. I wore a wrist-watch; all this in my view lent such weight to what I said that they had to listen to me respectfully. I too felt changed; I had ceased to be the old Railway Raju and I earnestly wished that I too could bury myself, as Rosie had done, under a new name. Fortunately it didn't make much difference. No one seemed to bother about my affairs as those in the immediate railway colony did, and even if they knew they seemed to have other things to remember than my career and its ups and downs. I never knew I could speak so fluently on cultural matters. I had picked up a little terminology from Rosie and put it to the best use. I described 'The Dancing Feet' and explained its significance word by word and almost performed the dance act myself.

They watched me in open-mouthed wonder. I threw a further bait to the committee: if they liked, they could go with me and see a sample of the show. They enthusiastically agreed. I mentioned her as a cousin who was on a visit, and who was famous in her own place.

The next morning Rosie had tidied up the hall so that it did not look too bad. She had decorated the place with flowers from a gold mohur-tree. She had stuck the bunch in a bronze tumbler, and kept it in a corner; it touched up our little home with some sort of beauty. She had also pushed away our rolls of bedding and other boxes, stools, and odds and ends to the farthest corner, thrown a *dhoti* over the heap, and covered it again cunningly with a striped carpet pulled from under a bed. This gave it a mysterious look. She had shaken the old mat and rolled it up so that the tattered portions were invisible. She managed to have ready cups of brown, steaming coffee. All this was an excellent preparation, calculated to win a public for her. The men, two of them, came and knocked on the door. When I opened it there they stood. Rosie had hung a printed sheet over the kitchen doorway and was behind it. I opened the door, saw the men there, and said, 'Oh, you have come!' as if I had thought they wouldn't. Somehow I felt it would be good to give it all a casual air. They smirked foolishly, realising they had come on an agreeable errand to watch a possible beauty.

I seated them on the mat, spoke to them of world politics for a moment, and said, 'You can spare a little time, I suppose? I'll ask my cousin if she is free.'

I walked through the kitchen curtain and she was standing there. I grinned at her and winked at her. She stood stock-still and grinned back at me. We were enjoying this piece of stage-management; we felt we had already begun to put on a show. She had tied her hair into a knot, decorated her forehead with a small vermilion dot, lightly sprinkled a little powder on her face, and clad herself in a blue cotton sari—an effect of simplicity produced with a lot of preparation. After five minutes of silent waiting, I nodded, and she followed me out.

The Secretary and the Treasurer gaped. I said, 'These are my friends. Sit down.' She smiled, and seated herself on a small mat—modestly away. I knew at that moment that her smile was an 'open sesame' to her future. There was an awkward pause for a moment and then I said, 'These are my friends. They are having a variety show in the College Union, and were wondering if you would do anything for them.'

She asked, 'Variety? What other items are you having?' and puckered her brow in a superior way.

They said apologetically, 'A few fancy-dress items, mimicry and such things.'

She said 'How can you fit my programme into that? How much time do you want to give me?' She was taking charge of their programme.

They said, greatly flustered, 'One hour, an hour and a half—anything you like.'

Now she delivered them a homily. 'You see, a dance programme is not like variety, it needs time to be built up. It's something that has to develop even as one is performing and one is watching.'

They agreed with her sentiments absolutely. I interrupted to say, 'Their main idea in coming now is to see you, and to see whatever bit of your art you can show them. Would you oblige us?'

She made a wry face and grumbled, looked hesitant, and gave us no reply.

'What is it? They are waiting for a reply from you. They are busy men.'

'Oh, no. No need to hustle the lady. We can wait.'

'How, how to—manage now—no accompaniments—without accompaniments I never like—' she was saying, and I said, 'Oh, this is not a full-dress show. Just a little— When there is a full-dress show we shall have accompaniments. After all, you are the most important item.' I cajoled her and the other two happily joined me; and Rosie agreed hesitantly, saying, 'If you are so keen, I can't refuse. But don't blame me if it is not good.' She went behind the curtain once again, returned bearing coffee on a plate, and set it down.

Out of formal politeness the gentlemen said, 'Why bother about coffee?' I pressed them to accept it.

As they sipped their coffee, Rosie began her dance, to the accompaniment of a song that she lightly sang. I ventured to beat time with my hands, like a very knowing one. They watched in fascination. She suddenly paused, wiped the perspiration from her brow, took a deep breath, and, before resuming again, said to me, 'Don't beat time; it misleads me.'

'All right,' I said, awkwardly grinning, trying not to look snubbed. I whispered, 'Oh, she is so precise, you know.' They shook their heads.

She finished her piece and asked, 'Shall I go on? Shall I do "The Dancing Feet"?'

'Yes, yes,' I cried, glad to be consulted. 'Go on. They will like it.'

When they recovered from the enchantment, one of them said, 'I must admit I have never cared for *Bharat Natyam*, but

[180]

watching this lady is an education. I now know why people are in raptures over it.'

The other said, 'My only fear is that she may be too good for our function. But it doesn't matter. I'll reduce the other items to give her all the time she wants.'

'We must make it our mission to educate the public taste,' I said. 'We must not estimate the public taste and play down to it. We must try to raise it by giving only the best.'

'I think up to the interval we shall have the variety and all such tomfoolery. After the interval this lady can take up the entire show.'

I looked up at her for a second as if waiting for her approval, and said, 'She'll, of course, be pleased to help you. But you must provide the drummer and accompanists,' and thus acquired at last the accompanists Rosie had been clamouring for all along.

9

MY activities suddenly multiplied. The Union function was the start. Rocket-like, she soared. Her name became public property. It was not necessary for me to elaborate or introduce her to the public now. The very idea would be laughed at. I became known because I went about with her, not the other way round. She became known because she had the genius in her, and the public had to take notice of it. I am able to speak soberly about it now—only now. At that time I was puffed up with the thought of how I had made her. I am now disposed to think that even Marco could not have suppressed her permanently; sometime she was bound to break out and make her way. Don't be misled by my present show of humility; at the time there was no limit to my self-congratulation. When I watched her in a large hall with a thousand eyes focused on her, I had no doubt that people were telling themselves and each other, 'There he is, the man but for whom—' And I imagined all this adulation lapping around my ears like wavelets. In every show I took, as a matter of right, the middle sofa in the first row. I gave it out that that was my seat wherever I might go, and unless I sat there Nalini would be unable to perform. She needed my inspiring presence. I shook my head discreetly; sometimes I lightly tapped my fingers together in timing. When I met her eyes, I smiled familiarly at her on the stage. Sometimes I signalled her a message with my eyes and fingers, suggesting a modification or a criticism of her performance. I liked the way the president of the occasion sat next to me, and leaned over to say something to me. They all liked to be seen talking to me. They felt almost as gratified as if they spoke to Nalini herself. I shook my head, laughed with restraint, and said something in reply, leaving the watching audience at our back to guess the import of our exchanges, although actually it was never anything more than, 'The hall seems to have filled.'

I threw a glance back to the farthest corner of the hall, as if to judge the crowd, and said, 'Yes, it's full,' and swiftly turned round, since dignity required that I look ahead. No show started until I nodded to the man peeping from the wings, and then the curtain went up. I never gave the signal until I satisfied myself that everything was set. I inquired about the lighting, microphone arrangements, and looked about as if I were calculating the velocity of the air, the strength of the ceiling, and as if I wondered if the pillars would support the roof under the circumstances. By all this I created a tenseness which helped Nalini's career. When they satisfied all the conditions and a performance began, the organisers felt they had achieved a difficult object. Of course, they paid for the dance, and the public was there, after paying for their seats, but all the same I gave the inescapable impression that I was conferring on them a favour by permitting the dance. I was a strict man. When I thought that the programme had gone on long enough I looked at the watch on my wrist and gave a slight nod of the head, and Nalini would understand that she must end the show with the next item. If anyone made further suggestions, I simply laughed them off. Sometimes slips of paper travelled down from the back of the hall, with requests for this item or that, but I frowned so much when a slip was brought near me that people became nervous to pass on such things. They generally apologised, 'I don't know. Someone from the back bench—it just came to me—' I took it with a frown, read it with bored tolerance, and pushed it away over the arm of the sofa; it fell on the carpet, into oblivion. I made it look as if such tricks should be addressed to lesser beings and that they would not work here.

One minute before the curtain came down, I looked for the Secretary and nodded to him to come over. I asked him, 'Is the car ready? Please have it at the other door, away from the crowd. I'd like to take her out quietly.' It was a false statement. I really liked to parade her through the gaping crowds. After the show, there were still people hanging around to catch a glimpse of the star. I walked ahead of her or beside her without much concern. At the end of the performance they presented her with a large garland of flowers, and they gave me one too. I accepted mine with protest. 'There is really no reason why you should waste money on a garland for me,' I said; I slung it carelessly on my arm or in the thick of the crowd dramatically handed it over to Nalini with 'Well, you really deserve two,' and made her carry it for me.

It was a world of showmanship till we reached the privacy of our house, when she would throw off the restraint and formality of hours and give me a passionate hug with 'Even if I have seven rebirths I won't be able to repay my debt to you.' I swelled with pride when I heard her, and accepted it all as my literal due. Methodically she started wrapping the flowers in a wet towel so that they might remain fresh in the morning.

On programme days she cooked our supper in the afternoon. We could easily have afforded to engage a cook, but she always said, 'After all, for two people, we don't need a cook moping around the house. I must not lose touch with my womanly duties.' She spoke of the evening show all through dinner, criticising some arrangement or the background accompaniment, how so-and-so just failed to catch up. She lived entirely in the memory of her evening show. Sometimes after food she demonstrated a piece. And then she picked up a book and read on till we went to bed.

In a few months I had to move out of my old house. The Sait managed to score a point of law and secured an attachment of the property before judgement. My lawyer came to me and said, 'Don't worry about it; it only means he will have to pay the house tax, with arrears, if any. Of course, your mother's signature may be required too, but I'll get it. It is just like mortgaging the house to him. You may have to give him rent—a nominal one if you stay here.'

'Paying rent for my own house!' I said. 'If I have to pay rent I prefer a better house.' For our growing stature the house was inadequate. No visitor could be entertained. No privacy. No place for my furniture. My father had designed this house for a shopkeeper, not for a man of consequence and status who had charge of a growing celebrity. 'Moreover, where is the place for you to practise in?' I asked Nalini when she demurred at the notion of moving out. Somehow she was deeply attached to the house, the place which first gave her asylum.

The lawyer went to the village and returned with my mother's signature on the document. 'How did she take it?' I could not help asking.

'Not badly, not badly,' said the adjournment expert. 'Well, of course, we cannot expect elderly people to take the same view as we do. I had to argue and persuade her, though your uncle proved a difficult man.'

Four days later my mother's letter came; she had written on a yellow paper with a pencil: '. . . I gave my signature not because I was happy about it but because otherwise the lawyer would not go from here, and your uncle would not let him stay in peace. It is all confusing to me. I'm sick of everything. I signed without your uncle's knowledge, when he was away in the garden, so that the lawyer might leave this place without any damage to his person. Anyway, what does it all mean? Your lawyer mentioned that you are looking for a new house for that woman. If it is so, I'll come back to live in my old house. After all, I wish to spend the rest of my days in my own house.' It was good of my mother to have set aside her own anger and written to me. I felt touched by her solicitude. I was troubled by her desire to come back. I could understand it, but I resisted the idea. It seemed best to let the Sait take the home and be done with it once for all. Who wanted this ramshackle house anyway? To have Mother live in the house, I should have to pay a rent to the Sait. Who would look after her? I was so busy. I rationalised in all possible ways and put away her letter without a reply. I moved to another house and became very busy, and in all the rush quietened my conscience. I felt sorry, but I rationalised: 'After all her brother is dear to her, and he will look after her. *Why* should she come here and live all alone?'

The stylish house at New Extension was more in keeping with our status. It was two-storied, with a large compound, lawns, garden, and garage. On the upper floor we had our bedrooms and a large hall where Nalini practised her dances. It was carpeted with a thick, deep blue, spun-silk carpet at one end, leaving a space of marble tiles for her to dance on. I had managed to fix up a pedestal and a bronze image of dancing

[186]

Nataraja in one corner. It was her office. I had now a permanent group of musicians—five of them: a flautist, a drummer, etc. She had a 'dance-master' whom I discovered in Koppal, a man who had steeped himself in the traditional dance for half a century and lived in his village home. I ferreted him out and brought him over to Malgudi and gave him an outhouse in our compound to live in. All kinds of people were always passing in and out of our house. I had a large staff of servants—a driver for our car, two gardeners for the garden, a Gurkha sentry at the gate with a dagger at his waist, and two cooks because our entertainments were beginning to grow. As I have said, a miscellaneous population was always passing in and out of the compound: musicians, their friends, those that came to see me by appointment, the servants, their friends, and so on. On the ground floor I had an office with a secretary-in-waiting, a young graduate from the local college, who dealt with my correspondence.

I had three or four grades of visitors. Some I received on the veranda; these were musicians or aspiring musicians who wanted a chance to accompany Nalini. I was offhand with them. About ten such asked for an interview with me every day. They were always waiting on the outer veranda to have a chance to speak to me. I went in and out, hardly noticing them. They respectfully rose at the sight of me and saluted, and if they intercepted me I kept up a show of giving them a hearing, and then said, 'Leave your address with my clerk there. If there is anything that can be done, I'll ask him to call you up.' When they flourished a batch of testimonials I snatched a brief look at them and said, 'Good good. But there is nothing I can do now. Leave your name in the office'—and I passed on. My outer veranda was cluttered with benches on which people sat and waited all day to have a chance to speak to me. I treated them with the scantiest attention. I left them to guess when I would come to my table. Sometimes obscure composers turned up with new songs especially created for Nalini's benefit. Sometimes when I sat at the office table I did not mind if they peeped in and took their chance to speak to me. I never offered this class of visitor a chair, but did not mind if he pulled one up and sat down. When I wanted to dispose of him, I pushed my chair back and went in abruptly, leaving it to my secretary to see him off. Sometimes I observed through the glass window in the hall, how big a crowd waited for me outside, and I made a strategic exit through a side door, straight on to the garage, and from there dashed to the gate, while the visitors looked on helplessly. I felt vastly superior to everyone.

Apart from those that came as supplicants, there were others who approached me with genuine offers of engagement. They were the higher grade of visitors. I received them on the hall sofa and rang the bell for coffee. I offered my inner circle of visitors coffee day and night. Our coffee bill alone amounted to three hundred a month, enough to maintain a middle-class family in comfort. The appointments in the hall were all expensive—brass-inlaid trays, ivory knick-knacks, group photographs with Nalini in the middle. Sitting in that hall and looking round, I had the satisfaction of feeling that I had arrived.

Where was Nalini in all this? Away out of sight. She spent a great part of the day in her rehearsal hall with her musicians. One could hear the stamping of feet and the jingle of anklets on the upper floor. After all, she was living the life she had visualised. Visitors had always a hope that they might get a glimpse of her passing in or out of the house. I knew what they were looking for, with their shifty looks darting at the inner doorway. But I took care to see that no one saw her. I had a monopoly of her and nobody had anything to do with her. If anyone ventured to ask for her I said, 'She is busy,' or 'No need to trouble her. You have told me; that is enough.' I resented anyone's wanting to make a direct approach to her. She was my property. This idea was beginning to take root in my mind.

There were, however, a few friends of the inner circle whom I took upstairs to her room. It was a very eclectic group. They had to be my intimates; I had had no friends at all formerly; my friendship was now sought after by others. I was on back-slapping terms with two judges, four eminent politicians of the district whose ward could bring ten thousand votes at any moment for any cause, and two big textile-mill owners, a banker, a municipal councillor, and the editor of *The Truth*, a weekly, in which an appreciation of Nalini appeared from time to time. These men could come into my hall without appointment, demand coffee, and ask loudly, 'Where is Nalini? Upstairs? Well, I think I'll see her for a moment and go.' They could go up, talk to her, order coffee, and stay on as long as they pleased. They addressed me as 'Raj', familiarly. I liked to hobnob with them because they were men of money or influence.

Apart from them, sometimes musicians or actors or other dancers called on Nalini and spent hours and hours with her. Nalini enjoyed their company immensely, and I often saw them in her hall, some lying on carpets, some sitting up, all talking and laughing, while coffee and food were being carried to them. I occasionally went up and chatted with them—always with a feeling that I was an interloper in that artistic group. Sometimes it irritated me to see them all so happy and

[189]

abandoned. I signalled to Nalini to come over to the bedroom, as if for a big, important aside, and when she closed the door I whispered, 'How long are they going to stay?'

'Why?'

'They have been here the whole day and may go on till night.'

'Well, I like their company. It's good of them to visit us.'

'Oh, as if we had no one else to visit us.'

'It's all right. How can I tell them to go? And it makes me happy to be with them.'

'Surely; I'm not denying it. But remember, you have to rest and we have a train journey ahead. You will have to pack up, and also practise. Remember you have promised new items for the Trichy show.'

'That's easy to manage!' she said, turning round and going back to her friends, shutting the door on me. I silently fretted. I liked her to be happy, but only in my company. This group of miscellaneous art folk I didn't quite approve. They talked too much shop and Nalini was likely to tell them all our business secrets. She never missed a chance to get a gathering of such friends, wherever she might be. She said, 'They are people with the blessing of Goddess Saraswathi on them, and they are good people. I like to talk to them.'

'You don't know the world—they'll be a jealous lot. Don't you know that the real artists never come together? These people come to you because they are your inferiors.'

'I'm tired of all talk of superior and inferior. What is so superior about us?' she asked in real indignation.

'Well, you know, you have more engagements than a hundred of them put together,' I said.

'That's more money,' she said. 'I don't care much for that sort of superiority.'

Gradually arguments began to crop up between us, and that, I said, put the final husband-wife touch on our relationship. Her circle was widening. Artists of the first and second rank, music-teachers, dilettantes of the town, schoolgirls who wanted ideas for their school functions, all kinds of people asked to see her. Wherever possible I turned them back, but if they managed to slip through and get upstairs, I could do nothing about it. Nalini kept them for hours and would hardly let them go back.

We had calls from hundreds of miles away. Our trunks were always packed and ready. Sometimes when we left Malgudi we did not return home for nearly a fortnight. Our engagements took us to all corners of South India, with Cape Comorin at one end and the border of Bombay at the other, and from coast to coast. I kept a map and a calendar and tried to plan out our engagements. I studied the invitations and suggested alternative dates, so that a single journey might combine several engagements. Arranging an itinerary for each period took up a lot of my energy. We were out of town for about twenty days in the month, and during the ten days we were in Malgudi we had one or two dates nearer home, and whatever was left over could be counted as rest. It was a strenuous programme, and, wherever I might be, my secretary kept me informed of the mail arriving each day and received instructions by phone. I was committed three months ahead. I had a large calendar on which I marked in red the dates of engagements, and hung it up at first in her rehearsal hall, but she protested, 'It's ugly. Take it away!'

'I want you to keep an idea before you of where you are going next.'

'Not necessary,' she cried. 'What am I going to do, looking at those dates?' She rolled it up and put it in my hand. 'Don't show it to me. It only frightens me to see so many engagements,' she said. When I told her to get ready for the train, she got ready; when I asked her to come down, she came down; she got in and out of trains at my bidding. I don't know if she ever noticed what town we were in or what *sabha* or under whose auspices a show was being held. It was all the same, I think, whether it was Madras City or Madura, or a remote hill town like Ootacamund. Where there was no railway, a car came to fetch us from the railhead. Someone met us at the platform, led us to a limousine waiting outside, and drove us to a hotel or a bungalow. Our circus of accompanying musicians was taken away in a bunch and berthed comfortably somewhere. I kept this lot in good humour by fussing about their comfort. 'They are our accompanists. I hope you have made proper arrangements for them too.'

'Yes, yes, sir. We've reserved two large rooms for them.'

'You must send them a car later to bring them over to our place.' I always made it a point to collect them and keep them handy two hours ahead of a show. They were a timeless lot, those instrumental players; they slept, or went shopping, or sat around playing cards—never looking at a clock. Handling them was an art—they had to be kept in good humour; otherwise they could ruin a whole evening and blame it on mood or fate. I paid them well. I kept up a show of looking after them, but I kept aloof. I was careful to see that they assumed no familiarity with Nalini.

If the show was at six, I generally insisted upon Nalini's resting until four o'clock in the afternoon. If we were guests in a house, she generally liked to sit around with the womenfolk and chat endlessly with them. But I went up to her and said with a good deal of firm kindness, 'I think you had better rest a while; the train journey last night was not very comfortable,' and she finished the sentence she was uttering or hearing and came up to our guest-room.

She felt annoyed at my interference. 'Why should you come and pull me out of company? Am I a baby?' I expostulated with her that it was for her own good that I did so. I knew it was only a partial truth. If I examined my heart I knew I had pulled her out because I did not like to see her enjoy other people's company. I liked to keep her in a citadel.

If there was a train to catch after the show, I managed to have a car waiting ready to take us to the station. I had food brought to us on the train in silver or stainless-steel vessels, and we had our supper in the privacy of our compartment. But it was a brief, short-lived relief, as it soon began all over again, getting down at another station, going through another performance, and off again. When we visited places of importance, she sometimes asked to be taken to see a famous temple or a shop or some local sight. I always replied, 'Yes, yes. Let us see if we can fit it in,' but it was never done, as I always had to catch another train so as to fulfil another engagement. We were going through a set of mechanical actions day in and day out—the same receptions at the station, fussy organisers, encounters, and warnings, the same middle sofa in the first row, speeches and remarks and smiles, polite conversation, garlands and flash photos, congratulations, and off to catch the train—pocketing the most important thing, the cheque. Gradually I began to say, not 'I am going to Trichy for a performance by Nalini,' but 'I am performing at Trichy on Sunday, on Monday I have a programme . . .' and then, 'I can dance in your place only on . . .' I demanded the highest fee, and got it, of anyone in India. I treated those that came to ask for a show as supplicants, I had an enormous monthly income, I spent an enormous amount on servants and style, and I paid an enormous amount of income tax. Yet I found Nalini accepting it all with a touch of resignation rather than bouncing contentment. She had seemed such a happy creature in our old house, even when my uncle was bullying her.

Nalini cherished every garland that she got at the end of a performance. Usually she cut it up, sprinkled water on it, and preserved it carefully, even when we were in a train. She said, holding up a piece of garland and sniffing the air for its fragrance, 'To me this is the only worth-while part of our whole activity.'

We were in a train when she said it. I asked her, 'What makes you say so?'

'I love jasmine.'

'Not the cheque that comes with it?'

'What is one to do with so much? All day long and all through the week you are collecting cheques, and more and more often. But when is the time coming when we can enjoy the use of those cheques?'

'Well, you have a big household, a big car and what not—is that not enjoyment of life?'

'I don't know,' she said, remaining moody. 'How I wish I could go into a crowd, walk about, take a seat in the auditorium, and start out for an evening without having to make up or dress for the stage!'

Some dangerous weariness seemed to be coming over her. I thought it best not to prod too much. Perhaps she wanted fewer engagements, but that was not possible. I asked, 'You are not saying that your legs are aching, are you?'

It had the desired effect. It pricked her pride and she said, 'Certainly not. I can dance for several hours at each show. Only you want me to stop.'

'Yes, yes; true,' I cried, 'Otherwise you would be fatiguing yourself.'

'Not only that; you also want to catch the train—though what will be lost if we catch the next day's, I don't know—'

I didn't allow her to finish her sentence. I called her flatteringly a shrewd girl, laughed and enjoyed it as a joke, fondled her, and made her forget the subject. I thought it was a dangerous line of thought. It seemed absurd that we should earn less than the maximum we could manage. My philosophy was that while it lasted the maximum money had to be squeezed out. We needed all the money in the world. If I were less prosperous, who would care for me? Where would be the smiles which greeted me now wherever I turned, and the respectful agreement shown to my remarks when I said something to the man in the next chair? It filled me with dread that I should be expected to do with less. 'If we don't work and earn when the time is good, we commit a sin. When we have a bad time no one will help us.' I was planning big investments as soon as possible—as soon as we could count on a little more margin. As it was, the style of living and entertaining which I had evolved was eating up all our resources.

Sometimes she said, 'Spending two thousand a month on just two of us. Is there no way of living more simply?'

'Leave that to me; we spend two thousand because we

have to. We have to maintain our status.' After a good deal of thought, I ran the bank account in her name. I didn't want my creditors to get at me again. My adjournment lawyer was proceeding at his own pace, sometimes coming to me for a signature or funds, and managing things without bothering me. Nalini signed any cheque I asked her to sign. One thing I must add: whenever I was in town I gathered a big circle of friends and we played cards practically twenty-four hours at a stretch. I had set apart a room for the purpose and I had two personal servants serving tea and coffee and even food on the spot; and we had surreptitious drinks too, although there was prohibition in force—well, the prohibition law was not for a man of my influence. I had managed to get a medical certificate to say that I needed alcohol for my welfare. Although I myself cared very little for drink, I hugged a glass of whisky for hours. 'Permit-holder' became a social title in our land and attracted men of importance around me, because the permit was a diffi-cult thing to acquire. I showed respect for law by keeping the street-window shut when serving drink to non-permit folk. All kinds of men called me 'Raj' and slapped my back. We played Three-Cards sometimes for two days at a stretch; I changed a two-thousand-rupee cheque for the purpose, and expected those who came there to meet me on equal terms. Through my intimacy with all sorts of people, I knew what was going on behind the scenes in the government, at the market, at Delhi, on the racecourse, and who was going to be who in the coming week. I could get a train reservation at a moment's notice, relieve a man summoned to jury work, reinstate a dismissed official, get a vote for a co-operative election, nominate a committee man, get a man employed, get a boy admitted to a school, and get an unpopular official shifted elsewhere, all of

[196]

which seemed to me important social services, an influence worth buying at the current market price.

In the glow of this radiant existence, I had practically overlooked the fact that Marco still existed. We hardly mentioned his name. I never took note of the fact that he still inhabited the globe, and I took the only precaution needed—I avoided any engagement near his house. I didn't want to run the risk of facing him again. I had no idea what Nalini had in mind. I believed she still felt embittered at the thought of him, and would rather not be reminded of him. I supposed that all associations with him were dim, fossilised, or had ceased to exist. I also thought that under her name Nalini she was safely out of range, but I was mistaken. We played for a whole week at Malgudi. The post one day brought us a book. Generally I received a miscellaneous collection of mail—catalogues, programmes, verse, and what not, all of which was seen and disposed of by my secretary. Some Tamil and English illustrated journals meant for Nalini were sent up. I hardly looked at anything except letters offering engagements, and certainly never at books and journals. I was a man of many preoccupations, and I found it impossible nowadays to sit down with any book and had instructed my secretary not to bother me with them. But one day he brought a packet, saying, 'Would you look at this, sir. I thought it might be of special interest.'

He held the book open. I snatched it from him. It was a book by Marco, a book full of illustrations and comments. 'See page 158' said a pencilled message. I turned it over, and there it was, the heading 'Mempi Cave Pictures'. At the head of the chapter was a brief line to say, 'The author is obliged to acknowledge his debt to Sri. Raju of Malgudi Railway Station for his help.' The book was from a firm of publishers in Bombay, with their compliments, sent by instructions of the author. It was a gorgeous book costing twenty rupees, full of art plates, a monograph on *The Cultural History of South India*. It was probably an eminent work on the subject, but beyond me.

I told the secretary, 'I'll keep it. It's all right.' I turned the pages. Why did the boy bring it up as a special matter? Did he know who was who? Or—? I dismissed the idea. It must have been because he was rather taken by the blue and gold of the binding and the richness of the material. He must have feared that if he didn't draw my attention to it, I might probably demand an explanation. That was all. So I said, 'Thank you, I'll read it.' And then I sat wondering what I should do about it. Should I take it upstairs to Nalini or—? I told myself, 'Why should she be bothered with this? After all, it is a piece of academic work, which has bored her sufficiently.' I turned it over again, to see if there was any letter enclosed. No. It was impersonal, like the electricity bill. I turned to page 158 and re-read his note. It was thrilling to see my name in print. But why did he do it? I lost myself in speculating on his motives. Was it just to keep his word because he had promised, or could it be to show that he'd not forgotten me so lightly? Anyway, I thought it would be best to put the book away. I carried it to my most secret, guarded place in the house—the liquor chest, adjoining the cardroom, the key of which I carried next to my heart—stuffed the volume out of sight, and locked it up. Nalini never went near it. I did not mention the book to her. After all, I told myself, 'What has she to do with it? The book is sent to me, and the acknowledgement is of my services.' But it was like hiding a corpse. I've come to the conclusion that nothing in this world can be hidden or suppressed. All such attempts are like holding an umbrella to conceal the sun.

Three days later Marco's photograph appeared in the *Illustrated Weekly of Bombay*, on the middle page. The *Illustrated Weekly* was one of the papers Nalini always read—it was full of wedding pictures, stories, and essays she enjoyed. The photograph was published along with a review of his book, which was called 'An epoch-making discovery in Indian cultural history.' I was looking through my accounts in the hall, free from all visitors. I heard footsteps clattering down in a great run. I turned and saw her coming with the magazine in her hand, all excitement. She thrust the page before me and asked, 'Did you see that?'

I showed appropriate surprise and told her, 'Calm yourself. Sit down.'

'This is really great. He worked for it all his life. I wonder what the book is like!'

'Oh, it's academic. We won't understand it. For those who care for such things, it must seem interesting.'

'I want so much to see the book! Can't we get it somewhere?' She suddenly called my secretary, an unprecedented act on her part. 'Mani,' she said and held the picture up to him, 'you must get me this book.'

He came nearer, read the passage, brooded for a moment, looked at me, and said, 'All right, madam.'

I hurriedly told him, 'Hurry up with that letter, and go in person to the post-office and remember to add a late fee.' He was gone. She still sat there. Unless she was called to meet visitors, she never came downstairs. What was this agitation that made her do these things? I wondered for a moment whether I ought not to bring the book out to her. But she would ask me for so many explanations. I simply suppressed the whole thing. She returned upstairs to her room. I noticed later that she had cut out the photo of her husband and placed it on her dressing mirror. I was rather shocked. I wanted to treat it as a joke, but could not find the right words, and so left it alone. I only averted my eyes when I passed the dressing mirror.

It was a long week in town; otherwise we should have been fully occupied in moving about, and probably would have missed that particular issue of the *Illustrated Weekly*. On the third day, while we were in bed, the very first question she asked me was, 'Where have you kept the book?'

'Who told you about it?'

'Why bother? I know it has come to you. I want to see it.'

'All right, I'll show it to you tomorrow.' Evidently Mani must be responsible. I had made it a convention in our establishment that my secretary should have no direct access to her, but the system was breaking down. I decided to punish him properly for his lapse.

She sat reclining on her pillow with a journal in her hand, to all appearances reading, but actually preparing herself for a fight. She pretended to read for a moment and suddenly asked, 'Why did you want to hide it from me?'

I was not ready for this, and so I said, 'Can't we discuss it all tomorrow? Now I'm too sleepy.'

She was out for a fight. She said, 'You can tell me in a word why you did it and go to sleep immediately.'

'I didn't know it would interest you.'

'Why not? After all—'

'You have told me that you never thought his work interesting.'

[200]

'Even now I'll probably be bored. But anything happening to him is bound to interest me. I'm pleased he has made a name now, although I don't know what it is all about.'

'You suddenly fancy yourself interested in him, that's all. But the book came to *me*, not to you, remember.'

'Is that sufficient reason why it should be hidden from me?'

'I can do what I please with my own book, I suppose? That's all. I'm going to sleep. If you are not reading, but are merely going to think, you can as well do it in the dark, and put out the light.'

I don't know why I spoke so recklessly. The light was put out, but I found that she was sitting up—and crying in the dark. I wondered for a second whether I should apologise and comfort her. But I decided otherwise. She had been bottling up a lot of gloom lately, it seemed to me. It would do her good to have it all out without my interference. I turned over and pretended to sleep. Half an hour passed. I switched on the light, and there she was, quietly crying still.

'What has come over you?'

'After all, after all, he is my husband.'

'Very well. Nothing has happened to make you cry. You should feel pleased with his reputation.'

'I am,' she said.

'Then stop crying and go to sleep.'

'Why does it irritate you when I speak of him?'

I realised it was no use trying to sleep. I might as well meet the challenge. I replied, 'Do you ask why? Don't you remember when and how he left you?'

'I do, and I deserved nothing less. Any other husband would have throttled me then and there. He tolerated my company for nearly a month, even after knowing what I had done.'

[201]

'You talk about a single incident in two different ways. I don't know which one I should take.'

'I don't know. I may be mistaken in my own judgement of him. After all, he had been kind to me.'

'He wouldn't even touch you.'

'Should you taunt me with that?' she asked with sudden submissiveness. I couldn't understand her. I had an appalling thought that for months and months I had eaten, slept, and lived with her without in the least understanding her mind. What were her moods? Was she sane or insane? Was she a liar? Did she bring all these charges against her husband at our first meeting just to seduce me? Would she be levelling various charges against me now that she seemed to be tiring of me—even to the extent of saying that I was a moron and an imbecile? I felt bewildered and unhappy. I didn't understand her sudden affection for her husband. What was this sudden mood that was coming over her? I did my best for her. Her career was at its height. What was it that still troubled her? Could I get at it and find a remedy? I had been taking too much for granted in our hectic professional existence.

'We must go on a holiday somewhere,' I said.

'Where?' she asked in a businesslike manner.

I was taken aback. 'Where? Anywhere! Somewhere.'

'We are always going somewhere. What difference is it going to make?'

'We'll go and enjoy ourselves on our own, without any engagement.'

'I don't think it's going to be possible until I fall sick or break my thighbone,' she said and giggled viciously. 'Do you know the bulls yoked to an oil-crusher—they keep going round and round and round, in a circle, without a beginning or an end?'

I sat up and told her, 'We'll go as soon as the present acceptances are finished.'

'In three months?'

'Yes. After they are finished we'll pause for a little breath.'
She looked so unconvinced of this that I said, 'Well, if you don't like an engagement, you can always say no.'

'To whom?'

'Why, of course, to me.'

'Yes, if you would tell me before you accept and take an advance.'

There was something seriously wrong with her. I went over to her bed, sat on it, shook her by the shoulder a little just to make it look personal, and asked, 'What is the matter with you? Are you not happy?'

'No. I'm not happy. What will you do about it?'

I threw up my arms. I really could not say anything. 'Well, if you tell me what is wrong, I can help. As far as I can see, there is nothing for you to be sorry about—you are famous, you have made money, you do what you like. You wanted to dance; you have done it.'

'Till the thought of it makes me sick,' she added. 'I feel like one of those parrots in a cage taken around village fairs, or a performing monkey, as he used to say—'

I laughed. I thought the best solvent would be laughter rather than words. Words have a knack of breeding more words, whereas laughter, a deafening, roaring laughter, has a knack of swallowing everything up. I worked myself into a paroxysm of laughter. She could not remain morose very long in the face of it. Presently she caught the contagion, a smirk developed into a chuckle, and before she knew what was what her body rocked with laughter, all her gloom and misgivings

[203]

exploded in laughter. We went to sleep in a happy frame of mind. The time was two hours past midnight.

Our life fell into a routine after this little disturbance. After a break of only three days, during which time I steeped myself in the card game, avoiding all discussions with her, our encounters were casual and slight. She was passing through a period of moodiness, and it was safest to keep out of her way and not to rouse her further. The engagements for the next three months were all-important, running, as they did, into the season of music and dance in South India, for which I had taken heavy advance payments. We had ahead of us a travel programme of nearly two thousand miles, from Malgudi back to Malgudi, and if we went through with it there was ample time for her to get over the mood, and then I could push her into another quarter-year of activity. I had no intention of slackening this programme. It seemed so unnecessary, so suicidal. My only technique was to keep her in good humour to the best of my ability from quarter to quarter.

We were getting through our engagements uneventfully. We were back in Malgudi. Mani was away for a couple of days and I was attending personally to an accumulation of correspondence on my table. Offers of engagements I piled up on one side. I had some misgivings about accepting any of them right away as I normally would. I felt I should do well to speak to her before replying. Of course she'd have to accept them, but I wanted to give her a feeling of being consulted. I sorted them out.

Suddenly I came upon a letter addressed to 'Rosie, alias Nalini'. It had on it the address of a lawyer's firm in Madras. I wondered what to do with it for a while. She was upstairs, probably reading one of her inexhaustible journals. I felt nervous about opening the letter. I had half an impulse to take it to her: a sensible part of me said, 'It must, after all, be her business. She is an adult, with her own affairs. Let her tackle it, whatever it may be.' But this was only fleeting wisdom. The letter had arrived by registered post some days ago and Mani had received it and kept it on the table. It had a big seal on its flap. I looked at it with misgiving for a while, told myself that I was not to be frightened by a seal, and just cut it open. I knew she would not mind my seeing her letters. The letter came from a lawyer and said, 'Madam, under instruction from our client, we are enclosing an application for your signature, for the release of a box of jewellery left in safe custody at the Bank of . . . . . ., in the marked place. After this is received we shall proceed to obtain the other signature as well, since you are aware that the deposit is in your joint names, and obtain the release of the said box, and arrange to forward it to you under insurance cover in due course.'

I was delighted. So this was going to bring in more jewellery for her? Of course she would be elated. But how big was the box? What were the contents worth? These were questions that agitated my mind for a while. I looked through the letter for some clue; but the lawyer was sparing of words. I took the letter and turned to go and give it to her. But on the staircase I paused. I returned to my room and sat in my chair, thinking. 'Well, let me think it over. Where is the hurry?' I asked myself. 'She has waited for this box so long. Just a couple of days more is not going to matter. Anyway, she never mentioned it, perhaps she doesn't care.' I took the letter to my drink casket and locked it up. A good thing Mani was not there. Otherwise he might have created a mess.

I had some visitors after this. I talked to them and went out

[205]

in the evening to see a few friends. I tried to distract my mind in various ways, but the packet bothered me. I returned home late. I avoided going upstairs. I heard her jingles upstairs, and knew that she was practising. I returned to my office table with the letter from the drink cabinet. I opened it carefully and read it again. I looked at the enclosed application. It was on a printed form; after her signature was going to be Marco's. What was the man's purpose in sending it now? Why this sudden generosity to return her an old box? Was he laying a trap for her, or what was it? Knowing the man as I did, I concluded 'that it might not be anything more than a correct disposal of his affairs, similar to his acknowledgement of my help in his book. He was capable of cold, machine-like rectitude; his vouchers were in order; he saw probably no sense in being responsible for Rosie's box any more. Rightly, too. The right place for Rosie's box was here. But how to release it? If Rosie saw this letter she would do God knew what. I had a fear that she would not view it calmly, in a businesslike manner. She would in all likelihood lose her head completely. She was likely to place the wildest interpretation on it and cry out, 'See how noble he is!' and make herself miserable and spoil for a fight with me. There was no knowing what would set off the trigger nowadays. His mere photo in the *Illustrated Weekly* drove her crazy: after that book incident I was very careful. I never showed her the book at all.

Next day I waited for her to ask for it, but she never mentioned it again. I thought it'd be safest to leave it there. I was very careful. I kept her in good humour and engaged, that was all; but I was aware that some sort of awkwardness had developed between us, and I kept myself aloof with extreme care. I knew that if I allowed more time she would be all right.

But I felt that to show her this letter would be suicidal. She might refuse to do anything except talk about his nobility. Or (who could say?) she might insist on taking the next train to his place, throwing up everything. But what was to be done with the letter? Just let it rest in the company of whisky bottles till it is forgotten,' I told myself and laughed grimly.

During dinner, as usual, we sat side by side and spoke of things such as the weather, general politics, the price and condition of vegetables, and so on. I kept the subject rigorously to inconsequential affairs. If we held on for another day, it'd be perfect. On the third day we should be on the move again, and the bustle and activity of travel would shield us from troublesome personal topics.

After dinner she sat down on the hall sofa to chew betel leaves, turned over the pages of a journal on the hall table and then went upstairs. I felt relieved. The swing was coming back to normal. I spent a little time in my office, looking into accounts. The income-tax statement was due to be sent in a couple of weeks. I was poring over my very personal account-book just to see where we stood, and how to prepare our expense-accounts. After brooding over this mystic matter for a while I went upstairs. I knew I had given her enough time either to be steeped in the pages of a book or to sleep. Anything to avoid talk. I was becoming uncertain of my own attitude nowadays. I feared I might blurt out about the letter. I laid my head on the pillow and turned over, with the formula, 'I'll sleep, I think. Will you switch off when you are done?' She grunted some reply.

How much jewellery might be in the box? Was it his present to her or her mother's or what? What a girl! She never gave it a thought! Perhaps they were antiquated and she did not care

[207]

for them. If so they might be sold now and converted into cash, and no income-tax officer would ever dream of its existence Must be a substantial lot if it had to be kept in safe custody. But who could say? Marco.was eccentric enough to do strange things. He was the sort of fellow to keep even a worthless packet at the bank, because that was the right thing—to—do—the—r-right thing to—do—I fell asleep.

Soon after midnight I awoke. She was snoring. An idea bothered me. I wanted to see if there was any time limit mentioned. Suppose I kept the letter secret and some serious consequences arose? I wanted to go down and examine the document at once. But if I got up, she would also wake up and ask questions. Or if I took no notice at all of it, what would happen? The box would continue to remain in safe custody; or the lawyer might write a reminder, which might come in when I was out and slip its way through to her, and then questions, explanations, scenes. This was proving a greater bother than I had at first thought. Nothing that that man did was ever quiet or normal. It led to unbelievable complexities. As I kept thinking of it, it magnified itself until I felt that I had dynamite in my pocket. I slept fitfully till about five o'clock, and then left my bed. I lost no time in going to the drink cabinet, pulling out the document, and examining it. I carefully read through the document, line by line, several times over. The lawyers said, 'Per return post,' which seemed to my fevered mind an all-important instruction. I took it over to the office desk. I found a scrap of paper and made a careful trial of Rosie's signature. I had her sign so many cheques and receipts each day that I was very familiar with it. Then I carefully spread out the application form and wrote on the indicated line: 'Rose, Nalini'. I folded it and put it in an addressed cover

which the lawyers had enclosed, sealed it, and I was the first to
appear at the window when our extension branch post-office
opened at seven-thirty.

The postmaster said, 'So early! You have come yourself!'

'My clerk is sick. I was out for a morning walk. Please
register this.' I had walked down for fear that opening the
garage door might wake her up.

I had no clear idea as to when or how the jewel box might
arrive, but I looked for it every day. 'Any parcel in the post,
Mani?' I asked constantly. This almost threatened to become
a habit. I expected it within the next two days. No signs of it.
We had to go out of town for four days. Before leaving I
instructed Mani, 'There may be an insured packet coming.
Tell the postman to keep it in deposit till we are back on
Tuesday. They keep such things, don't they?'

'Yes, sir. But if it is only a registered parcel, I can sign for
you.'

'No, no. This is an insured parcel and it will have to be signed
for by one of us. Tell the postman to bring it again on Tuesday.'

'Yes, sir,' said Mani, and I left him abruptly; otherwise he
might have started expanding on the subject.

We were back on Tuesday. The moment Rosie went upstairs
I asked Mani, 'Did the parcel arrive?'

'No, sir. I waited for the postman, but there was nothing.'

'Did you tell him that we were expecting an insured parcel?'

'Yes, sir, but there was nothing.'

'Strange!' I cried. 'Per return', the lawyers had written.
They probably wanted the signature, that was all. Perhaps
Marco planned to appropriate the box himself and had tried
this ruse. But as long as that lawyer's letter was with me, I

H

could hang them; none of their tricks was going to succeed. I went to my drink cabinet and re-read the letter. They had committed themselves clearly. 'We shall arrange to forward, under insurance cover . . .' If it meant nothing in a lawyer's letter, where was it going to mean anything? I felt somewhat puzzled, but told myself that it would ultimately arrive; banks and lawyers' offices could not be hustled; they had their own pace of work, their own slow red-tape methods. Slow-witted red-tapeists—no wonder the country was going to the dogs. I put the letter back and locked it up safely. I wished I didn't have to go to the drink cabinet every time I wanted to read the letter; the servants, knowing the contents, might begin to think that I took a swill of whisky every few minutes. My desk would be the right place for the letter, but I'd a suspicion that Mani might see it; if he caught me studying the letter so often, he was sure to want to take a look at it by stealing up at my back and pretending to have some question to ask. He had worked for me for months and months without my noticing anything against him, but now he and everyone around appeared sinister, diabolical, and cunning.

That evening we had an engagement at Kalipet, a small town sixty miles away. The organisers were providing a van for the musicians, and a Plymouth for me and Nalini, so that we might fulfil the engagement and return home the same night. It was a benefit show for building a maternity home, and they had collected seventy thousand rupees. The price of tickets ranged from two hundred and fifty rupees in a kind of fancy scale, and officials persuaded businessmen and merchants to contribute. Businessmen ungrudgingly paid up on condition that they were given the nearest seats in the first row. They wanted to sit as near the performer as possible, with a chance of being noticed. In their thoughts, Nalini, while dancing, noted their presence and later inquired, 'Who were those important men in the front row?' Poor creatures, they hardly knew how Nalini viewed her audience. She often remarked, 'They might be logs of wood for all I care. When I dance I hardly notice any face. I just see a dark well in the auditorium, that's all.'

This was a very large-scale function because of official interest in it. The officials were interested because the chief man of the place, who was behind all the shows, was a minister of the state cabinet, and it had been his ambition in life to build a first-rate maternity centre in this area. Knowing the circumstances, I had moderated my demand to a thousand rupees for expenses, which meant it was free of income tax. After all, I too liked to contribute to a social cause, and certainly we would not come out of it too badly anyway. But it was all the same for Nalini. Instead of travelling by train, we were going by car, that was all. She was pleased that we should be returning home the same night.

The show was held in an immense pavilion specially constructed with bamboos and coconut matting and decorated with brilliant tapestry, bunting, flowers, and coloured lights. The stage itself was so beautifully designed that Nalini, who generally ignored everything except the flowers at the end, cried, 'What a lovely place. I feel so happy to dance here.' Over a thousand people were seated in the auditorium.

She began her first movement, as usual, after a signal from me. She entered, carrying a brass lamp, with a song in praise of Ganesha, the elephant-faced god, the remover of impediments. Two hours passed. She was doing her fifth item—a snake dance, unusually enough. I liked to watch it. This item always interested me. As the musicians tuned their instruments and played the famous snake song, Nalini came gliding onto the stage. She fanned out her fingers slowly, and the yellow spotlight, playing on her white, upturned palms, gave them the appearance of a cobra hood; she wore a diadem for this act, and it sparkled. Lights changed, she gradually sank to the floor, the music became slower and slower, the refrain urged the snake to dance—the snake that resided on the locks of Shiva himself, on the wrist of his spouse, Parvathi, and in the ever-radiant home of the gods in Kailas. This was a song that elevated the serpent and brought out its mystic quality; the rhythm was hypnotic. It was her masterpiece. Every inch of her body from toe to head rippled and vibrated to the rhythm of this song which lifted the cobra out of its class of an underground reptile into a creature of grace and divinity and an ornament of the gods.

The dance took forty-five minutes in all; the audience watched in rapt silence. I was captivated by it . . . She rarely chose to do it indeed. She always said that a special mood was needed, and always joked that so much wriggling twisted her up too much and she could not stand upright again for days. I sat gazing as if I were seeing it for the first time. There came to my mind my mother's remark on the first day, 'A serpent girl! Be careful.' I felt sad at the thought of my mother. How much she could have enjoyed watching this. What would she have said if she could have seen Rosie now, in her shining costume and diadem? I felt a regret at the rift that had developed between me and my mother. She occasionally wrote me a postcard, and I sent her small sums of money now and then, dashing off a few lines to say I was well. She often asked

[212]

when I'd get back the house for her—well, that involved a big sum and I told myself I'd attend to it as soon as I had some time. Anyway, what was the hurry? She was quite happy in the village; that brother of hers looked after her very well. Somehow I could never fully forgive her for her treatment of Rosie on that fateful day. Well, we were now on cordial terms, but far away from each other, the best possible arrangement. I was watching Nalini and at the same time thinking of my mother. At this moment, one of the men of the organisation came up to me unobtrusively and said, 'You are wanted, sir.'

'Who wants me?'

'The District Superintendent of Police.'

'Tell him I'll be with him as soon as this act is over.'

He went away. The District Superintendent! He was one of my card-playing mates. What did he want to see me about now? Of course, the officials were all here, expecting the Minister (a sofa was kept vacant for him), and extra police were posted to control the crowd and the traffic. After this act, when the curtain came down, thunderous applause broke out, and I went out. Yes, the District Superintendent was there. He was in plain dress.

'Hello, Superintendent, I didn't know you were coming; you could have come with us in the car,' I cried.

He plucked my sleeve and drew me aside because there were too many people watching us. We went to a lonely spot under a lamp outside, and he whispered, 'I'm awfully sorry to say this, but I've a warrant for your arrest. It has come from headquarters.'

I smiled awkwardly, partly disbelieving him. I thought he was joking. He pulled out a paper. Yes, it was a true and good warrant for my arrest on a complaint from Marco, the charge being forgery. When I stood ruminating, the Inspector asked, 'Did you sign any recent document for—the lady?'

'Yes; she was busy. But how can you call that forgery?'

'Did you write "For" or just write her name?' He plied me with questions. 'It's a serious charge,' he said. 'I hope you will pull through, but for the moment I have to take you in custody.'

I realised the gravity of the situation. I whispered, 'Please don't create a scene now. Wait until the end of the show, and till we are back home.'

I'll have to be with you in the car, and after the warrant is served you can arrange for a surety bond till the case is taken up. That will leave you free, but first I'm afraid you will have to go with me to the magistrate. He has to sanction it. I have no powers.'

I went back to my sofa in the hall. They brought me my garland. Somebody got up and made a speech thanking the dancer and Mr Raju for their help in getting the collection to over seventy thousand rupees. Incidentally he spun out a lot of verbiage around the theme of the dance in India, its status, philosophy, and purpose. He went on and on. He was a much-respected president of the local high-school or some such thing. There was tremendous applause at the end of his speech. More speeches followed. I felt numb, hardly hearing anything. I didn't care what they said. I didn't care whether the speech was long or short. When it was over, I went to Nalini's dressing-room. I found her changing. A number of girls were standing around her, some waiting for autographs, and some just looking on. I said to Nalini, 'We will have to hurry.'

I went back to the Superintendent in the corridor, composing my looks, trying to look cheerful and unconcerned. A lot of the first-row men surrounded me to explain their appreciation in minute detail. 'She just towers above all others,' someone said. 'I have seen dancers for a half-century—I'm the sort of man who will forgo a meal and walk twenty miles to see a dance. But never have I seen,' etc. etc. 'This maternity home, you know, will be the first of its kind. We must have a wing named after Miss Nalini. I hope you will be able to come again. We would like to have you both for the opening ceremony. Could you give us a photograph of her?... We'd like to enlarge it and hang it in the hall... That'll be a source of inspiration for many others, and, who knows, in this very building may be born a genius who may follow the footsteps of your distinguished wife.'

I didn't care what they said. I simply nodded and grunted till Nalini came out. I knew that the men surrounded and talked to me only in the hope of getting a close view of Nalini. As usual, she had her garland; I gave her mine. The Superintendent led the way unobtrusively to our Plymouth waiting outside. We had to walk through a crowd buzzing around us like flies. The driver held the door open.

'Get in. Get in,' I said impatiently to Nalini. I sat beside her. Her face was partially illuminated by a shaft of gaslight from a lamp hanging on a tree. Thick dust hung in the air, churned up by the traffic; all the vehicles, cars, bullock-carts, and *jutkas* were leaving in a mass, with a deafening honking of horns and rattle of wheels. A few policemen stood at a discreet distance and saluted the Superintendent as our car moved away. He occupied the front seat next to the driver. I told her, 'Our friend, the District Superintendent, is coming back with us to the city.'

It was about two hours' journey. She talked for a while about the evening. I gave her some comments on her performance. I told her something of what I had heard people say about her snake-dance. She said, 'You are never tired of it,' and then lapsed into silence and drowsiness, only waiting for our destination, as our car whizzed along the country highway, past long rows of bullock-carts with their jingling bells. 'They sound like your anklets,' I whispered to her clumsily.

The moment we reached our home, she threw a smile at the Superintendent, murmured 'Good night,' and vanished into the house. The Superintendent said to me, 'Let us go now in my jeep.' It was waiting at the gate.

I sent away the Plymouth. I said, 'I say, Superintendent, give me a little time, please. I want to tell her about it.'

'All right. Don't delay. We must not get into trouble.'

I went up the staircase. He followed. He stood on the landing while I went into her room. She listened to me as if I were addressing a stone pillar. Even now I can recollect her bewildered, stunned expression as she tried to comprehend the situation. I thought she would break down. She often broke down on small issues, but this seemed to leave her unperturbed. She merely said, 'I felt all along you were not doing right things. This is *karma*. What can we do?' She came out to the landing and asked the officer, 'What shall we do about it, sir? Is there no way out?'

'At the moment I have no discretion, madam. It's a nonbailable warrant. But perhaps tomorrow you may apply for reconsideration of bond. But we can do nothing till tomorrow, till it's moved before the magistrate.' He was no longer my friend, but a frightful technician.

10

I HAD to spend a couple of days in the lock-up, among low criminals. The District Superintendent ceased to be friendly the moment we were in the Central Police Station. He just abandoned me to the routine care of the station officer.

Rosie came to see me in the police lock-up and wept. I sat for the first time with my eyes averted, in the farthest corner of the cell. After a while I recovered my composure and told her to go and see our banker. All that she asked was, 'Oh, we had so much money! Where is it all gone?'

I went back home three days later, but the old, normal life was gone. Mani worked in a mechanical manner, with bowed head, in his own room. There was no work for him to do. Fewer letters arrived for me. There was a sepulchral quietness about the house. Nalini's feet were silent upstairs. No visitors came. She had had to scrape up a bail bond for ten thousand rupees. If I had lived as a normal man of common sense, it would not have been difficult to find the amount. As it was, I had tied up whatever was left over in several foolish share certificates, on which the banks would not advance any money, and the rest I had spent in showy living, including the advances taken for future engagements.

I suggested to Rosie, 'Why don't you go through with your engagements for the next quarter? We should receive the balance of the fees.' I caught her at dinner, because nowadays I spent all my time downstairs and left her alone. I lacked the

[217]

confidence to face her alone in her room. I even spent my sleeping hours on the hall sofa.

She did not answer. I repeated my question, at which she muttered, when the cook went in to fetch something, 'Must we discuss it before the cook?' I accepted the snub meekly.

I was now a sort of hanger-on in the house; ever since she had released me from police custody, the mastery had passed to her. I fretted inwardly at the thought of it. When the first shock of the affair had subsided, she became hardened. She never spoke to me except as to a tramp she had salvaged. It could not be helped. She had had to scrape together all her resources to help me. She went through her act of help in a sort of cold, businesslike manner. I ate my food in silence. She deigned to spend some time in the hall after food. She came and sat down there. She had a tray of betel leaves by her side on the sofa. I pushed it off and dared to seat myself by her side. Her lips were reddened with betel juice. Her face was flushed with the tingling effect of betel leaves. She looked at me imperiously and asked, 'Now, what is it?' Before I opened my mouth, she added, 'Remember, you should speak nothing before the cook. The servants are gossiping too much. On the first of the month I'm going to send one of them away.'

'Wait, wait. Don't rush,' I began.

'What should I wait for?' Her eyes glistened with tears; she blew her nose. I could do nothing about it but just watch. After all, the mastery had passed to her and if she thought fit to cry, it was her business. She had enough strength in her to overcome it if she thought it necessary. It was I that needed comforting. I was overwhelmed with a sudden self-pity. Why should she cry? She was not on the threshold of a prison. She had not been the one who had run hither and thither creating glamour and a public for a dancer; it was not she who had been fiendishly trapped by a half-forgotten man like Marco—an apparent gazer at cave-paintings, but actually venomous and vindictive, like the cobra lying in wait for its victim. I can now see that it was a very wrong line of thought to adopt. But how could I help it? It was only such perverse lines of thought and my excessive self-pity that enabled me to survive those moments; one needed all that amount of devilry to keep oneself afloat. I could give no time for others. I could not bother to think of her own troubles, of the mess she had been led into, of the financial emptiness after all those months of dancing and working, of the surprise sprung upon her by my lack of—what should we call it, judgement? No, it was something much lower than that. Lack of ordinary character! I see it all now clearly, but at that time I still clung to my own grievances, and could watch without much perturbation her emotional tantrums. I allowed her to have her cry as usual. She wiped her eyes and asked, 'You said something when we were eating?'

'Yes; but you wouldn't let me proceed,' I said petulantly. 'I was asking why you should not go through with the programmes, at least those for which we have received an advance.'

She remained in thought for a while and said, 'Why should I?'

'Because we received only an advance, while what we desperately need is the full fee in every case.'

'Where is all the money?'

'You should know. The account is all in your name, and you may see the bankbook if you like.' It was a cruel thing to say. Some devil was wagging his tongue within my skull. I was suddenly racked with the feeling that after all I had done for her she was not sufficiently sympathetic to my cause.

She spurned continuing this perverse discussion. She merely said, 'Please tell me what those engagements are and I'll return them all their money.'

I knew that this was just a brave statement. Where would she find the amount to refund? 'Why should you? Why should you not go through with them?'

'Is money your only consideration? Don't you see how I can't face the public again?'

'Why not? If I'm under arrest, I'm under arrest; that is all. Not you. Why should you not go about your business normally?'

'I can't; that is all. I can say nothing more.'

I asked coldly, 'What do you propose to do in future?'

'Perhaps I'll go back to him.'

'Do you think he will take you back?'

'Yes; if I stop dancing.'

I laughed in a sinister manner. 'Why do you laugh?' she asked.

'If it were only the question of dancing, he might.'

Why did I talk like this? It hurt her very much. 'Yes; you are in a position to say such a thing now. He may not admit me over the threshold, in which event it is far better to end one's life on his doorstep.' She remained moody for a while. It gave me a profound satisfaction to see her imperiousness shattered after all. She added, 'I think the best solution for all concerned would be to be done with this business of living. I mean both of us. A dozen sleeping pills in a glass of milk, or two glasses of milk. One often hears of suicide pacts. It seems to me a wonderful solution, like going on a long holiday. We could sit and talk one night perhaps, and sip our glasses of milk, and maybe we should wake up in a trouble-free world. I'd propose it this very minute if I were sure you would keep the pact, but I fear that I may go ahead and you may change your mind at the last second.'

'And have the responsibility of disposing of your body?' I said, which was the worst thing I could have said. Why was I speaking like this again and again? I think I was piqued that she would not continue her dancing, was a free creature, while I was a jailbird.

I said, 'Is it not better to keep dancing than think these morbid thoughts?' I felt I must take charge of her again. 'Why won't you dance? Is it because you think I won't be there to look after you? I'm sure you can manage. And it may after all be only for a short time. Oh, there is nothing in this case of ours. It'll just break down at the first hearing. You take my word for it. It's a false charge.'

'Is it?' she asked.

'How can they prove anything against me?'

She merely ignored this legal rambling and said, 'Even if you are free, I'll not dance in public any more. I am tired of all this circus existence.'

'It was your own choice,' I said.

'Not the circus life. I visualised it as something different. It's all gone with that old home of yours!'

'Oh!' I groaned. 'And you wouldn't let me rest then. You drove me hard to help you come before the public, and now you say this! I don't know, I don't know, you are very difficult to satisfy.'

'You don't understand!' she cried, and got up and went upstairs. She came down a few steps to say, 'It does not mean I'm not going to help. If I have to pawn my last possession, I'll do it to save you from jail. But once it's over, leave me once and for all; that's all I ask. Forget me. Leave me to live or die, as I choose; that's all.'

She was as good as her word. A sudden activity seized her. She ran about with Mani's help. She sold her diamonds. She gathered all the cash she could, selling under par all the shares. She kept Mani spinning around. She sent him to Madras to pick up a big lawyer for me. When the stress for cash·became acute and she found we would have a lot to make up, she became somewhat more practical-minded. She swallowed her own words and went through her engagements, shepherding the musicians herself, with Mani's help, making all the railway arrangements, and so forth. I taunted her as I saw her moving around. 'You see, this is what I wanted you to do.'

There was no dearth of engagements. In fact, my present plight, after a temporary lull, seemed to create an extra interest. After all, people wanted to enjoy a show, and how could they care what happened to me? It hurt me to see her go through her work, practice, and engagements unconcernedly. Mani was very helpful to her, and those that invited her gave her all assistance. Everything went to prove that she could get on excellently without me. I felt like telling Mani, 'Be careful. She'll lead you on before you know where you are, and then you will find yourself in my shoes all of a sudden! Beware the snake woman!' I knew my mind was not working either normally or fairly. I knew I was growing jealous of her self-reliance. But I forgot for the moment that she was doing it all for my sake. I feared that, in spite of her protestations to the contrary, she would never stop dancing. She would not be able to stop. She would go from strength to strength. I knew, looking at the way she was going about her business, that she would manage—whether I was inside the bars or outside, whether her husband approved of it or not. Neither Marco nor I had any place in her life, which had its own sustaining vitality and which she herself had underestimated all along.

Our lawyer had his own star value. His name spelled magic in all the court-halls of this part of the country. He had saved many a neck (sometimes more than once) from the noose; he had absolved many a public swindler in the public eye and in the eye of the law; he could prove a whole gang of lawless hooligans to be innocent victims of a police conspiracy. He set at naught all the laboriously built-up cases of the prosecution; he made their story laughable; he picked the most carefully packed evidence between his thumb and forefinger and with a squeeze reduced it to thin air; he was old-fashioned in appearance, with his long coat and an orthdox-style *dhoti* and turban and over it all his black gown. His eyes scintillated with mirth and confidence when he stood at the bar and addressed the court. When the judge's eyes were lowered over the papers on his desk, he inhaled a deep pinch of snuff with the utmost elegance. We feared at one stage that he might refuse to take our case, considering it too slight for his attention; but fortunately he undertook it as a concession from one star to another—for Nalini's sake. When the news came that he had accepted the brief (a thousand rupees it cost us to get this out of him), we felt as if the whole case against me had been dropped by the police with apologies for the inconvenience caused. But he was expensive—each consultation had to be bought for cash at the counter. He was in his own way an 'adjournment lawyer'. A case in his hands was like dough; he could knead and draw it up and down. He split a case into minute bits and demanded as many days for microscopic examination. He would keep the court fidgeting without being able to rise for lunch, because he could talk without completing a sentence; he had a knack of telescoping sentence into sentence without pausing for breath.

He arrived by the morning train and left by the evening one, and until that time he neither moved off the court floor nor let the case progress even an inch for the day—so that a judge had to wonder how the day had spent itself. Thus he prolonged the lease of freedom for a criminal within the available time, whatever might be the final outcome. But this meant also for the poor case-stricken man more expense, as his charges per day were seven hundred and fifty rupees, and he had to be paid railway and other expenses as well, and he never came without juniors to assist him.

He presented my case as a sort of comedy in three acts, in which the chief villain was Marco, an enemy of civilised existence. Marco was the first prosecution witness for the day, and I could see him across the hall wincing at every assault mounted against him by my star lawyer. He must have wished that he had not been foolhardy enough to press charges. He had his own lawyer, of course, but he looked puny and frightened.

The first part of the comedy was that the villain wanted to drive his wife mad; the second part of the comedy was that the wife survived this onslaught, and on the point of privation and death was saved by a humble humanitarian called Raju, who sacrificed his time and profession for the protection of the lady and enabled her to rise so high in the world of the arts. Her life was a contribution to the prestige of our nation and our cultural traditions. When the whole world was thirsting for *Bharat Natyam*, here was this man slighting it, and when she made a big name for herself, someone's gorge rose. Someone wanted to devise a way of blowing up this whole edifice of a helpless lady's single-handed upward career, Your Honour. And then the schemer brought out the document—a document which had been forgotten and lain in concealment for so many years. There was some other motive in involving the lady by getting her to sign the document—he would go into it at a later part of the argument. (It was his favourite device to make something look sinister; he never found the opportunity to return to it later.) Why should anyone want to trot out a document which had been kept back for all those years? Why did he leave it alone so long? Our lawyer would leave the point for the present without a comment. He looked about like a hound scenting a fox. The document, Your Honour, was returned without signature. The idea was not to get involved, and the lady was not the type to get caught by jewellery; she cared little for it. And so the document was unsigned and returned, the good man Raju himself carrying it to the post-office in order to make sure of its dispatch, as the postmaster would testify. So it was a big disappointment for the schemer when the document went back unsigned. So they thought of another trick: someone copied the lady's signature on it and took it to the police. It was not his business to indicate who could have done it; he was not interested in the question. He was only interested to the extent of saying categorically that it was not his client who had done it; and unhesitatingly he would recommend that he should be immediately discharged and exonerated.

But the prosecution case was strong, though unspectacular. They put Mani in the box and examined him till he blurted out

[225]

that I was desperately looking for an insured parcel every day; the postmaster was cross-examined and had to admit that I had seemed unusual, and finally it was the handwriting expert who testified that it could reasonably be taken to be my handwriting: he had detailed proofs from my writings on the backs of cheques, on receipts and letters.

The judge sentenced me to two years' imprisonment. Our star lawyer looked gratified, I should properly have got seven years according to law books, but his fluency knocked five years off, though, if I had been a little careful . . .

The star lawyer did not achieve this end all at once, but over a period of many months, while Nalini worked harder than ever to keep the lawyer as well as our household going.

I was considered a model prisoner. Now I realised that people generally thought of me as being unsound and worthless, not because I deserved the label, but because they had been seeing me in the wrong place all along. To appreciate me, they should really have come to the Central Jail and watched me. No doubt my movements were somewhat restricted: I had to get out of bed at an hour when I'd rather stay in, and turn in when I'd rather stay out—that was morning five and evening five. But in between these hours I was the master of the show. I visited all departments of the prison as a sort of benevolent supervisor. I got on well with all the warders: I relieved them in their jobs when other prisoners had to be watched. I watched the weaving section and the carpentry sheds. Whether they were murderers or cut-throats or highwaymen, they all listened to me, and I could talk them out of their blackest moods. When there was a respite, I told them stories and philosophies and what not. They came to refer to me as *Vadhyar*—that is,

Teacher. There were five hundred prisoners in that building and I could claim to have established a fairly widespread intimacy with most of them. I got on well with the officials too. When the jail superintendent went about his inspections, I was one of those privileged to walk behind and listen to his remarks; and I ran little errands for him, which endeared me to him. He had only to look ever so slightly to his left, and I knew what he wanted. I dashed up and called the warder he was thinking of calling; he had only to hesitate for a second, and I knew he wanted that pebble on the road to be picked up and thrown away. It pleased him tremendously. In addition, I was in a position to run ahead and warn warders and other subordinates of his arrival; and that gave them time to rouse themselves from brief naps and straighten out their turbans.

I worked incessantly on a vegetable patch in the back-yard of the superintendent's home. I dug the earth and drew water from the well and tended it carefully. I put fences round, with brambles and thorns so that cattle did not destroy the plants. I grew huge *brinjals* and beans, and cabbages. When they appeared on their stalks as tiny buds, I was filled with excitement. I watched them develop, acquire shape, change colour, shed the early parts. When the harvest was ready, I plucked them off their stalks tenderly, washed them, wiped them clean to a polish with the end of my jail jacket, arranged them artistically on a tray of woven bamboo (I'd arranged to get one from the weaving-shed), and carried them in ceremoniously. When he saw the highly polished *brinjals*, greens, and cabbage, the superintendent nearly hugged me for joy. He was a lover of vegetables. He was a lover of good food, wherever it came from. I loved every piece of this work, the blue sky and sunshine, and the shade of the house in which I sat and worked, the feel of

[227]

cold water; it produced in me a luxurious sensation. Oh, it seemed to be so good to be alive and feeling all this; the smell of freshly turned earth filled me with the greatest delight. If this was prison life, why didn't more people take to it? They thought of it with a shudder, as if it were a place where a man was branded, chained, and lashed from morning to night! Medieval notions! No place could be more agreeable; if you observed the rules you earned greater appreciation here than beyond the high walls. I got my food, I had my social life with the other inmates and the staff, I moved about freely within an area of fifty acres. Well, that's a great deal of space when you come to think of it; man generally manages with much less. 'Forget the walls, and you will be happy,' I told some of the newcomers, who became moody and sullen the first few days. I felt amused at the thought of the ignorant folk who were horrified at the idea of a jail. Maybe a man about to be hanged might not have the same view, nor one who had been insubordinate, or violent; but short of these, all others could be happy here. I felt choked with tears when I had to go out after two years, and I wished that we had not wasted all that money on our lawyer. I'd have been happy to stay in this prison permanently.

The superintendent transferred me to his office as his personal servant. I took charge of his desk, filled his inkwells, cleaned his pens, mended his pencil, and waited outside his door to see that no one disturbed him while he worked. If he so much as thought of me, I went in and stood before him, I was so alert. He gave me file-boxes to carry to his outer office; I brought in the file-boxes that they gave back to his table. When he was away, the newspapers arrived. I took charge of them and glanced through their pages before taking them to him. I don't think he ever minded; he really liked to read his paper in bed, after his lunch, in the process of snatching a siesta. I quietly glanced through the speeches of world statesmen, descriptions of the Five Year Plan, of ministers opening bridges or distributing prizes, nuclear explosions, and world crises. I gave them all a cursory look.

But on Friday and Saturday I turned the last page of the *Hindu* with trembling fingers—and the last column in its top portion always displayed the same block, Nalini's photograph, the name of the institution where she was performing, and the price of tickets. Now at this corner of South India, now there, next week in Ceylon, and another week in Bombay or Delhi. Her empire was expanding rather than shrinking. It filled me with gall that she should go on without me. Who sat now on that middle sofa? How could the performance start without my signal with the small finger? How could she know when to stop? She probably went on and on, while others just watched without the wit to stop her. I chuckled to myself at the thought of how she must have been missing her trains after every performance. I opened the pages of the paper only to study her engagements and to calculate how much she might be earning. Unless she wrote up her accounts with forethought, super-tax would swallow what she so laboriously piled up with all that twisting and writhing of her person! I would have suspected Mani of having stepped into my shoes, and that would have provided more gall for me to swallow, but for the fact that in the early months of my stay Mani came to see me on a visitor's day.

Mani was the only visitor I had in prison; all other friends and relatives seemed to have forgotten me. He came because he felt saddened by my career. He wore a look of appropriate gloom and seriousness as he waited for me. But when I told him, 'This is not a bad place. You should come here, if you can,' he looked horrified and never saw me again. But in the thirty minutes he was with me he gave me all the news. Nalini had cleared out of the town, bag and baggage. She had settled down at Madras and was looking after herself quite well. She had given Mani a gift of one thousand rupees on the day that she left. She had a hundred bouquets of garlands presented to her on the railway platform. What a huge crowd had gathered to see her off! Before her departure she had methodically drawn up a list of all our various debts and discharged them fully; she had all the furniture and other possessions at our house turned over to an auctioneer. Mani explained that the only article that she carried out of the house was the book— which she came upon when she broke open the drink cabinet and had all the drink thrown out. She found the book tucked away inside, picked it up, and took it away carefully.

'That was my book. Why should she take it?' I cried childishly. I added, 'She seems to think it a mighty performance, I suppose!... Did it please him? Or did it have any useful effect?' I asked devilishly.

Mani said, 'After the case, she got into the car and went home, and he got into his and went to the railway station: they didn't meet.'

'I'm happy at least about this one thing,' I said. 'She had the self-respect not to try and fall at his feet again.'

Mani added before going away, 'I saw your mother recently. She is keeping well in the village.' At the court-hall my mother had been present. She had come on the last day of the hearing, thanks to our local 'adjournment lawyer', who was my link generally with her, as he continued to handle the tortuous and prolonged affair of half my house being pledged to the Sait. He had been excited beyond words at the arrival of the glamorous lawyer from Madras, whom we put up at the Taj in the best suite.

Our little lawyer seemed to have been running around in excitement. He went to the extent of rushing to the village and fetching my mother—for what purpose he alone knew. For my mother was overcome with my plight as I stood in the dock; when Rosie approached her to say a few words in the corridor, her eyes flashed, 'Now are you satisfied with what you have done to him?' And the girl shrank away from her. This was reported to me by my mother herself, whom I approached during the court recess. My mother was standing in the doorway. She had never seen the inside of a court-hall, and was overwhelmed with a feeling of her own daring. She said to me, 'What a shame you have brought on yourself and on all known to you! I used to think that the worst that could happen to you might be death, as when you had that pneumonia for weeks; but I now wish that rather than survive and go through this . . .' She could not complete her sentence; she broke down and went along the corridor and out before we assembled again to hear the judgement.

11

RAJU'S narration concluded with the crowing of the cock. Velan had listened without moving a muscle, supporting his back against the ancient, stone railing along the steps. Raju felt his throat smarting with the continuous talk all night. The village had not yet wakened to life. Velan yielded himself to a big yawn, and remained silent. Raju had mentioned without a single omission every detail from his birth to his emergence from the gates of the prison. He imagined that Velan would rise with disgust and swear, 'And we took you for such a noble soul all along! If one like you does penance, it'll drive off even the little rain that we may hope for. Begone, you, before we feel tempted to throw you out. You have fooled us.'

Raju waited for these words as if for words of reprieve. He looked on Velan's silence with anxiety and suspense, as if he waited on a judge's verdict again, a second time. The judge here seemed to be one of sterner cast than the one he had encountered in the court-hall. Velan kept still—so still that Raju feared that he had fallen asleep.

Raju asked, 'Now you have heard me fully?' like a lawyer who has a misgiving that the judge has been wool gathering.

'Yes, Swami.'

Raju was taken aback at still being addressed as 'Swami'. 'What do you think of it?'

Velan looked quite pained at having to answer such a question. 'I don't know why you tell me all this, Swami. It's very

[232]

kind of you to address at such length your humble servant.'
Every respectful word that this man employed pierced Raju
like a shaft. 'He will not leave me alone,' Raju thought with
resignation. 'This man will finish me before I know where I
am.'

After profound thought, the judge rose in his seat. 'I'll go
back to the village to do my morning duties. I will come back
later. And I'll never speak a word of what I have heard to
anyone.' He dramatically thumped his chest. 'It has gone
down there, and there it will remain.' With this, he made a deep
obeisance, went down the steps and across the sandy river.

A wandering newspaper correspondent who had come to the
village picked up the news. The government had sent a commission to inquire into the drought conditions and suggest
remedies, and with it came a press correspondent. While
wandering around he heard about the Swamiji, went to the
temple across the river, and sent off a wire to his paper at
Madras, which circulated in all the towns of India. 'Holy
man's penance to end drought,' said the heading, and then a
brief description followed.

This was the starting point.

Public interest was roused. The newspaper office was
besieged for more news. They ordered the reporter to go back.
He sent a second telegram to say 'Fifth day of fast'. He described the scene: how the Swami came to the river's edge,
faced its source, stood knee-deep in the water from six to
eight in the morning, muttering something between his lips,
his eyes shut, his palms pressed together in a salute to the gods,
presumably. It had been difficult enough to find knee-deep
water, but the villagers had made an artificial basin in sand and,

[233]

when it didn't fill, fetched water from distant wells and filled it, so that the man had always knee-deep water to stand in. The holy man stood there for two hours, then walked up the steps slowly and lay down on a mat in the pillared hall of the temple, while his devotees kept fanning him continuously. He took notice of hardly anyone, though there was a big crowd around. He fasted totally. He lay down and shut his eyes in order that his penance might be successful. For that purpose he conserved all his energy. When he was not standing in the water, he was in deep meditation. The villagers had set aside all their normal avocations in order to be near this great soul all the time. When he slept they remained there, guarding him, and though there was a fair-sized crowd, it remained totally silent.

But each day the crowd increased. In a week there was a permanent hum pervading the place. Children shouted and played about, women came carrying baskets filled with pots, firewood, and foodstuffs, and cooked the food for their men and children. There were small curls of smoke going up all along the river bank, on the opposite slope and on this bank also. It was studded with picnic groups, with the women's bright-coloured saris shining in the sun; men too had festive dress. Bullocks unyoked from their carts jingled their bells as they ate the straw under the trees. People swarmed around little water-holes.

Raju saw them across his pillared hall whenever he opened his eyes. He knew what that smoke meant; he knew that they were eating and enjoying themselves. He wondered what they might be eating—rice boiled with a pinch of saffron, melted *ghee*—and what were the vegetables? Probably none in this drought. The sight tormented him.

This was actually the fourth day of his fast. Fortunately on the first day he had concealed a little stale food, left over from the previous day, in an aluminium vessel behind a stone pillar in the innermost sanctum—some rice mixed with buttermilk, and a piece of vegetable thrown in. Fortunately, too, he was able on the first day to snatch a little privacy at the end of the day's prayer and penance, late at night. The crowd had not been so heavy then. Velan had business at home and had gone, leaving two others to attend on the Swami. The Swami had been lying on the mat in the pillared hall, with the two villagers looking on and waving a huge palmyra fan at his face. He had felt weakened by his day's fasting. He had suddenly told them, 'Sleep, if you like; I'll be back,' and he rose in a businesslike manner and passed into his inner sanctum.

'I don't have to tell the fellows where I am going or why or how long I shall be gone out of sight.' He felt indignant. He had lost all privacy. People all the time watching and staring, lynx-eyed, as if he were a thief! In the inner sanctum he briskly thrust his hand into a niche and pulled out his aluminium pot. He sat down behind the pedestal, swallowed his food in three or four large mouthfuls, making as little noise as possible. It was stale rice, dry and stiff and two days old; it tasted awful, but it appeased his hunger. He washed it down with water. He went to the back-yard and rinsed his mouth noiselessly— he didn't want to smell of food when he went back to his mat.

Lying on his mat, he brooded. He felt sick of the whole thing. When the assembly was at its thickest, could he not stand up on a high pedestal and cry, 'Get out, all of you, and leave me alone, I am not the man to save you. No power on earth can save you if you are doomed. Why do you bother me with all this fasting and austerity?'

It would not help. They might enjoy it as a joke. He had his back to the wall, there was no further retreat. This realisation helped him to get through the trial with a little more resignation on the second day of his penance. Once again he stood up in water, muttering with his face to the hills, and watching the picnic groups enjoying themselves all over the place. At night he left Velan for a while and sneaked in to look for leftover food in his aluminium vessel—it was really an act of desperation. He knew full well that he had finished off the vessel the previous night. Still he hoped, childishly, for a miracle. 'When they want me to perform all sorts of miracles, why not make a start with my own aluminium vessel?' he reflected caustically. He felt weak. He was enraged at the emptiness of his larder. He wondered for a moment if he could make a last desperate appeal to Velan to let him eat—and if only he minded, how he could save him! Velan ought to know, yet the fool would not stop thinking that he was a saviour. He banged down the aluminium vessel in irritation and went back to his mat. What if the vessel did get shattered? It was not going to be of any use. What was the point of pampering an empty vessel? When he was seated, Velan asked respectfully, 'What was that noise, master?'

'An empty vessel. Have you not heard the saying, "An empty vessel makes much noise"?'

Velan permitted himself a polite laugh and declared with admiration, 'How many good sentiments and philosophies you have gathered in that head of yours, sir!'

Raju almost glared at him. This single man was responsible for his present plight. Why would he not go away and leave him alone? What a wise plan it would have been if the crocodile had got him while he crossed the river! But that poor old thing, which had remained almost a myth, had become dehydrated. When its belly was ripped open they found in it ten thousand rupees' worth of jewellery. Did this mean that the crocodile had been in the habit of eating only women? No, a few snuff-boxes and ear-rings of men were also found. The question of the day was: Who was entitled to all this treasure? The villagers hushed up the affair. They did not want the government to get scent of it and come round and claim it, as it did all buried treasure. They gave out that only a couple of worthless trinkets had been found inside the crocodile, although in actual fact the man who cut it open acquired a fortune. He had no problems for the rest of his life. Who permitted him to cut open the crocodile? Who could say? People didn't wait for permission under such circumstances. Thus had gone on the talk among the people about the crocodile when it was found dead.

Velan, fanning him, had fallen asleep—he had just doubled up in his seat with the fan in his hand. Raju, who lay awake, had let his mind roam and touch the depths of morbid and fantastic thought. He was now touched by the sight of this man hunched in his seat. The poor fellow was tremendously excited and straining himself in order to make this penance a success, providing the great man concerned with every comfort—except, of course, food. Why not give the poor devil a chance? Raju said to himself, instead of hankering after food which one could not get anyway. He felt enraged at the persistence of food-thoughts. With a sort of vindictive resolution he told himself, 'I'll chase away all thought of food. For the next ten days I shall eradicate all thoughts of tongue and stomach from my mind.'

This resolution gave him a peculiar strength. He developed on those lines: 'If by avoiding food I should help the trees

[237]

bloom, and the grass grow, why not do it thoroughly?' For the first time in his life he was making an earnest effort; for the first time he was learning the thrill of full application, outside money and love; for the first time he was doing a thing in which he was not personally interested. He felt suddenly so enthusiastic that it gave him a new strength to go through with the ordeal. The fourth day of his fast found him quite sprightly. He went down to the river, stood facing upstream with his eyes shut, and repeated the litany. It was no more than a supplication to the heavens to send down rain and save humanity. It was set in a certain rhythmic chant, which lulled his senses and awareness, so that as he went on saying it over and over again the world around became blank. He nearly lost all sensation, except the numbness at his knees, through constant contact with cold water. Lack of food gave him a peculiar floating feeling, which he rather enjoyed, with the thought in the background, 'This enjoyment is something Velan cannot take away from me.'

The hum of humanity around was increasing. His awareness of his surroundings was gradually lessening in a sort of inverse proportion. He was not aware of it, but the world was beginning to press around. The pen of the wandering journalist had done the trick. Its repercussions were far and wide. The railways were the first to feel the pressure. They had to run special trains for the crowds that were going to Malgudi. People travelled on footboards and on the roofs of coaches. The little Malgudi station was choked with passengers. Outside, the station buses stood, the conductors crying, 'Special for Mangala leaving. Hurry up. Hurry up.' People rushed up from the station into the buses and almost sat on top of one another. Gaffur's taxi drove up and down a dozen times a day.

[238]

And the crowd congregated around the river at Mangala. People sat in groups along its sandbank, down its stones and steps, all the way up the opposite bank, wherever they could squeeze themselves in.

Never had this part of the country seen such a crowd. Shops sprang up overnight, as if by magic, on bamboo poles roofed with thatch, displaying coloured soda bottles and bunches of bananas and coconut-toffees. The Tea Propaganda Board opened a big tea-stall, and its posters, green tea plantations along the slopes of blue mountains, were pasted all around the temple wall. (People drank too much coffee and too little tea in these parts.) It had put up a tea-bar and served free tea in porcelain cups all day. The public swarmed around it like flies, and the flies swarmed on all the cups and sugar-bowls. The presence of the fly brought in the Health Department, which feared an outbreak of some epidemic in that crowded place without water. The khaki-clad health inspectors sprayed every inch of space with DDT and, with needle in hand, coaxed people to inoculate themselves against cholera, malaria, and what not. A few youngsters just for fun bared their biceps, while a big crowd stood about and watched. There was a blank space on the rear wall of the temple where they cleaned up the ground and made a space for people to sit around and watch a film show when it grew dark. They attracted people to it by playing popular hits on the gramophone with its loudspeakers mounted on the withering treetops. Men, women, and children crowded in to watch the film shows, which were all about mosquitoes, malaria, plague, and tuberculosis, and BCG vaccination. When a huge close-up of a mosquito was shown as the cause of malaria, a peasant was overheard saying, 'Such huge mosquitoes! No wonder the people get malaria in those countries.

Our own mosquitoes are so tiny that they are harmless,' which depressed the lecturer on malaria so much that he remained silent for ten minutes. When he had done with health, he showed a few Government of India films about dams, river valleys, and various projects, with ministers delivering speeches. Far off, outside the periphery, a man had opened a gambling booth with a dart-board on a pole, and he had also erected a crude merry-go-round, which whined all day. Pedlars of various kinds were also threading in and out, selling balloons, reed whistles, and sweets.

A large crowd always stood around and watched the saint with profound awe. They touched the water at his feet and sprinkled it over their heads. They stood indefinitely around, until the master of ceremonies, Velan, begged them to move. 'Please go away. The Swami must have fresh air. If you have had your *darshan*, move on and let others have theirs. Don't be selfish.' And then the people moved on and enjoyed themselves in various ways.

When the Swami went in to lie on his mat in the hall, they came again to look at him and stood about until Velan once again told them to keep moving. A few were specially privileged to sit on the edge of the mat very close to the great man. One of them was the schoolmaster, who took charge of all the telegrams and letters that were pouring in from all over the country wishing the Swami success. The post-office at Mangala normally had a visiting postman who came once a week, and when a telegram came it was received at Aruna, a slightly bigger village seven miles down the river course, and was kept there until someone could be found going to Mangala. But now the little telegraph office had no rest—day and night messages poured in, just addressed, 'Swamiji', that was all.

They were piling up every hour and had to be sent down by special messengers. In addition to the arriving telegrams, there were many going out. The place was swarming with press reporters, who were rushing their hour-to-hour stories to their papers all over the world. They were an aggressive lot and the little telegraph-master was scared of them. They banged on his window and cried, 'Urgent!' They held out packets and packed-up films and photographs, and ordered him to dispatch them at once. They cried, 'Urgent, urgent! If this packet does not reach my office today . . .' and they threatened terrifying prospects and said all sorts of frightening things.

'Press. Urgent!' 'Press. Urgent!' They went on shouting till they reduced the man to a nervous wreck. He had promised his children that he would take them to see the Swamiji. The children cried, 'They are also showing an Ali Baba film, a friend told me.' But the man was given no time to fulfil his promise to his children. When the pressmen gave him respite, the keys rattled with incoming messages. He had spent a fairly peaceful life until then, and the present strain tore at his nerves. He sent off an SOS to all his official superiors whenever he found breathing space: 'Handling two hundred messages today. Want relief.'

The roads were choked with traffic, country carts, buses and cycles, jeeps and automobiles of all kinds and ages. Pedestrians in files with hampers and baskets crossed the fields like swarms of ants converging on a lump of sugar. The air rang with the music of a few who had chosen to help the Swami by sitting near him, singing devotional songs to the accompaniment of a harmonium and *tabala*.

The busiest man here was an American, wearing a thin bush-shirt over corduroys. He arrived in a jeep with a trailer, dusty,

I

rugged, with a mop of tousled hair, at about one in the afternoon on the tenth day of the fast and set himself to work
immediately. He had picked up an interpreter at Madras and
had driven straight through, three hundred and seventy-five
miles. He pushed everything aside and took charge of the scene.
He looked about for only a moment, driving his jeep down to
the hibiscus bush behind the temple. He jumped off and strode
past everyone to the pillared hall. He went up to the recumbent
Swami and brought his palms together, muttering, '*Namasté*'—
the Indian salute, which he had learned the moment he landed
in India. He had briefed himself on all the local manners.
Raju looked on him with interest; the large, pink-faced arrival
was a novel change in the routine.

The pink visitor stooped low to ask the schoolmaster, sitting
beside the Swami, 'Can I speak to him in English?'

'Yes. He knows English.'

The man lowered himself on to the edge of the mat and
with difficulty sat down on the floor, Indian fashion, crossing
his legs. He bent close to the Swami to say, 'I'm James J.
Malone. I'm from California. My business is production of
films and TV shows. I have come to shoot this subject, take it
back to our country, and show it to our people there. I have in
my pocket the sanction from New Delhi for this project. May
I have yours?'

Raju thought over it and serenely nodded.

'Okay. Thanks a lot. I won't disturb you—but will you let
me shoot pictures of you? I wouldn't disturb you. Will it
bother you if I move a few things up and fix the cable and
lights?'

'No; you may do your work,' said the sage.

The man became extremely busy. He sprang to his feet,

[242]

pulled the trailer into position, and started his generator. Its throbbing filled the place, overwhelming all other noises. It brought in a huge crowd of men, women, and children to watch the fun. All the other attractions in the camp became secondary. As Malone drew the cables about, a big crowd followed him. He grinned at them affably and went about his business. Velan and one or two others ran through the crowd, crying, 'Is this a fish market? Get away, all of you who have no work here!' But nobody was affected by his orders. They climbed pillars and pedestals and clung to all sorts of places to reach positions of vantage. Malone went on with his job without noticing anything. Finally, when he had the lights ready, he brought in his camera and took pictures of the people and the temple, and of the Swami from various angles and distances.

'I'm sorry, Swami, if the light is too strong.' When he had finished with the pictures, he brought in a microphone, put it near the Swami's face, and said, 'Let us chat. Okay? Tell me, how do you like it here?'

'I am only doing what I have to do; that's all. My likes and dislikes do not count.'

'How long have you been without food now?'

'Ten days.'

'Do you feel weak?'

'Yes.'

'When will you break your fast?'

'Twelfth day.'

'Do you expect to have the rains by then?'

'Why not?'

'Can fasting abolish all wars and bring world peace?'

'Yes.'

[243]

'Do you champion fasting for everyone?'

'Yes.'

'What about the caste system? Is it going?'

'Yes.'

'Will you tell us something about your early life?'

'What do you want me to say?'

'Er—for instance, have you always been a Yogi?'

'Yes; more or less.'

It was very hard for the Swami to keep up a continuous flow of talk. He felt exhausted and lay back. Velan and others looked on with concern. The schoolmaster said, 'He is fatigued.'

'Well, I guess we will let him rest for a while. I'm sorry to bother you.'

The Swami lay back with his eyes closed. A couple of doctors, deputed by the government to watch and report, went to the Swami, felt his pulse and heart. They helped him to stretch himself on the mat. A big hush fell upon the crowd. Velan plied his fan more vigorously than ever. He looked distraught and unhappy. In fact, keeping a sympathetic fast, he was now eating on alternate days, confining his diet to saltless boiled greens. He looked worn out. He said to the master, 'One more day. I don't know how he is going to bear it. I dread to think how he can pull through another day.'

Malone resigned himself to waiting. He looked at the doctor and asked, 'How do you find him?'

'Not very satisfactory; blood pressure is two hundred systolic. We suspect one of the kidneys is affected. Uremia is setting in. We are trying to give him small doses of saline and glucose. His life is valuable to the country.'

'Would you say a few words about his health?' Malone

asked, thrusting his microphone forward. He was sitting on the head of a carved elephant decorating the steps to the pillared hall.

The doctors looked at each other in panic and said, 'Sorry. We are government servants—we cannot do it without permission. Our reports are released only from headquarters. We cannot give them direct. Sorry.'

'Okay. I wouldn't hurt your customs.' He looked at his watch and said, 'I guess that's all for the day.' He approached the schoolmaster and said, 'Tell me, what time does he step into the river tomorrow?'

'Six a.m.'

'Could you come over and show me the location?' The schoolmaster got up and took him along. The man said, 'Wait, wait. You'll not mind understudying him for a minute. Show me where he starts from, how he gets up, and where he steps and stands.'

The teacher hesitated, feeling too shy to understudy the sage. The man urged him on. 'Come on; be co-operative. I'll take care of it, if there is any trouble.'

The teacher started from the pedestal. 'He starts here. Now follow me.' He showed the whole route down to the river, and the spot where the Swami would stop and pray, standing in water for two hours. The crowd followed keenly every inch of this movement, and someone in the crowd was joking, 'Oh! The master is also going to do penance and starve!' And they all laughed.

Malone threw a smile at them from time to time, although he did not know what they were saying. He surveyed the place from various angles, measured the distance from the generator, shook the schoolmaster's hand, and went back to his jeep. 'See you tomorrow morning.' He drove off amidst a great roar and puffing of his engine as his jeep rattled over the pits and ditches beyond the hibiscus, until he reached the road.

The eleventh day, morning. The crowd, pouring in all night, had nearly trebled itself because it was the last day of the fast. All night one could hear voices of people and the sound of vehicles rattling over the roads and pathways. Velan and a band of his assistants formed a cordon and kept the crowd out of the pillared hall. They said, 'The Swami must have fresh air to breathe. It's the only thing he takes now. Don't choke the air. Everyone can have his *darshan* at the river, I promise. Go away now. He is resting.' It was an all-night vigil. The numerous lanterns and lamps created a criss-cross of bewildering shadows on all hedges, trees, and walls.

At five-thirty in the morning the doctors examined the Swami. They wrote and signed a bulletin saying: 'Swami's condition grave. Declines glucose and saline. Should break the fast immediately. Advise procedure.' They sent a man running to send off this telegram to their headquarters.

It was a top-priority government telegram, and it fetched a reply within an hour: 'Imperative that Swami should be saved. Persuade best to co–operate. Should not risk life. Try give glucose and saline. Persuade Swami resume fast later.'

They sat beside the Swami and read the message to him. He smiled at it. He beckoned Velan to come nearer.

The doctors appealed, 'Tell him he should save himself. Please, do your best. He is very weak.'

Velan bent close to the Swami and said, 'The doctors say—'

In answer Raju asked the man to bend nearer, and whispered, 'Help me to my feet,' and clung to his arm and lifted himself.

[246]

He got up to his feet. He had to be held by Velan and another on each side. In the profoundest silence the crowd followed him down. Everyone followed at a solemn, silent pace. The eastern sky was red. Many in the camp were still sleeping. Raju could not walk, but he insisted upon pulling himself along all the same. He panted with the effort. He went down the steps of the river, halting for breath on each step, and finally reached his basin of water. He stepped into it, shut his eyes, and turned towards the mountain, his lips muttering the prayer. Velan and another held him each by an arm. The morning sun was out by now; a great shaft of light illuminated the surroundings. It was difficult to hold Raju on his feet, as he had a tendency to flop down. They held him as if he were a baby. Raju opened his eyes, looked about, and said, 'Velan, it's raining in the hills. I can feel it coming up under my feet, up my legs—' He sagged down.